THE CAGE

SCOTT MARIANI

Published by Sifu's Hut Publishing

Cover design by Authorbytes
www.authorbytes.com

We do not strive towards, desire or long for a thing because we deem it to be good; but on the contrary, we deem it a good thing because we strive, wish, desire or long for it.

Benedict Spinoza

His dreams had been of the half-remembered life he'd known, long ago, before this. Now, as the awful reality returned, he found himself once more wakening up to the darkness so profound and complete that it made no difference whether you opened your eyes or kept them shut. The maddening silence of his prison was broken only by the drip-drip of water echoing off the bare brick walls and the squeak and scuttle of the rats, deep in the impenetrable shadows the other side of the bars.

The man in the cage had given up screaming for help a long time ago.

His head was pounding and nausea racked his body. Now that he was awake the fog in his mind began to dissipate gradually, but consciousness seemed unable to ever fully return. It was hard to focus his thoughts properly, as though his brain had only half a grip on reality. He had no idea how long he had been here. Weeks or months? Who knew? He had lost all track of time – had lost track of almost everything; could barely even remember his own name any longer.

All he knew was that he was a prisoner in this terrible place. And with that knowledge came the terrifying belief that he would remain incarcerated here for the rest of his life. How long would that be? He'd given up trying to imagine what the future held for him. All that existed now were the cold and the hunger and the rawness of the fear that occupied his waking mind from one instant to the next.

The man's heart fluttered as he heard the footsteps descending towards the cellar door – because he knew enough to have understood that was where he was, in a cellar. He listened, holding his breath, as the steps reached the bottom and paused outside. His blood chilled to the rattle of keys, the turn of the lock, the metal door swinging open with a grinding squeal that sounded like a blade being sharpened on a whetstone. He knew what these sounds meant, because he'd already had his food dish refilled with the disgusting things he was made to eat and his slop bucket taken away that day, earlier, while he was sleeping. There could only be one other reason why his captor could be returning.

The man in the cage blinked as the cellar's single light bulb, filmed with dust and dead insects, flickered into life. As his eyes adjusted to the glare he stared through the grimy iron bars of his prison and watched his captor walk inside the cellar. The person he hated and feared more than anyone or anything else in this world, dressed all in black like always. Those implacable eyes watching him through the slits in the mask.

The prisoner struggled weakly to his feet. The cage ceiling was just high enough to allow him to stand bent, knees crooked. 'What do you want with me? What are you going to do to me?' He'd begged for the answers to those questions so many, many times, sometimes in a demented scream, other times in a croaking sob, before he'd realised there would never be a reply. His captor hadn't spoken to him a single time. To be deprived of hearing the sound of another human voice for so long was a torture in itself.

But there were other kinds of torture, too. The man had known for a long time that it was coming. On the bare pine table in the corner of the cellar were the implements, laid out in a row. Some glittered in the dim light, while others were black with grime and rust. The man swallowed as he watched his captor walk slowly towards the table. Was today going to be the day, at last, after all this terrible waiting? 'No,' he tried to say. 'Please.' But the words only came out as a dry croak.

The captor reached out with a black-gloved hand and drew the gleaming sabre blade from the row of implements. Then, with slow, deliberate movements, turned back towards the cage. The sword was wickedly curved to a needle point, and easily long enough to penetrate all the way through the cage from one side to the other. The man shrank away towards the far side, the cold steel bars pressing into his back. The captor might have been smiling, but the mask hid all human expression. The sword tip passed through the bars and slowly, slowly, came closer, heading inexorably for his belly. There was no escape from it.

The man in the cage tried not to imagine what it was going to feel like for the cold, sharp steel to sink through his innards, but in this moment he could think of nothing else. Every muscle in his body was rigid. He let out a whimper of terror as the tip of the blade suddenly changed course and pointed towards his face. It touched his cheek, the razor edge scraping on his whiskers. He screwed his eyes tight shut, waiting for the shock of the slash. The flesh opening up, the warm blood welling out.

But the captor just held it there, as if teasing him with its touch.

The man felt its hard, sharp point move slowly down his face. Its gentle pressure caressed the trembling flesh of his throat. Down to his chest.

The man almost wanted to be cut, sliced open. Let something happen. End this now. His whimpering became a groan. He barely recognised his own voice. He sounded like an animal.

Then the blade's cutting edge scraped against steel as the captor drew it abruptly away. The man stared at the curved tip receding between the bars. The captor stepped back from the cage, returned to the table and placed the sword back among the other implements. The black-gloved hand seemed to linger there for a moment, as though the captor was considering picking up another.

But no. It wasn't to be today. The captor turned from the table and began walking back towards the cellar door.

'Why are you doing this?' the man moaned, collapsing to his knees on the bare cage floor. 'Who are you?'

Silence. The metal door creaked open again and the captor stepped through it, switching out the light. The lock turned. The footsteps padded away.

And then the man in the cage was alone again, with the darkness and the rats, and the horror of what tomorrow might bring.

CHAPTER ONE

It was a fine Saturday evening in one of the warmest summers Oxfordshire had seen in years, and Tom McAllister was driving fast through the countryside, his headlights burning through the dusk as he raced to get to his destination. He was a man on a mission, because time was running out and any moment now old Alfie would be closing up shop, pulling down the shutters and shuffling off to bed. Once he'd got his hearing aids off there would be no rousing him.

Tom snatched out his phone. 'Alfie, it's Tom. Listen, I got held up at work but I'm just ten minutes out. Do me a favour and stay open until I get there, will you? I'll make it worth your while.'

The old man chuckled. 'Because it's you, Tom. I know how much you love your Langtree Hundred.'

'You're a saviour.'

Tom hustled the rest of the way, the throaty rasp of the big American V8 blatting off the Cotswold stone houses as he reached the village of Bampton. His dog Radar was riding in the back as usual, a big German shepherd head poking through the gap in the front seats with two huge triangular ears sticking straight up.

'Yeah, yeah, I know what you're thinking,' Tom said to him. 'You're thinking what an eedjit I am, getting in a twist over something as daft as running out of beer. It's a human thing. You wouldn't understand.'

The dog said nothing, but his disapproval was tangible.

At last, Tom reached the narrow, dark street on the edge of the village where Alfie Birtwhistle had been running his little wine shop and off-license when Tom was still a schoolboy growing up in Belfast. Alfie was pushing eighty now and a widower, but he had no plans to retire. Tom was a friend and a regular customer, and Langtree Hundred was the local craft ale that he regularly ordered by the crateload from Alfie. To run out of the stuff would be a calamity, at the best of times. For the supply to have dried out on a Saturday, when Alfie would be closed all day tomorrow, was unthinkable. Alfie was one of the last traders in the country who still honoured the old traditions. Which Tom regarded as pretty much a good thing, as long as it didn't threaten to cut off his lifeblood. He'd finished his last bottle of it late last night, after a long and difficult day at work.

Tom didn't really want to think about work right now.

He pulled up outside the shop and his sharp powers of observation instantly drank in something unusual about the scene. In all the years that Tom had been his customer, he'd never known Alfie to close the blinds on the windows. But they were closed now, even though the sign on the door still read OPEN. It looked like Alfie had another late-evening customer in there, too. There was a car parked outside the shop door. A rough old hot hatch with worn-out tyres and a taped-up headlamp. Though Tom didn't live in the village he knew most of its residents' cars by sight, and this wasn't one of them.

Tom muttered to the dog, 'What do you think, Radar?'

Radar drew his lips into a snarl, eyes fixed on the shop doorway. Tom replied, 'That's what I'm thinking, too.'

Tom was a big, broad-shouldered man but he could move with surprising speed and agility. He slipped out of the car, the shepherd trailing him like a silent shadow. Tom motioned the 'wait' command and the dog instantly dropped down to the pavement, alert and ready. Tom tiptoed up to the window and peered in through a slit in the blind. What he saw was more or less what he'd expected. Two little goblins inside, skinny and narrow-shouldered, probably late teens or early twenties, ripped jeans, hoodies, balaclavas. One of them toting a sawn-off shotgun in old Alfie's face while the other one had hopped over the counter to raid the till.

Around the back of the shop was an alley with a rear trade entrance that doubled as the door to Alfie's little flat. Tom had sometimes helped the old guy bring in deliveries, as a way of thanking him for stocking all his crates of ale. It was never locked.

Tom skirted the corner, stalked quickly up the alley and let himself in the rear door. Pausing, he could hear raised voices coming from inside the shop. Alfie was a tough old bird and things could get ugly.

Tom hesitated a moment, then slipped inside the flat. Alfie had been a star of the local cricket team, back in the day. He was still the undefeated wicket-taker of the West Oxon league and his lucky bat hung on the living room wall. Tom took it down and hefted it in his hand. A fine piece of white willow, light and strong.

Tom moved faster now. From the storeroom he entered the shop via the door that said STAFF ONLY, clutching the bat like a sword. The two armed robbers had their backs to him and were too busy terrorising Alfie and stealing his money to notice. Tom strode straight up behind the one with the gun

3

and in a huge, wide, furious one-handed swing of the bat swept his legs out from under him. The guy went up in the air and then hit the floor like a sandbag, and the shotgun spun across the tiles. Tom snatched it up with his empty hand, loomed over him pointing the gun in his masked face and said, 'Don't get up.'

At the same instant the second crook was leaping back over the counter, scattering banknotes as he went, and racing for the front door.

Which wasn't such a great idea.

As the little crook burst out into the street, Radar instantly closed on him and stopped him in his tracks, reared up full height and pinning him to the shop window with a paw on each shoulder and his long fangs bared about three inches from the guy's boggling eyes. He would hold him there for hours, or until Tom gave him the 'leave' command. They usually pissed themselves in fear after the first couple of minutes.

'You assaulted me,' the robber on the floor yelped up at Tom. 'I'm calling the police!'

Another little goblin who thought he was a lawyer.

Tom broke open the shotgun, ejected the cartridges and tossed the weapon away. He said, 'No need for that. They're already here. And you're under arrest.'

CHAPTER TWO

Monday morning dawned bright and warm. Tom lived alone in a remote rural cottage in the west of the county, a stone's throw from the banks of the winding, meandering, tree-shaded River Thames. He had taken Radar for his early morning walk down by the water's edge, past the old semi-ruined mill that sat on Tom's half acre of riverside. It was going to be too hot a day to bring the dog into work with him, and so Tom had arranged for Ken Sparrowhawk to come and feed him lunch. Sparrowhawk was a local odd-bod, a reclusive character who lived on a river boat and floated downstream now and then to help Tom look after the place.

After a snatched breakfast – coffee from freshly-ground beans and home-baked croissants – Tom carefully watered the jungle of plants that filled the cottage's little conservatory, jumped into his work clothes and was off, rumbling through the lanes. He couldn't profess to know everything about his fellow Thames Valley Police officers, but he was fairly certain that he was the only cop in the force who drove a 1970 Plymouth Barracuda muscle car that was as long and wide as a river boat, sounded like a tank battalion in full charge, drank more fuel than a Boeing 747 and made the cruisers and pursuit cars in the police pool look like minis.

Some time later, Tom climbed the familiar steps up to the floor of the Oxford police station where he worked when he wasn't at the Kidlington HQ or tramping his hunting grounds around the city and surrounding areas. As he walked into the office area he was greeted with a mixture of praise, some of it sincere and some jokey: 'Good for you, Tom.' 'Well done, mate.' 'Hey there, Wyatt Earp.'

The story of the Thames Valley cop who had foiled the wine shop robbery had had time during Sunday to spread all over the local news. Even old Alfie Birtwhistle had made an appearance on TV, making Tom sound like a Greek god. The real stars of the show, one Gavin Tribe and his partner in crime Dougie Biggar, were in custody awaiting their first court hearing.

Tom was heading for his cubicle when the door of the office at the far end of the open-plan space swung open and a small, reedy figure stepped out of it to survey him with a scowl of undisguised disapproval. Then again, that was pretty much the only expression Tom had ever seen on the waspish, mean-looking face of Detective Chief Superintendent Alan Forbes, universally known as Forbsie.

'In my office, McAllister.'

Here we go, Tom thought.

'Close the door,' Forbes snapped as Tom walked in. Tom always deliberately left it open, just to annoy him.

Forbes stalked around to the reclining throne behind his desk and threw himself down into it. Tom remained standing.

'So, McAllister, how do you propose to explain yourself this time?' The moustache was bristling like the hairs on the back of an angry cat.

'I was scared they might steal my beer,' Tom said. 'I really like that beer.'

'You pointed a gun at Mr Tribe.' *Mr Tribe.*

Tom shrugged. 'Only for a second. I wasn't actually intending to shoot him.'

'He didn't know that.'

'He'd have known about it, if I had,' Tom replied.

Forbes wasn't amused. 'You scared the living daylights out of a member of the public.'

'A member of the public who'd just been pointing the same gun at a seventy-nine-year-old man. Didn't seem to bother him that Alfie could've dropped dead of a heart attack. I just gave him a taste of his own medicine.'

Forbes shook his head, drumming his fingers on the desk. 'I'm not happy with the way you handled this, McAllister. Why didn't you call in a rapid response unit?'

'Because they're not rapid enough, sir. And besides, I didn't need them. I had help.'

Forbes sneered. 'Ah, yes. I was coming to that. That dog of yours is not authorised to carry out police duties.'

'He was making a citizen's arrest,' Tom said.

'There are rules, McAllister. Even for you, as I seem to recall was pointed out to you at your last disciplinary tribunal, not so very long ago.'

'What are you going to do, arrest him for impersonating an officer? I can see the headlines: "Vigilante hound takes law into its own paws".'

'Watch your lip, Detective Inspector. Quite frankly, I'm getting tired of your attitude. Consider this a warning. I can only hope it'll sink into your head this time, because we all know where you're headed otherwise. Don't we?'

'Fine. Can I go now? I've got work to do. Sir.' Tom often added the 'sir' only as an afterthought, and this time left a longer pause than usual.

'Yes, you certainly have. Need I ask if there have been any updates to the Jameson investigation? No, of course not.

You're too busy running around the county buying beer and using disproportionate force against minor offenders, when you have a killer on the loose. Now get out of here and bring me some actual results.'

A fine start to the day, Tom was thinking as he left the office, making sure to leave Forbes's door wide open on his way out. He was skulking moodily back to the bomb site of his three-sided workstation when he was met with the brightest thing he'd seen all morning. That was the smiling face of Detective Sergeant Billie Flowers. She'd seen him emerge from Forbes's lair and knew what was up. Billie always seemed to know what was up. Tom wished he had her good sense.

'Hey, cheer up. You'll always be my hero.' Billie talked with the same voice that she sang with, smoke and honey and melted chocolate. Her people were of Afro-Dominican origin and her old man had been a semi-famous reggae artist in his day, but mellow, bluesy jazz was Billie's music. Tom sometimes went to hear her perform at local clubs, on those rare occasions when they were both off duty.

'Aye, well, you can call me a hero after I solve this frigging Jameson case,' he grumped, hanging his jacket over the back of the chair and settling at his desk.

'Here,' she said, handing him a little package. 'A gift for my favourite law enforcer.'

'Can I open it?' He ripped at the paper, delved inside and found a box of little brown savoury cookies. He plucked one out, tossed it in his mouth and chewed vigorously. 'Hmm. Not too bad. Need seasoning.'

Billie frowned. 'That's because they're dog biscuits, silly. For Radar.'

'Sure, I knew that.'

'You want some coffee?'

'I'll pass. Thanks for the biscuits.'

'Save some for the dog,' she muttered, and went off, leaving him to his work. Not that he was much looking forward to getting stuck back into the Jameson case, a major headache of which he'd been put in charge as chief investigating officer.

Almost two weeks ago on a sunny Tuesday morning, a single, unmarried local resident named Raymond Jameson, fifty-five years of age, had been mysteriously gunned down while taking a quiet stroll through Florence Park, in East Oxford. The sole witness to the killing had been a council worker mowing the grass, a guy called Bob Sell, who had barely taken much notice of Jameson walking past until he'd suddenly keeled over stone dead with blood pouring out of him. Neither Sell nor anyone else in the vicinity had heard the shot and the killer had got away unnoticed.

Thirteen days on, Tom still had relatively little to go on. The police forensic team had recovered a spent rifle cartridge case ninety metres away across the park, the other side of a copse of trees, which was their best indication of the shooter's position. The empty casing happened to match perfectly up to the mangled thirty-calibre conical bullet that had been dug out of the victim. The projectile had passed cleanly through the trees and hit Jameson in the base of the skull, rattling around inside and turning his brain into mush.

One shot, one kill, a neat and highly proficient job. The fact that nobody had heard the gunshot made sense, in light of the forensic evidence. The lab team had determined from the case and bullet that the murder weapon was something called a .300 Blackout, using subsonic ammunition capable of being silenced to the point where it was no louder than a handclap. The relatively low-powered cartridge accounted for the way the bullet hadn't gone straight through the victim's head, in one side and out the other.

But what didn't make sense to Tom was that not a single eyewitness had seen a man with a rifle enter the park, carry out the deed or make his escape afterwards. Florence Park was generally a quiet, peaceful place on weekdays. The kids were still in school, most folks were at work in the morning; but even so it seemed to defy credibility that not one sighting had been reported, thirteen days after the event.

'The frigger's some kind of ghost,' Tom muttered under his breath, not for the first time.

Combing the internet for every type of rifle he could find that was chambered for the .300 Blackout cartridge, not one of them was the usual bolt-action type that civilians could own under the UK's strict gun laws. Instead he found himself looking at image after image of military-style black rifles, highly utilitarian semiautomatic devices with extendable stocks and high-capacity magazines. That class of firearm had been made off-limits to law-abiding British shooters a long, long time ago. Which meant the murder weapon was unregistered, and would be much harder to trace. The Firearms Department database had yielded zilch, little to Tom's surprise.

Meanwhile the shooting had stunned the city and sent Thames Valley Police into an uproar. This was Oxford, not Chicago. While crime and even violent crime weren't exactly unknown in the City of the Dreaming Spires, shootings were a rare event, and it certainly wasn't every day that a sniper equipped with serious military-style ordnance went around taking pot-shots at citizens. The revelation that Raymond Jameson was on the Convicted Sex Offenders List, a habitual child molester recently released from prison, had caused no less of a stir.

For the sake of solving one murder, the web of investigation had quickly grown into a sprawling great logistical mess. Tom, Billie and a task force of investigating officers both within Thames Valley and other police forces all up and down the country had faced the task of identifying, assessing and interviewing a large number of potential male suspects associated with Raymond Jameson's past victims. Over the last twenty-two years the man had been responsible for wrecking the lives of more than a dozen underage girls – and two boys – all over England, whose various fathers, brothers, cousins and uncles comprised a long list now made larger by the present-day partners and spouses of those victims who had now reached adulthood, not to mention an unknowable quantity of friends and boyfriends. The task force's job had been to sift through as many of them as they could find, looking for possible candidates who might have both the motive and the ability to carry out a revenge killing on their loved one's behalf, even years after the fact.

Tom had started out with a list of forty-eight names. First to be eliminated were the dead, the seriously sick, and those who had emigrated abroad and not recently returned to the UK. Next, those with a plausible alibi. Of those remaining, the investigation had planned to focus on anyone with a history of violence, or military experience, or known firearms expertise as a civilian. Best of all, anyone who might, in front of witnesses, have expressed a desire to punish Ray Jameson for his past misdeeds.

Needless to say, police work was never quite as easy as that.

Billie had been working the phone like a demon and firing off emails in all directions day after day, whittling the list down until it was now shrunk away almost entirely. An uncle of one of Jameson's early victims had served in the army but was now living in Tasmania. Abi Smith, a girl he'd raped in Leeds in 1996, had a cousin called Donnie Marshall who was a volatile character known to police – had once tried to strangle a transvestite with a length of chain – but it turned out he was serving a two-year stretch for car theft. And on, and on, until there were more crossings-out on the list than names, and finally no names left at all.

In short, Tom and his team had one very dead paedophile

on their hands and not the slightest whiff of a real suspect to show for it so far. Forbes was on him like a ton of manure. The media were going wild too, in particular Suzie Green, an especially persistent reporter for the Oxford Mail who wouldn't leave him alone. Which, Tom had to admit to himself if to nobody else, was partly his fault. He and Suzie had dated a few times. Not seriously enough to call it a 'relationship'; he didn't know what you'd call it. 'Torrid fling' might suit better, but it didn't sound so good either.

As Tom sat scowling at his computer screen, thinking that maybe if he stared at it hard enough it would yield up the answers he needed, the phone on his desk rang. He snatched it up. Talk of the devil. Should never have given her his direct number.

'Hello, lover,' Suzie Green purred in his ear. She could hiss like a viper, too, when provoked.

'God give me strength. If it isn't my favourite journalist, Lois Lane. What did I do to deserve this?'

'Don't be like that, McAllister.'

'What do you want, Suzie?'

'Be cool, I'm not asking you for a date or anything like that. I want what everyone else wants, to talk to the hero of the late-night off-licence robbery. And to get the latest on the paedo killer. Give me an exclusive, for old times' sake. I'll make it worth your while. I promise.'

'Is that a threat?'

'Come on McAllister, stop fooling around. Truth is, I'm going stir crazy working for this lousy provincial rag. I need a scoop. A big one.'

'Sorry, Suzie, I've nothing for you. Go away,' Tom said, put the phone down and went back to thinking. He was still pondering the whole mystery an hour later when Billie put her head around the side of his cubicle and said softly in his ear, 'Hey. Don't forget your eleven o'clock appointment.'

Startled, Tom jumped back from his screen and looked at his watch. 'Shite!'

'Don't want to be late, sir. First impressions, and all that.'

'Why didn't you remind me?'

'I just did.'

Tom grabbed his jacket and raced out of the office. On the way out of the station he bumped into another DI he knew, a guy named Morley. 'Christ, McAllister. You look like you're off to your own funeral.'

'That would be bad enough,' Tom replied. 'Where I'm going is worse.'

CHAPTER THREE

Second floor up, third door on the left, Billie had told him.

Tom paused at the door before he knocked. The building was old and a little rundown. He could sniff mildew, mixed with the scent of ethnic cooking that lingered on the stairway. He could hear the Cowley Road traffic through the dusty window on the landing. The carpet under his feet was thin against the boards and the door in front of him was old and pitted and battered.

He glanced again at the business card in his fist and checked the name against the one on the imitation brass plaque that was held by a single screw to the door. The name on it was H.R. Pepper B.Sc (Hons). Under the name were a bunch of professional designations Tom didn't recognise.

He breathed out long and slow through his nose. Nervous. He wanted to turn away and head back down the creaky stairs, but it was too late now. He heard footsteps from the other side; then the handle turned and the door opened.

Tom had dealt with a few psychologists in his job. They were always austere-looking, chinless, tweedy guys with thinning grey hair and narrow shoulders, who had an annoying way of peering at you over their spectacles. Harvey Pepper was pretty much the opposite of one of those. The shrink ran his fingers through his unruly black hair and flipped back a comma that hung low across his left eye. He was maybe five years younger than Tom, somewhere in his mid-thirties, and at around five-seven he was a good six inches shorter. One side of his shirt hem was hanging out from the bulging waistband of his jeans and he wore no shoes. One sock red, the other blue. He was puffing on a slim roll-up cigarette and he hadn't shaved in the last couple of days.

Unconventional.

'Dr Pepper,' Tom said. 'Like the drink.'

'Call me Harvey. And I'm not a Dr. Come on in.'

Tom stepped into the office and navigated around a precarious pile of books that teetered in the middle of the floor. 'Sorry about the state of the place,' Harvey said. 'I just moved in last week.'

Tom looked around him. There was no desk. Some cardboard boxes piled in a corner. Two battered leather armchairs facing one another across the worn rug, at an angle so client and therapist wouldn't have to sit staring at each other. He figured that would be too confrontational for psychotherapy. To the right of each armchair was a small table, square and low. On one table was a box of tissues and a glass of water. He guessed that was the patient's chair. On the other table was a notepad and pen and an ashtray.

'I thought you had to lie on a couch,' Tom said.

Harvey smiled. 'That's not the way I do things.'

'It's what happens in all the movies I've seen.'

'So this is your first time?'

Tom nodded. 'I haven't done anything like this before.' He sat in the designated armchair and pointed at the box of tissues. 'Do they cry a lot?' he asked.

'Buckets,' Harvey said.

'I'll have to try not to let that happen.'

Harvey flopped down opposite and threw his chubby legs out in front of him. He reminded Tom of a German shepherd pup: round and roly but the eyes were sharp. They settled on Tom for a few seconds. 'Tell me a bit about yourself. Why are you here?'

'Don't you already know why?'

'I'd like to hear it in your own words.'

Tom sighed. *OK, straight out with it.* 'I've been told I have a problem with anger.'

'But you don't agree.'

'How can you tell I don't agree?'

'I'm a psychologist. I know things about people.'

'Are you a good psychologist?'

Harvey raised an eyebrow. 'You're avoiding the question.'

Tom shrugged. 'As far as I'm concerned, I'm a paragon of sweetness and light. Most of the time, at any rate.'

'That's a good start.' Harvey reached out to the table next to him, snatched up the pad and pen. He scribbled a note, holding the cigarette in the corner of his mouth. It wagged up and down when he spoke. 'So who thinks you have a problem?'

'My DS. The one who suggested I see you. Well, actually it was the higher-up brass who ordered me to get therapy. But it was Billie who looked you up and found you.'

Harvey's eyes had widened somewhat. 'DS as in—'

'As in Detective Sergeant Billie Flowers of the Thames Valley force.'

Harvey paused a beat, laid down his pad and pen. He plucked the cigarette from his lips and tossed it into the ashtray, like a naughty schoolboy caught in the act. 'You're police?'

Tom made a noncommittal gesture. 'I'm a DI. Detective Inspector. And don't worry about the cigarette.'

'I thought there were rules about that.'

'There are, but some rules I don't mind breaking. Or so I'm told.'

Harvey picked up the cigarette and went on smoking. 'That's a relief. What do I call you? Inspector?'

'Whatever you like. God knows I've been called most things in my time.'

'Maybe that would be another part of why you're here?'

'You tell me,' Tom said.

'All right. Let's try and unpack this a little. Why does she, Billie, Detective Sergeant Flowers, think you needed to see me?'

'How'd you know it's a she? Could be Billy with a *y*.'

'The way you talk about her. A certain tone in your voice, change of body language. So I'm guessing it's Billie with an *ie*. Like Billie Holliday. You like her.'

'Maybe you really are a good psychologist,' Tom said. 'Anyhow, it's not a man-woman thing. Billie's just a colleague.'

'But she went to the trouble of helping you find a therapist.'

'She worries that I might get suspended.'

'Why would you be suspended?'

Tom shrugged again. 'Certain behaviour.'

'Such as?'

'You really want to know?'

'That's what we're here for,' Harvey said.

'We could be here a long time.'

'How about starting with the most recent example?'

'That would be a few weeks back, on a typical Saturday night. A gentleman was brought in on a domestic abuse charge. Two in the morning, off his face on booze and drugs and covered in blood. The blood belonging to his girlfriend, who he'd kicked the shit out of earlier that evening because his team lost, and put her in the hospital, where it later turned out she was three months pregnant. She lost the baby. Meanwhile, his nibs is sitting in a cell shouting his mouth off about his rights. I was working late, went to get some coffee. I could hear the little gobshite swearing at Billie. Called her by an ethnophaulism.'

'That's a fancy word. I take it your colleague Billie is a person of colour?'

'I'm not really up to speed with what they prefer to be called nowadays. But I'm pretty sure it's not "jungle bunny". Which pissed me off slightly. Actually it was more than slightly. Put it together with the reason he was in the cells in the first place, I sort of lost it a little.'

Harvey nodded slowly. 'Can we be specific about what exactly made you so angry at that moment? Racial prejudice? Social injustice? Misogynistic abuse?'

'No, I just hate violent little bastards who think they can throw their weight around and bleat about it afterwards,' Tom said.

Harvey made a note. 'Okay. And how did you react?'

Tom flexed his right fist and looked at it.

'You hit him?'

'No. Or I'd have lost my job. But I let him think I was going to. He was quiet afterwards.'

'Obviously not that quiet,' Harvey said. 'I'm assuming he made a complaint. So now you've been threatened with suspension?'

Tom nodded.

'Serious threat? Anything imminent?'

'Just a warning. Not the first.'

'How many times has this kind of thing happened before?'

'I've had the occasional brush with the board,' Tom said. 'I'm insubordinate. Not a team player. Maverick. All that kind of crap.'

'And are you?'

'You're the shrink,' Tom said. 'You decide.'

Harvey made another note. 'How long have you been out of Ireland? What's that accent, Belfast?'

'I haven't been back there in a long time,' Tom said. 'Twenty-two years with Thames Valley Police. But the accent never faded. That must mean something, no? Psychologically?'

'It's something we can discuss at a later date. Why Oxford and not Belfast?'

'Wrong side of the fence,' Tom said. 'A Catholic boy can't join the Royal Ulster Constabulary without becoming a very unpopular guy. Bad enough to be hated by one half of the population.'

'You're religious?'

'Nope. But in Northern Ireland even the non-believers still have to belong to one club or the other. Catholic atheist, or Protestant atheist. Take your pick. My lot were Catholic atheist.'

'Sounds like you must have been highly motivated to become a cop,' Harvey observed.

'Aye, I was a right daftie at that age,' Tom said.

'Let's talk about your life now. Are you married? Children?'

'I live alone,' Tom said. 'Just me and the dog. His name's Radar.'

'What about women?'

'You ask a lot of questions.'

'It's my job.'

'Mine too,' Tom said. 'Women? No serious relationships. Nothing involved or committed. When one of us gets fed up and wants to move on, there are no hard feelings. Things don't get sticky. Only one rule. I don't date colleagues.'

'That works for you?' Harvey said.

'Every time. It's exactly what I need out of life.'

'So it's not your love life that makes you angry.'

'I already told you what makes me angry,' Tom said. 'Why are we talking about love?'

'Have you ever been in love?'

'I don't go in for big emotions.'

'Yes, you do,' Harvey said. 'Love and hate. Peaches and cream. You're capable of one, you're capable of the other.' He looked at his watch. 'And there endeth the lesson, I think.'

'Jeez, that was quick.'

'Time flies when you're having fun,' Harvey said. 'I'd like to see you again in – let's see – how about two days from now, Wednesday, same time?'

'I thought this was going to be a weekly thing. Why so soon?'

"Cause you're an angry so-and-so.'

'Provoke the client – that part of the way it works?'

'Only in the most desperate cases.'

'Thanks a heap.'

Harvey gave a mischievous grin. 'I like to start off intense, then reduce the number of sessions as we go forward. I can do evenings if that's not convenient, or we can even talk on the phone. Your choice.'

'Wednesday should be fine, unless something comes up. I'll let you know. How many sessions am I going to need? Don't answer that.'

Just then, Tom felt a pulse of vibration from the phone in his pocket. 'I need to take this,' he said. He pulled out the phone and answered, 'McAllister.'

The low, smooth voice on the other end was Billie's.

'Tom,' she said. 'There's been another one.'

20

The old man had died exactly three minutes after he walked inside the gates.

The children's play area was on the edge of an Oxfordshire village called Stanton Harcourt. It was just gone eleven on what was growing into a hot, hazy day and the sky was intense blue.

A tranquil, happy scene. Some kids were knocking a football around the grassy patch, a couple of younger children were clambering up a slide and scooting down the chute, shrieking with delight. An overweight woman had her fat terrier on a leash and was letting it snuffle and root around in the unmown grass near a line of gnarly oak trees that fringed one edge of the park. Over on the other side of the play area, a young mother was seated on a bench beside her little daughter. The girl was four years old, and her hair was golden in the sunshine. She was clutching a floppy teddy bear to her side.

The mother smiled at the old man as she saw him stroll down the footpath and into the play area. She lived in a terraced house close by and had often seen him here during the last couple of months, in his gleaming patent-leather shoes and the long beige raincoat he wore whatever the weather. He smiled back at her, wished her a polite good morning; and as he passed he reached out a thin, long-fingered hand and patted the little girl fondly on the head. The child beamed up at him.

The mother thought he looked like a kindly sort of man. A little sad around the eyes. Lonely. A widower, maybe, in his mid-seventies or thereabouts. She wondered if he'd recently moved to the village, and what his name was.

The old man walked on by and paused to watch the older kids playing football, standing with his hands clasped behind his back and a benevolent expression on his face. You could tell he loved children, the young mother thought. The little girl tugged at her sleeve and said something, distracting her attention for a second.

That was the moment it happened. The old man was still standing watching the football knock-around when he snapped rigid with his spine arched. It was as though he'd remembered something terribly

21

important, or he'd fallen asleep on his feet and then jolted abruptly awake, in an exaggerated and almost comical way. People around the play area turned to look, curiosity quickly turning to alarm as they realised that something was wrong. The old man staggered in a half-circle, the shiny shoes kicking up dust. He seemed to hang in space for an instant. Then he dropped to the ground, suddenly limp and formless, like an empty suit of clothes that had been cut from a washing line.

He never made a sound. Lay there in the grass, his face half-hidden. His legs jerked in a spasm and then went still. The terrier barked, the fat woman gasped, the kids forgot about their ball. One of the kids on the chute let out a scream.

The young mother told her little girl to stay there and don't move, leapt up from the bench and ran over to him. She was thinking heart attack, stroke, brain aneurism, all of the things that can wipe out an old man from one instant to the next. Or heatstroke, maybe, in this fierce sun.

She got to him and knelt in the grass. It was dry and prickly against her bare knees. She sensed other people running towards her. She reached out a hand to his inert body and laid her fingertips tentatively on his shoulder. Nudged him once, twice, no response. 'Sir? Are you all right? Can you hear me? Sir?'

She became aware of the crowd gathering around. She remembered reading something about the first aid recovery position. What were you meant to do?

Then she saw the blood that was welling fast out of the ragged hole under his right shoulder blade.

CHAPTER FOUR

Tom hustled away from Cowley Road, crossed over Magdalen Bridge and headed up the High Street into the heart of Oxford. The main Thames Valley force HQ was situated in Kidlington, seven miles north of the city, but Tom spent most of the administrative part of his job working out of the station in St Aldate's, just off the centre. Compared with the sprawling modern complex of the main headquarters, the crumbly old sandstone building was a chaotic warren of narrow corridors and tiny cluttered offices. There was endless talk of refurbishment, even of closure, but Tom liked it the way it was and hoped they didn't change it. The Thames flowed past nearby, and the rear of the building overlooked Christ Church Meadow.

Billie was waiting for him outside a side exit off Floyd's Row as he pulled up with a screech of tyres. He reached across and threw open the passenger door for her and she hopped in, pointedly glancing at her watch. Tom swung the car around and hit the gas hard.

'I still can't understand whatever possessed you to buy this thing,' Billie commented over the engine roar as the acceleration pressed her into her seat.

Tom looked at her as though she'd lost her mind, and said, 'I've told you a thousand times, I won it in a poker game. I'd never have bought it, sure.'

'Maybe you are capable of being sensible, after all,' she said dryly.

'But I kind of like it now. It grows on you. Radar likes it, too.'

'So I've noticed,' she replied, plucking tan German shepherd hairs off her sleeve. Every square inch of the car's interior was plastered with them. 'So how did your session with the psychologist go? Or is that confidential?'

Tom shrugged. 'Weirdest shrink I've ever come across, so he is. Not that I'm much of an expert.'

They were piling into the lumbering mid-afternoon traffic. Tom headed south and then turned onto Thames Street, slicing across the city towards St Giles' and then the Northern Bypass and the A40. Their destination was the village of Stanton Harcourt, a twenty-minute drive into the West Oxfordshire countryside. Tom knew where they were going and had a pretty good idea why, but she hadn't had time to explain much on the phone. He said, 'So fill me in.'

'It looks a lot like the first one,' Billie replied.

'Pattern?'

'I'd say that's a fair bet.'

With the news of a second killing, the complexity of his case hadn't just doubled, but multiplied exponentially with the quest for a suspect with connections to not one dead paedophile, but two of them. Loose ends that were previously inches apart were now separated by miles, and the mystery had deepened into a bottomless trench.

'Great,' Tom muttered. 'Okay, I'm listening.'

'Star of the show this time around is one Mr Eddie Blake,'

Billie said. 'Seventy-three years of age, released three months ago after serving eighteen for child abuse, and placed into a one-bedroom rental in Stanton Harcourt. Wasn't his first offence.'

Tom's fists tightened on the steering wheel. He shook his head. 'Holy crap. Since when does a habitual child abuser get off with eighteen months?'

'Early release on health grounds. He had chronic emphysema.'

'Until our boy put the dirty pervert out of his misery.'

Billie shot him a sideways look of disapproval.

'If you won't say it, then I will,' Tom said. 'If someone's tracking down and executing convicted sex offenders that the system let go with a slap on the wrist, then good luck to him. These sickos gave up their right to walk this earth a long time ago.'

'Be sure to let Forbsie hear you say that. It'll really impress him.'

Tom made an impatient gesture, as though Forbes were a mosquito he'd just whisked out of the car window. 'Anyway, I'll bet whoever the shooter is, he isn't finished yet.'

'Unless we catch him first,' Billie said. 'That's what we're here for, isn't it?'

'Aye, it's a crappy job we have, and no mistake.'

'And something tells me it's about to get crappier.'

Tom and Billie arrived at the crime scene just as Eddie Blake's body was being taken off to the coroner's mortuary at the John Radcliffe hospital in Headington. The children's play park where the shooting had taken place was situated to the side of a narrow footpath on the edge of the village, closed to regular traffic and barely wide enough for the ambulance. Police cars and vans were parked single-file all along the path and Tom had to roll the Barracuda up onto the sloping grass verge to let the ambulance leave. He and Billie got out, walked down the grassy slope and passed under the cordon of police tape that had been erected all around the edge of the park. The crime scene was full of bustle and activity: cops everywhere, a photographer going around snapping the park from every angle, the forensic people examining the area where the victim died. A group of witnesses stood gathered to one side, some of them looking visibly shaken and upset and being attended to by trauma officers.

Tom was taking in the scene when someone he'd preferred to have avoided stepped up and grinned in his face, showing a load of crooked teeth.

'Hello, McAllister. What are you doing here?'

DI Niall Bates was Tom's opposite number in the West Oxfordshire division. For the last few years Thames Valley Police had been divided into a dozen different LAPs, local policing areas, each with its own divisional team assigned to that jurisdiction. Stanton Harcourt fell under West Oxfordshire while Tom and Billie's main stamping ground was the city itself.

Tom replied, 'I might have known you West Ox boys would try to poke your noses in.'

Bates flushed, stabbed a finger towards the ground and replied, 'What are you talking about? This is my LAP. My case.'

'Sorry, Niall, you can't have it,' Tom said. 'The first victim was shot within city limits. That makes it mine.'

'You don't know for sure this one's connected.'

'Call it telepathy. Didn't anyone tell you I have the gift?'

Bates looked pissed off, but he knew Tom was probably right and didn't try to press the issue. He turned and slunk off without saying more.

But if this was Tom's case, it also belonged to his boss. Just when Tom was thinking there were already enough idiots hanging around this crime scene, he caught sight of the unmarked car driven by Detective Superintendent Forbes rolling up to park on the grassy verge behind the Barracuda. 'Oh, Christ,' Tom groaned, loudly enough to be heard by everyone around him. 'This is all I need.'

Billie jabbed him in the ribs with her elbow. 'Shh. Keep your voice down.'

The vulturine shape of Superintendent Forbes emerged from the car and he strutted over, instantly working the scene like a general marshalling his troops. Tom and Billie both slipped away: Billie to go and talk to the small gathering of witnesses, Tom to meet someone he didn't want to avoid. Crossing the grassy patch past the spot where Eddie Blake had died, he walked over to the row of gnarly oaks that ran alongside the edge of the park.

'How are we doing, Thins?'

Nobody could remember what wag in the force had come up with that nickname for Harry Waller, Thames Valley's senior forensic pathologist, in homage to the jazz great Fats Waller, but it had stuck because it was so appropriate. His face was greyer than his hair and the backs of his bony hands were mapped out with veins, blue through translucent skin. Tom had known him for years. He was crazy but he knew his shit.

Waller barely looked up and offered no more than a grunt of greeting as he crouched by a tree, working slowly and methodically, sweltering under the hot sunshine but apparently not caring. He and two of his forensic team had traced the path of the bullet to where it had buried itself in the oak's thick trunk. After carefully stripping away a small section of bark, Thins was now wrestling with a pair of long needle-nosed pliers to yank it out. It was a thousand-to-one shot they'd even found it, but old Thins could smell these things out like a polar bear smells a seal through a metre of ice.

'Got the bugger,' he announced with satisfaction as it came

free at last. He scrutinised it for a moment, looked pleased, and dropped it into a plastic evidence bag.

Tom said, 'Sure, you're a frigging genius, Thins.'

'Tell that to my wife. She needs to hear it from someone other than me.'

'What've we got?'

'Here's our culprit.' Waller held up the evidence bag to show Tom the twisted, flattened remains of what had been a conical rifle bullet, before it went punching through human organs and flesh and then came to an abrupt stop inside the tree. 'Another inch deeper and we'd have had to cut half the bloody trunk away to get at it.'

'Didn't come from a BB gun, that's for sure,' Tom said, peering closely at the bag.

'Looks like your typical thirty-calibre copper-jacketed rifle projectile. Fairly heavy bullet; I'd say it was a 220-grainer.'

'Same kind the .300 Blackout uses.'

Waller nodded, and a bead of sweat fell from his nose. 'Especially for subsonic loads fired with a silencer. That would account for the lack of an audible gunshot.'

'Just like Florence Park.'

'Maybe, but we won't know for sure until we do the lab work and compare it to the one we pulled out of Raymond Jameson. With a bit of luck, there'll be enough rifling striations left intact on the jacket to confirm whether or not they came out of the same barrel.'

'Fifty quid says they did,' Tom said.

'You know I'm not a betting man, McAllister. But my instinct tells me it would seem like a bit of a coincidence for two separate shootings to take place in the same county within a matter of days and employing such a similar MO, and not be connected. Looks like you've got your hands full. Can't say that I envy you much.'

'Me neither,' Tom said.

'It also means that your killer, assuming we are talking about a single killer, has access to some pretty useful hardware. Certainly did enough damage to the victim. Entry wound in the right pectoral muscle of the chest, exit wound below the left scapula. He didn't have as much meat on him as the first victim, or else it might have stuck in his ribcage. From the amount of blood, looks like it went straight through the heart, though again we won't know that until we open him up for a poke-around inside. You're welcome to come and spectate.'

Tom had been present at a couple of Thins' autopsies and didn't relish a repeat experience. He asked, 'Do we know where the shot came from?'

'Still working on that one.' Waller pointed past Tom's shoulder, across the park towards a thicker patch of woodland in the distance, beyond the western edge of Stanton Harcourt. 'For now, my best guess is your shooter was using the cover of those trees over there. Possibly climbed halfway up one for a better shot, judging from the angle. That's where I'd have done it from.'

Tom turned to gaze at the faraway trees and said, 'Seems like a hell of a long way.'

Waller nodded. 'It's a fair old distance. A long range shot like that indicates a lot of training. A skilled marksman, at any rate.'

'Military?' Tom wondered.

'Maybe. Maybe not. There are plenty of civilian shooters who could do the job. Hunters, stalkers, the target sports brigade who go down to Bisley to punch bullseyes at a thousand metres.' Waller gave a shrug. 'Then again, I could be wrong. The shot might not have come from there at all. It's virtually impossible to calculate the trajectory from this end, since the projectile could have been deflected way off course by the first impact.' He looked gravely at Tom. 'Forensic ballistics is a dark and mysterious art, Inspector. More so than some of you fellows seem to appreciate.'

Tom appreciated it, but a moment later they were joined by someone who didn't. Forbes had caught the last few words of their conversation as he came striding over, and now butted in like the smart-arse he was. 'That woodland must be five hundred yards away. Much too far for a shot like that.'

'Three hundred and eighty,' Thins corrected him. 'Unless you have a more accurate eye than my laser rangefinder, Superintendent.'

Forbes shook his head. 'Still, it's quite unfeasible. My bet is he was over that way instead.' He motioned towards a row of nearby houses, making a line with his arm that was twenty degrees north of the distant trees. 'Probably hid in someone's garden.'

'I'm inclined to agree with Thins,' Tom said. 'The woodland cover would have given him a better shot and less chance of being spotted. Not to mention a clean egress. He could be miles away before anyone knew what was happening.'

'It's nothing more than a wild guess,' Forbes replied acidly. 'I don't suppose you've had the gardens searched, have you, Inspector?' he added, fixing Tom with a cold stare.

'I just got here. Sir.'

'Then it's just as well I turned up, isn't it? Get it done right away.' Forbes marched off to oversee his legions.

'How that man ever came to achieve the rank he has,' Waller said, shaking his head as he watched him go, 'I shall never comprehend. The Freemasons, I expect.' He looked at Tom with an amused twinkle. 'So, Inspector, are you going to take heed of your superior's wisdom and have those gardens checked?'

'I'm going with your idea of those woods first, Thins. If I dispatch a couple of PCs up there, can you spare a few of your team to check the place out for evidence?' If they could find a spent cartridge case among the trees, it would be one in the eye for Forbsie, and no mistake.

Waller smiled. 'Consider it done.'

Tom left him to his work and collared a couple of uniforms to delegate his orders to. He had too much on his own plate to spend time trudging around in the woods. Then he walked over to rejoin Billie, who was finishing up taking a statement from one of the witnesses: the young mother who'd been closest to the victim when he was shot. The woman was anxious to leave, red-eyed and upset and tightly clutching her little girl's hand. The child was clutching a floppy teddy to her side. Billie spoke gently and reassuringly. She was single with no kids of her own, but had a good way with children.

Tom kept at a distance until Billie had finished, and a female uniformed officer led the mother and child to a car to take them the short distance to their home.

Tom had seen enough of this place. He said to Billie, 'Let's go.'

CHAPTER FIVE

On the drive back to the office Billie filled him in on what she'd learned. 'Mrs Byrne – that's the little girl's mother – didn't have a lot to tell us that we don't already know. She'd seen Eddie Blake in the children's play area a few times before. No indication that he was up to anything suspicious. She thought he seemed like a sweet old man.'

'It's the sweet ones you need to look out for,' Tom said. 'Did anyone in the village know about his background?'

'His neighbours certainly didn't. A couple of constables have been over and talked to them. I don't think the local residents would have been so well disposed towards dear sweet Eddie if they'd known they had a convicted kiddie molester in their midst.'

'You can say that twice,' Tom said. 'But it's one thing to take a dim view of them, and another thing to start going around picking them off like fish in a barrel with a high-powered rifle.'

They'd got back to St Aldate's and were walking from the car when Tom's mobile buzzed. It was Thins Waller, sounding immensely pleased with himself as he delivered news that stopped Tom dead in his tracks.

'Bingo. We found it in the woods, right where we said. A shiny brass .300 Blackout ejected casing, freshly fired and smelling of burnt powder. I do love a whiff of nitrocellulose, don't you?'

The discovery of an ejected casing indicated that the bullet that punched Eddie Blake's ticket had come from a semiautomatic rifle. It also confirmed, beyond much doubt, Tom's belief that the two killings had been carried out by the same shooter. Comparing the bullets for a match would be just a formality now. 'Jesus, that was fast work.'

'Chance discovery. It was buried among the leaves a couple of feet from the tree that I reckon he made the shot from. I'm sure he wouldn't have left it there on purpose, but he didn't have time to hang around hunting for it. Our boy may very well have slipped up there.'

'Prints?' Tom asked hopefully.

'None visible, but we might get a DNA trace. I'm on it.'

'When will you know?'

'This is science, dear boy. Not to mention, the lab's got a backlog as long as your arm. Could take a few days.'

'Keep me posted.'

An hour later, seated at his desk, Tom grabbed his coffee mug and took a long swig. The coffee was nasty and cold, but he needed the fortification for what he was about to read. Across the open-plan office space Billie was sitting quietly absorbed in her screen. Now and then she tapped at her keyboard, her fingers skipping over the keys like an organist's. Tom distractedly watched her for a moment, then took a breath and opened up the file on Eddie Blake.

The man's life story was a squalid little journey through the heart of darkness. Once upon a time he'd been a primary school teacher in Bristol, until his unsavoury predilection for little girls had come to the notice of the educational authorities and he'd been fired. This early disgrace had been kept secret from his first wife, Moira, whom Blake married after retraining as a litho printer and moving to High Wycombe. That marriage had produced no kids, and then had come to an end after Blake's first conviction for possessing child pornography.

From there it was the usual sordid tale of prison spells followed by further offences, followed by more prison spells. But Eddie seemed to be one of those individuals who could wile and charm their way around people, and despite his repulsive track record he'd managed to seduce a second wife, Jacqui, into believing that he was a reformed character. Jacqui, who had come into the relationship with a little daughter from a prior marriage, found the truth out when she caught him interfering with eight-year-old Melanie in her bedroom. Another divorce; another prison stretch; and out he'd come again, apparently cured of his sickness and eager to rejoin society as a responsible and trustworthy citizen. He'd managed to carry off that act for a long time, as nearly fifteen years had gone by with no further arrests or convictions. Even his estranged ex-wife Jacqui and his former victim Melanie, now in her early twenties and a single parent living in the south Oxfordshire town of Didcot with her mother, had found it within their hearts to forgive him, let him back into their lives and even allowed him to visit their home.

Not a smart move, as it turned out. One summer's morning in 2019 when Melanie was at work and Jacqui was alone in the house looking after her toddler granddaughter, Eddie came a-calling. While Jacqui went to the kitchen to make tea, Eddie slipped into the room where one-year-old Shona was sleeping peacefully in her cot, unzipped his trousers and began to set about his old ways.

Thankfully, he'd been caught in the act before things had

gone too far. When the police showed up to arrest Eddie, they had to physically restrain Jacqui from murdering him with a kitchen knife.

Tom puffed his cheeks and rubbed his eyes. What were you supposed to do with these people? Apart from drill them through with a bullet, that was. He briefly wondered whether he should bring in Jacqui or Melanie, to find out what more they might be able to tell him. But then he dismissed the idea. Short of considering two ordinary women as suspects in a skilled sniper assassination, it seemed pretty unlikely they'd be able to shed any significant light on the case. Nor were they likely to shed any tears over the deceased. Tom pictured himself asking them if they knew of anyone who might have wanted to harm poor, sweet Eddie. No line of questioning could be more lame, and nothing could be more predictable than their reply: 'Anyone with a child would be his enemy. I'm glad he's dead. He had it coming, and I only wish someone would have done it years ago.'

Tom was still deep in thought when Billie came over to his desk, waving a printout of a police statement that had just pinged across to her terminal. 'Sorry to interrupt. Something's come in. You should read this.'

'I'm sick of reading. Summarise it for me.'

Mark and Mandy Whitworth, a couple from Stanton Harcourt who had been out walking their dog along the paths close to the village shortly after eleven that morning, had come forward to report hearing a strange popping sound coming from the woods, like a muffled crow banger or a balloon bursting. Moments later, they'd seen a strange figure running down a lane, about quarter of a mile from the play park.

Tom's ears pricked up. Quarter of a mile was four hundred yards, give or take. He asked, 'The woods where Thins found the cartridge?'

Billie nodded. 'He was carrying something in a long bag

and they thought he was a fisherman at first. It's not far from the river. But something about his behaviour seemed odd. After they heard what had happened, they called the police.'

'Description?'

'Bit of a discrepancy between their statements,' Billie said, frowning at the printout. 'Mandy Whitworth says he was tall, over six foot, and heavily built. Mark Whitworth reckons he was smaller, say five-nine, and lighter. They agreed he was dressed unusually heavily for the hot weather, some kind of padded or quilted jacket. He was wearing a baseball cap but they couldn't agree on what colour. He says black, she says blue.'

Tom nodded. It was the usual story from the helpfully observant public. Eyewitness accounts could be wildly conflicting. 'Did they see which way he went?'

Billie shook her head. 'Said he was some way away and they had the sun in their eyes. They only saw him for a moment, then he was gone.'

'If he was heading back to his car he could have gone anywhere.'

'So he knows his way around the lanes and footpaths. Local guy?'

'Or just a fisherman,' Tom said. 'Who's now sitting watching this on the TV news same as everyone else. Not a lot to go on, is it?'

'Something else, too,' Billie said. 'I was about to tell you, when the Whitworths' statement came in.'

'Tell me what?'

She handed him another sheet of paper. 'Take a look at this. I've been doing a bit of digging and it turns out that both Jameson and Blake attended Metcalfe House at around the same time.'

Tom knew the place. It was a halfway house in Summertown, to the north of Oxford city, that discreetly posed as a rehabilitation clinic to disguise its real purpose. Which was to take in newly-released sex offenders, subject them to various psychological assessments and then reintegrate them back into the community, fully rehabbed and clean as a whistle. Just like Eddie Blake. Tom felt like making an acerbic remark, but held his tongue.

'I'm wondering if maybe they knew each other?' Billie suggested.

'Or someone else knew both of them, more to the point,' Tom said. 'Good work, Billie. Get on the phone and see if there's someone there I can go and talk to.'

'Already taken care of it,' Billie replied, allowing herself a little smirk of satisfaction. 'I spoke to an assistant for a Dr Fielding, one of their chief clinical psychologists. They were happy to give you an interview this afternoon.'

'Over in Summertown?'

'No, at E Wing at Bullingdon. Dr Fielding runs sessions there twice a month.' Billie was talking about the special Edgware Unit of HM Prison Bullingdon, located in Arncott, about fourteen miles northeast of Oxford. E Wing was home to several hundred 'vulnerable prisoners' who were required to take part in SOPT or Sex Offender Treatment Programme therapy during their incarceration.

Tom groaned. 'This afternoon? It's an hour round trip to Bullingdon and it takes almost that bloody long to get inside.'

'Sorry, boss. Couldn't be helped. Dr Fielding's schedule is chock-a-block and that was the only slot they could fit us in.'

'Okay,' he grumped. 'What time?'

'Three o'clock.'

He looked at his watch. 'Christ, then I'd better shift my arse over there pronto.'

CHAPTER SIX

Tom met with heavy traffic on the way to Bullingdon. An articulated lorry had overturned on a roundabout on the Oxford ring road and spilled its cargo all across both lanes, causing a logjam that went on for miles and made him wish he was driving a real police car. There was nothing like blues and twos for cutting a swathe through traffic. Running badly late, he sped through the prison gates and impatiently endured the reception process for a visiting police officer, surrendering his phone to the gate officer and then being escorted inside.

Tom's meeting with Dr Fielding had been arranged to take place in an office on the fourth floor of E Wing's administrative section. Whether it was the warm, muggy weather or his flustered state after rushing to get here, he was pouring with sweat and his shirt was sticking to his back as he hurried across a lobby towards the lift. He reached it just as the door was closing, put on a spurt of speed and managed to force through the gap just in time.

'Jesus,' he muttered to himself, jabbing the button for the fourth floor; then he realised that he wasn't alone in the lift.

His fellow passenger was a woman – a particularly

attractive woman, he found it impossible not to notice – smartly dressed and carrying a briefcase. She was tallish, about five-eight in her low heels. She was wearing a dark suit crimped at the middle to show a slim waist. He noticed that the collar of her crisp white blouse was high, kind of oriental-style. It was open enough at the neck to show a glint of a fine gold chain. As the door glided shut and the lift began to rise, she smiled at him and nodded a polite greeting. White teeth, perfectly even. Hazel eyes. Chestnut hair with reddish highlights, shoulder-length and shimmering under the centre panel light in the lift ceiling.

Tom smiled back, then realised that he was staring and turned away to gaze studiously at the floor indicator panel on the wall. Neither of them spoke. The lift climbed on. First floor; silence. Second floor; silence.

Then the lift chugged to a sudden, faltering stop between floors. In the next moment, the ceiling light and wall panel both went out and the lift was plunged into total darkness.

'Shit,' Tom said. 'I don't believe it.'

He heard the woman's voice close by in the dark. 'Don't worry,' she said calmly. 'This happens sometimes. It's an old building.'

'I'm not worried about the lift,' he replied. 'I'm late for my three o'clock appointment.'

'They'll get it going in a minute,' she said in the same level, reassuring voice. Tom liked the sound of it. It seemed to soothe his agitated state of mind. Her calmness was infectious.

'Funny thing about lifts,' he said after a pause. 'When they're running smoothly everybody's a stranger. The thing stops dead and the lights go out, suddenly we're talking.'

'Survival mechanism,' she said. 'Sense of community. We're in it together now.'

'I'm okay with that,' he said. 'You work here?'

'Sometimes,' she said.

'There's no way you're a prison officer,' he said.

'You can tell that in the dark?' She chuckled. He liked the sound of that, too. 'What was your appointment?' she asked.

'Oh, I've come to meet some egghead clinical psychologist.'

'"Egghead" is an interesting choice of words,' she commented. 'You have an issue with psychologists?'

'*Issue* sounds like a psychology term,' he said.

'So you know all about it. But you don't like them.'

Now Tom sensed a gentle challenge in her voice that he didn't find quite as soothing as before. 'I have no problem with them,' he replied, trying not to sound defensive. 'As a matter of fact I'm seeing one myself. A different kind. More like a shrink, I suppose you'd call him.'

'Good for you. How's that working out?'

'I've only had the one session,' he answered. 'Too early to say.' He was astonished at the candour of his reply. He never normally opened himself up to strangers. He felt strangely naked, exposed, even in the darkness.

'So what seems to be the problem?' she asked.

He paused a long time, aware of the half-joking tone in her question but wondering if she was making fun of him. He hovered on the brink of snapping back something like 'Mind your own frigging business, lady,' but that might have sounded confrontational. 'I don't think I have that much of a problem,' he said. After a beat he added, 'Some folks at work think I have a problem with anger.'

'I see. And do you?'

This was beginning to sound like therapy with Harvey Pepper, Tom thought.

He should have twigged the reason why, but he didn't.

'Depends what you mean by anger,' he said. 'Like wanting to tear people's arms out of their sockets angry? Not really. Only now and then.'

'Interesting,' she said. 'I'm wondering what side of the bars

40

you belong on. If this is a clever prison break, shouldn't you be heading down instead of up?'

'Nothing like that,' he said. 'I'm a cop.'

'Ah, that explains everything. It's okay for you, you have the law on your side.'

'I'm sorry I said it,' he said after another pause. 'I don't know why I did,' he added truthfully. He felt like an idiot for revealing so much of himself.

Just then, the lights came back on and the lift jerked into motion with a whoosh of hydraulics.

'Here we go,' she said. 'Told you it wouldn't take long. So what's this egghead called?'

'Fielding. He works at the rehab centre in Summertown, runs some kind of SOPT sessions here at Bullingdon.'

'As it happens, I know Dr Fielding. Pretty well, in fact.'

Now Tom felt even more of an idiot. 'Shit. You'll keep the egghead bit quiet, I hope.'

'Don't worry about it, Detective Inspector McAllister. I won't breathe a word.'

He stared at her. 'Are you Dr Fielding's assistant?'

She looked back at him. A smile. 'No, I work even more closely with Dr Fielding than that. I'm him. Or more correctly speaking, I'm her. Wouldn't like to misgender myself.'

'*You're* Dr Fielding?'

'I'm Desdemona Fielding. But maniacs and rapists call me Desi.'

'So what do I call you?'

'You can call me *Dr*.' She smiled again. The lift juddered to a halt. They'd reached the fourth floor. 'This is me,' she said.

'Me too,' he said.

'Then I guess I'll see you later, Detective Inspector.'

'Can't we talk now?'

She looked at her watch, shook her head. 'Sorry. It so happens I'm running late myself. Can you wait until my session

41

is over? It's just thirty minutes. You're welcome to observe, if you like. They've got a little viewing booth with two-way glass. Just tell the guard and they'll let you in.'

'What kind of session is it?' he asked.

'Today I'll be speaking with a Mr Driscoll. One of my more recalcitrant repeat offenders. He's currently on his fourth consecutive stay here at Bullingdon. Here, tell you what.' She opened up her briefcase and pulled out a card folder. 'Some background reading. You might find it interesting.'

'Thanks,' he said, not sure if he really wanted to know.

'Afterwards, I'm all yours.'

'Have fun,' Tom said. She gave him a last smile before she headed briskly off down a corridor, where a guard was waiting. He watched her go.

And if he'd known at that moment what lay in store for him, he'd have turned around and walked away, right then. And maybe got himself a different job, while he was at it.

CHAPTER SEVEN

Tom watched through the two-way mirror as Dr Desi Fielding sat across a laminate table from a prisoner dressed in standard-issue sweatshirt and jogging pants. Desi's blouse was buttoned all the way up to the neck now. The eye of a video camera was surveilling the interview and a speaker grille by the glass relayed the audio from a microphone into the viewing room.

Tom didn't much care for the way the interview was set up. The prisoner had his back to the only door in the square, stark room. The nearest prison officer was six feet away on the other side of it, a long way away from Desi. Tom glanced again at the file she'd given him. It was thirty pages long. Just glancing through it cursorily had made him wince. And he'd thought he was used to this crap.

The prisoner's name was Clive Driscoll. He was white, born in Essex, brown hair, brown eyes, thirty two years old, five-six, whippy and lean, and he was a paedophile two years into his current sentence. The oldest child on his long list of victims was eleven. The youngest was three.

The session had been underway for just fifteen minutes,

and already Tom couldn't wait for it to end. His mouth was dry and his muscles were clenched.

'I dreamed about Kirsty again last night,' Driscoll was saying. A quick dart of pink as he ran his tongue across his lips. His body language was full of confidence and swagger.

'Kirsty. She was the third little girl you raped. In 2013.' Desi Fielding didn't need to refer to her notes.

'Yes, that's right,' Driscoll said, quite openly and without any trace of remorse in his tone. He smiled. He fell silent and seemed to be playing the memory back in his mind.

'We can learn a lot from our dreams,' Desi said. 'Perhaps you'd like to describe it to me?' Her voice sounded calm, controlled, neutral.

'No, I wouldn't,' Driscoll answered. There was a dangerous flare in his eyes as he said it.

'That's fine, Clive,' Desi replied patiently. 'Then tell me instead, how does it make you feel to remember Kirsty – when you think about what happened?'

Driscoll wiped his lips with his sleeve. 'Makes me feel good. I remember it like yesterday. I think about it all the time.'

'Then let's talk about that. If you're comfortable with it.' Like she was challenging him and luring him at the same time, yet all the time keeping him in his safe zone. Dr Fielding certainly knew how to play this game.

Driscoll shrugged, happy to retell the story. 'I was staying with a friend. He was divorced and he had custody of his daughter for the weekend. She was eight. So sweet. But she could be a right little bitch. She did things...' his voice trailed off. His face gave a twitch.

'What things, Clive?' Desi asked.

'Things that pissed me off,' he went on. 'Like the thing she did with the spoon. She had this cup of tea. It was like that herbal stuff, raspberry or something. No milk. You just add hot water. You have to wait for it to cool before you can drink it.

She left a spoon in it. Metal spoon. The spoon got hot. Hot enough to burn you, know what I mean? I was sleeping on the couch. I think I'd been watching the TV. She came over to me and took the spoon out of the cup and pressed it against my face. Here. Look. See?'

Driscoll pointed to his right cheekbone, as though he had some terrible scar to show. There was nothing there.

'You felt that she'd hurt you,' Desi said. 'Crossed the line, is that right?'

'Oh yeah, and it made me very angry. I didn't do anything, I didn't say anything to her. I waited until later. That night I had a few more beers with her dad. He was drunk, but I stayed sober. When he was asleep I crept up the stairs. I sneaked into her room and I raped her in her bed. It went on for a long time. I kept my hand over her mouth to make her stay quiet.' Driscoll's voice had sunk to a whisper. It trailed off into silence. He licked his lips and moved his eyes from side to side, as though he was imagining with relish the details of what he'd done.

'You ripped her,' Desi said through the silence. 'Caused permanent damage to her little body. She won't be able to have children, Clive. Not ever, in her whole life. Because of what you did. What do you think about that?'

Driscoll's face darkened. He said nothing for a minute. Then he smiled as though a thought had occurred to him. 'You want to know what I'm thinking?' he said.

'That's what I'm here for.'

'All right, then I'll tell you what I'm thinking.' Driscoll reclined comfortably in his plastic chair. He would have rocked it back on its hind feet, but it was bolted to the floor. He stretched his legs out in front of him and meshed his fingers together across his chest. 'I'm thinking that you have nice thick hair,' he said. 'And how I could get my fingers into it. I could curl my fingers tight, tight, tight into those lovely locks.

Then I'd smash your head down on this table, very hard. And I'd keep doing it until the screaming stopped. What do *you* think about that?'

Tom felt his heart quicken and his fingertips whitened on the edge of the file. The door stayed shut. *Where was the frigging officer?* Come on, people! Dr Fielding was in a closed room with a prisoner whose record said he had a habit of attacking anyone he felt was annoying him. He was between her and the door, and there was no way she could get past him without him grabbing her. The door was still shut. The guard outside seemed a million miles away.

Tom waited, almost breathless, to see how she would react. Her body language stayed the same, but he could see a tiny change in her eyes. He knew that if she said the wrong thing to Driscoll, he was coming over the table at her. She knew it too: Tom could see it in her expression. He'd be on her before the guard could come in. By the time they pulled him off, he could have seriously injured her.

She looked coolly across the table at the rapist, then reached out and pressed a buzzer button on her side. 'I think that's it for today, Clive. Session's over.'

She stood up and gathered up her things. The door opened and the prison officer, joined by another, came in to escort Driscoll back to his cell. As they led him away he kept staring back over his shoulder at her, the look on his face halfway between a sneer and a glower. Desi followed, calm, maintaining eye contact with him.

And Tom was able to start breathing again. Something felt loose in his hands. He looked at the file he'd been clutching, and saw that it was torn in half.

CHAPTER EIGHT

'How do you handle it?' Tom asked her. They'd decided to shift their meeting from the office to a nearby staff canteen, and were sitting at a small corner table with Styrofoam cups of coffee that was as foul as the stuff the vending machine at the police station vomited out. The plastic chairs were identical to the ones in the interview room, except that they weren't bolted down.

It was hot in the canteen, sunlight burning through the broad windows. Beyond the perimeter fence, the fields rolled away into the distance. Tom was sweating. Desi had taken off her jacket and draped it neatly over the back of her chair. He kept his eyes away from the slender figure he could see under her blouse. Her forearms were tanned and toned. She emptied two containers of cream and two paper tubes of Demerara sugar into hers and stirred it up with a plastic spoon. Tom approved of the fact that she didn't use artificial sweetener.

'It's part of my job,' she replied to his question. 'I don't like hearing what they have to say, but you have to let them talk. It's what therapy is all about.'

'So they're supposed to just talk themselves better?' he said. 'Accessing the unconscious mind, that kind of idea?'

'Something like that,' she replied. 'Sometimes we do one-to-one like today; sometimes it's group therapy where they're encouraged to share their feelings with the others, like a support group. In low-risk situations we sometimes bring in the victims, and they talk about what happened. It can get very emotional.'

'It all sounds very cosy. But do they get better?'

'Some do,' she said.

'And the scumbag you were talking to today, will he get better?' Tom asked. He was still fuming from watching Driscoll threaten her, and remembering the smirk on the guy's face when they'd led him off back to his cell. 'Looks to me like he's spent the last two years enjoying the same old fantasies that put him in here this time around, and the time before, and the time before that, and rehearsing in his mind what he'll do all over again when he gets out.'

'You can't know that for sure.'

'You've seen the reoffence stats. I'd say it's a fair bet that the likes of Driscoll aren't going to be cured by some touchy-feely therapy programme. Then it becomes the police's job to put the bastard back inside again, but only after three, maybe four, maybe a dozen more little girls have paid the price of his freedom. And maybe it's just a question of time before we find a dead one in the boot of his car.'

If she was offended by the frankness of his views, she didn't show it as she sipped her coffee, eyeing him thoughtfully over the brim of the foam cup. He watched the way her slender fingers were pinching the sides of the cup in. Her nails were perfect and shiny red. As she raised her arm to drink, a tiny gold watch slipped down her wrist and caught the sunlight from the window.

She replied, 'We can only do what we can, Inspector. In my

line of work you learn to accept the fact that the Clive Driscolls of this world will always exist, no matter what we try to do to rehabilitate them. The system doesn't always produce perfect results, but it's the only system we have. What else are we supposed to do, march them out at dawn and put them in front of a firing squad with a hood over their head?'

'Wouldn't be a bad idea,' Tom said. 'Except I wouldn't let them have the hood.'

'Are you serious?'

'If it takes these scumbags out of the game permanently, it gets my vote. Show me a better way to guarantee a zero reoffence rate.'

'You wouldn't be the only one who thinks that way,' she said. 'Like the person you're supposed to be trying to catch, for instance. Maybe you think he's doing the world a favour.'

Tom shrugged. 'Just because it's my job to catch him, doesn't mean I can't privately approve.'

'You're honest, at least. Perhaps a little too honest, Inspector. Should you really be telling me this?'

'Doesn't matter what I think,' Tom said. 'I've still got a job to do, and this guy is going down.'

'Confident as well as honest,' she said with a half-smile. 'So, how is the investigation going?'

'I'm close,' he replied.

'No, you're not. You're nowhere near close.'

He looked at her. 'What makes you think that?'

'Because you're here talking to me,' she replied. 'When you could be knocking on doors and hauling in suspects for interrogation. I'm assuming there aren't any, at this point?'

'I'm simply pursuing every line of inquiry,' Tom told her, aware of sounding a little officious.

'From what I've read and heard about this case, it sounds as though you're dealing with a pretty smart operator. Maybe he's too smart to let himself get caught so easily.'

'Not that smart,' Tom said. 'He's already made one mistake.'

Desi Fielding raised a curious eyebrow. 'Really? I hadn't heard that. What kind of mistake?'

Tom told her about the cartridge case found at the scene of the second murder, and the possibility of getting a DNA trace.

'DNA records are pretty sketchy,' she said. 'We're still a long way from having complete government files on every citizen in the country, thank God. I'm not sure I'd want to live in that world.'

'True, but once we have a suspect, we might get a match-up,' Tom explained. 'It's a start.'

'But until then, you don't have any idea who you're looking for.'

Tom nodded. 'Nope,' he admitted. 'Right now I haven't got a clue who he could be. All I know is that he's two up, both of them registered paedos, he's a skilled shooter with an untraceable weapon and he's leaving them where he finds them.'

'There's an interesting question,' she said. '*How* is he finding them?'

'That's what I hoped you could help me with,' he said. 'You knew both victims, didn't you?'

'Yes, I conducted therapy sessions with Eddie Blake and Ray Jameson at Metcalfe House, individually and within a group context. Their periods of residency there overlapped by a couple of months, so both men were present at a few of those sessions.'

'How well did they know one another?'

'I don't recall that they ever sat together in a group session,' Desi Fielding replied. 'Nor did I get the impression they were particular friends, but who can tell? As to whether they kept in touch afterwards, I wouldn't be able to say. Why do you ask?'

'Just in case there might be some common denominator

here,' Tom said. 'Apart from them both being convicted perverts.'

'That's not the word we use, Inspector.' Gently berating him.

Tom brushed that off and asked, 'Did they ever talk about any threats made against them? Express any fears that anyone might harm them?'

'That's a pretty common concern for any former sex offender about to be released into the community,' she said. 'None of them have any illusions about the reception they'd get, if their record became local knowledge. It's a highly inflammatory subject with the public, not surprisingly. But if you're asking about specific threats, then no, neither Eddie nor Raymond ever said anything to me about that. You should talk to the families. They might be able to tell you more. I suppose, in your shoes, I'd be looking at the victims' families too. Though I guess that the chances of a vengeful relative targeting both victims must be pretty slim. Then of course it still doesn't explain how the killer was able to track them down.'

'We're working on it,' Tom said, perhaps a little too curtly.

'Sorry. Not trying to tell you your job. From my angle, the concern here is that someone on the outside clearly has access to extremely sensitive information. The details of where rehabilitated sex offenders are relocated in the community are meant to be highly confidential, for obvious reasons. So the question is, where did the leak come from? Not from within my organisation, that's for sure. We work hard to protect our people.'

'Even after what they've done,' Tom said.

'Even after what they've done. Absolutely. If you can't believe in human redemption, in the capacity for even the worst sinner to repent and mend their ways, then what can you believe in?'

'You really mean that?' he asked her.

'Of course I do,' she replied. Her expression was completely earnest.

He shook his head. 'I couldn't do your job.'

'That makes two of us, because I wouldn't want yours either,' she said with a smile. 'Sounds like you've got your work cut out for you, Inspector McAllister.'

'Call me Tom, Dr Fielding.'

'Okay, Tom. And you call me Desi.'

'Like the rapists and the maniacs.'

'I do have friends, as well,' she said.

'It was nice to meet you, Desi.'

'And you. I'm sorry I couldn't be of any more use.'

'Not at all,' he replied. 'You've been very helpful. And it's good to get out of the office.'

'Speaking of which,' she said, glancing at her watch. 'I should be getting back to Summertown.'

'And it's back to the cop shop for me,' Tom replied sadly. He regretted that their meeting was over. Even though he'd never met her before, he felt comfortable in her company and he could have sat for hours talking to her about everything under the sun that wasn't work-related.

They left the cafeteria. Tom had been hoping that they'd ride back down in the lift together. He was even hoping that it might break down again, trapping them inside for a few more hours. But it wasn't to be. Pausing outside in the corridor, Desi said she had to have a word with one of the prison administrators before she left. Tom reluctantly said goodbye, gave her a card and asked her to call him if she thought of anything. As they parted ways, he headed alone towards the lift feeling strangely saddened and lonely. Reaching the lift he turned to see her disappearing up the corridor.

And that, he supposed, was the last he would see of Dr Desi Fielding.

CHAPTER NINE

Tom got home just before sunset that evening, feeling frustrated and restless over his lack of progress with the case. But as much as his head was filled to bursting point with all the unanswered questions that he knew would keep him from sleep that night, what seemed to dominate his thoughts even more was the memory of his meeting with Desi Fielding.

He didn't seem to be able to shut her out. What was up with that? It puzzled him. Normally, when Tom felt drawn to a woman, his impulses weren't particularly subtle or hard to interpret. It was just a matter of asking her out, and whether she was up for it. Yes or no. Black and white. No messing around. That was how it had been with Suzie Green and all the others. But with Desi Fielding it was different, somehow.

Psychology stuff, he thought to himself. Maybe he was going soft in the head. He wondered whether he should mention it to Harvey Pepper at their next session. Harvey might have some useful insights. Maybe even a cure.

It was a peaceful evening. It was always peaceful here. Tom changed out of his work clothes and took Radar for a walk down the grassy riverbank from the cottage. He stood by the river awhile, watching the last of the rich sunset colours ripple on the water and make shimmering reflections against the stones of the old watermill. He had plans for the watermill. One day he was going to make them happen. One day.

He sighed and tried to savour the moment as he listened to the birds' evensong before they curled up to sleep in their nests, and to the restful slurp and slosh of the water against the riverbank. He wanted to drink in the tranquillity, let it absorb into his soul. He needed all the tranquillity he could get, because tomorrow was another day.

As darkness fell, he walked back up to the cottage and thought about dinner.

Tom's greatest passion wasn't for policing, for solving crimes, not even for bringing justice to the world. He was too jaded to believe much in that any more. No, his one true love was cooking, and his dream was to quit the force one day and go pro. Few of his colleagues knew his secret, apart from Billie, on whom he occasionally tried out a new recipe.

Tonight, though, he was just too dog tired and preoccupied to do anything fancy. In his rustic and slightly chaotic but very well-equipped kitchen he poured himself a pint of his beloved Langtree Hundred ale in a stone tankard and drank half of it down with extreme relish. Smacking his lips, he grabbed one of his expensive Misono chef knifes from the block and set about expertly dicing an onion into perfect little cubes. With the onion set aside he trimmed four rashers of unsmoked back bacon. He put a big pot of water on the range to boil, salted just right. Then started gently frying the onion cubes in olive oil. When they were soft he added the bacon. A little seasoning, a dash of wine.

He paused to admire the colour. Looking good already. He beat a free-range egg, yesterday's egg from the farm up the lane, into a bowl along with some fresh double cream and a judicious grind of sea salt and black pepper. When the water was boiling he grabbed a fistful of spaghetti and plonked it into the pot, all sticking out like straw, and swirled it around with a fork. As he waited for the pasta to cook he finished his Langtree and poured more of the wine into a glass. A special-reserve Cabernet, much too good to cook with, really.

Now it was action stations as he heated up the bacon and onion mixture, strained off the spaghetti, tossed a heap of it into the pan and then threw in the beaten egg, whisking it around quickly with the fork before it curdled, so that the pasta was all nicely coated in that lovely glistening texture. Spaghetti alla carbonara, one of the quickest pasta dishes to whiz up, and just about the best, in his book. Some people were freaked out by the raw egg – but they just didn't appreciate proper food. He grated a sprinkling of parmesan cheese over his dish and carried it over to his table in the living room, with his wine.

And in that moment, Detective Inspector Tom McAllister was in heaven.

Next morning was a different story. He was up early, fed the dog, slurped a coffee, then put on his best suit and jumped into the Barracuda. He was dreading the morning, because today, in the wake of the second murder, a big press conference was being held at St Aldate's station, and he was going to be firmly in the limelight.

Tom wasn't nervous because of the public speaking, or the TV cameras – you got used to that. It was knowing that the conference was going to be splashed all over social media and streamed live on YouTube. It was sure to receive millions of views, by far the biggest audience he'd ever appeared in front of. One dramatic paedophile murder had been a big enough media story. As the news of a second spread across the internet and TV networks like wildfire, the press hounds were going berserk.

Billie greeted him at the station. 'Ready for your big appearance?'

'As ready as I'll ever be. How do I look?'

'Like classic Liam Neeson meets Brendan Gleeson,' she said. 'Hold on, let me straighten your tie for you.'

'Brendan Gleeson's an old fat guy.'

'It's the rugged look. Women love it.'

'Do they?'

'Nervous?'

'A little bit,' he admitted.

'You'll be fine. Just try not to blow up at anyone.'

'Oh, thanks for reminding me. Maybe I should call Harvey over for a quick anger management refresher session, to get me through it.'

'Sounds like you value his input,' Billie said, smiling. 'That's good.'

'He says I'm a desperate case.'

She put on a look of feigned sympathy. 'Oh, you poor thing. Is there no hope for you at all?'

A constable appeared. 'Detective Inspector, they're asking for you.'

Tom nodded. Took a deep breath. 'Right, let's do this.'

Billie walked with Tom along a corridor where Forbes met them, looking impatient and irascible and his usual charming self. 'You'll be doing most of the talking, Inspector, so try and make a good impression, will you?'

'On my very best behaviour. Sir.'

The conference was being held in a room set up specially for the event. A screen with the Thames Valley Police crest emblazoned on each side stood behind a table covered in fluffy microphones and trailing wires. A BBC camera crew were making their final sound and lighting adjustments, while a gang of IT techies were fiddling with monitors and webcams and whatever it was they needed to do for the livestreaming of the event. Dozens of plastic chairs had been brought in for the press, but there were more reporters than chairs crammed as far as the back wall, filling the room with a hubbub of excitement. Perched in a ringside seat, all revved up, dyed blond hair teased to perfection and her face plastered in makeup as though she was the one appearing in front of the world, was the ever-eager Suzie Green of the Oxford Mail.

Tom, Billie and Forbes entered the room to the sound of clamour. Forbes approached the table first, glowered at the sea of faces like a stern headmaster at school assembly and asked for silence. When the buzz had died down he leaned towards the microphones and offered up the usual platitudes about shocking crimes and no stone being left unturned in the hunt for the perpetrator, etc. He managed to keep the meaningless hyperbole going for a whole minute and a half, and then handed the floor over to Tom.

Tom took his place in front of the mikes, cleared his throat and introduced himself to the room and to the world at large. 'I'm Detective Inspector Tom McAllister and I'm leading this investigation.'

In plain and dispassionate language, he laid out the bare facts of the case as they currently stood. 'Following the recent murder of Raymond Jameson we can confirm that a second similar incident occurred in the county yesterday morning, resulting in the death of Edward Blake, a seventy-three-year-old resident of Stanton Harcourt. Thames Valley Police, in association with other police forces across the country, are pursuing multiple lines of inquiry and I'm fully confident that we'll bring this case to a swift and decisive resolution.'

The questions came at him like artillery fire. The first one was predictable enough: 'Andrea Dixon, *Daily Mail*. Do Thames Valley Police have a suspect for these killings?'

Tom replied, 'As I say, we are pursuing multiple avenues of inquiry. At this time we have not narrowed our investigation to a specific suspect.' And I wouldn't tell you if we had, you daft minger, he could have added.

Suzie Green's hand had shot up to reach quivering for the ceiling, but Tom very deliberately passed her over in favour of a sharp-suited young male reporter in the third row. 'Aarush Kumar, the *Express*. Can you confirm that both attacks were carried out by the same person? Could the second be a copycat murder?'

You've been watching too many movies, Tom thought. He said, 'We're open to all possibilities here, but our forensic findings suggest a single individual at work. Next?'

'Justin Bowyer, the *Independent*. Detective Inspector, are the general public at risk from this attacker?'

Tom replied, 'We believe, based on the available evidence, that these attacks are being specifically targeted against convicted sex offenders. Hence there's no reason to be concerned that the wider public are in any danger at this time.'

'How was this person able to obtain an assault rifle? Don't Thames Valley Police have a duty to protect their citizens?'

'There's no suggestion that an assault rifle was used. And yes, of course we want to protect our citizens. That's why we're trying to catch him. Next question.' Tom pointed at another raised hand in the front row. Suzie Green was fuming.

'Brett Lucas, from the *Guardian*,' said the androgynous ginger-haired creature Tom had picked out. 'Do you feel it's irresponsible for the police to describe the victims as sex offenders, given that both Raymond Jameson and Edward Blake paid their debt to society and were rehabilitated, law-abiding citizens?'

'If I'd thought it was irresponsible I wouldn't have bloody said it, would I?' Tom nearly replied. Instead he said, in his most neutral-sounding voice, 'From the perspective of the killer, we're taking the view that he regards them very much as sex offenders, whether rehabilitated or not. That seems to be the only possible motive here. Next question?'

But Brett Lucas hadn't finished yet. 'But aren't you just stirring up hate with these inflammatory labels, Inspector? Shouldn't Thames Valley Police be taking a more progressive and responsible approach?'

'Next question,' Tom repeated more firmly, casting a look at Brett Lucas that made him shut up at last.

'Daisy Honeyghan, for the BBC. How did the killer know the whereabouts of the victims? Isn't that information meant to be kept secret?'

'I'm afraid I'm not in a position to answer that,' Tom said.

'Meaning that you don't know?' Daisy was a pushy one.

'Meaning that this is a murder inquiry and the police are limited in what we can reveal. Another question?'

Tom couldn't hold Suzie Green on her leash any longer. She blurted out, 'Detective Inspector McAllister, would it be accurate to describe this person as a vigilante killer?'

Right on the nose as usual, Suzie, Tom thought. 'That's a little too speculative for me to comment on. And I think that's enough for now. Thank you for your questions.'

CHAPTER TEN

The media were still baying for more as Tom and Billie filed out of the room. Forbes was already long gone.

'Phew. How was I?' he whispered.

'You were fine. Surprisingly calm, I thought. The therapy must be working.'

Back at his desk, Tom peeled off his jacket and slumped in his chair to check his morning deluge of emails. He'd been half-hoping he might have been sent some feedback from Thins Waller at the forensics lab, but there was nothing. Across the office space, Billie was at her cubicle looking at the conference livestream on YouTube. 'You should see this,' she called over to him.

'I don't want to see it.'

'I don't mean your stellar performance, I mean the comments.'

Tom reluctantly heaved himself from his chair and went over. She'd turned the sound off, so mercifully he didn't have to listen to his own voice. Just seeing himself on the screen was bad enough. He unconsciously put a hand against his stomach and sucked his belly in. Too much spaghetti alla carbonara.

'They started coming in the instant the video started streaming,' Billie said, shaking her head in amazement. 'Look at it. There are thousands of them. And more still pouring in so fast you can't keep up. Listen to this one: "Why are the police wasting taxpayer money chasing this man? He's a hero." And this one: "Vigilante paedo killer for Prime Minister!" "This guy gets my vote. He's cleaning up our streets. Bring it on." There's more and more. "Cops are after the wrong guy. Let him do his thing and rid the world of these evil dirtbags." "Disgusting that UK citizens aren't allowed to know if we're living on the same street as a paedophile. Bring back the death penalty!"'

'Any variations on that theme?' Tom asked.

'Not a lot that I can see,' Billie replied. 'They all seem to share pretty much the same views on the matter. It goes on and on. "These people have no right to live. Kill 'em all." "Police are protecting perverts." "Shooting's too good for these lowlifes. Hang them!" This one says, "Castrate them." Then another comes in with, "I wouldn't castrate them, I'd chop their tallywhackers off."' She looked up at Tom with innocent eyes. 'What's a tallywhacker?'

'I think you've a pretty good idea,' Tom said. 'Unless you want me to draw you a picture. Any more?'

Billie returned to the screen, smiling. 'Another's just come in. Says, "This guy McAllister—"' Her smiled dropped. 'Hm. You might not want to hear that one.'

Tom felt a hot prickle on his cheeks. 'This guy McAllister what?'

'"Should be ashamed of himself. He's probably a paedo himself."'

'That's just great.' Tom had heard enough. Fists clenched, he stumped heavily back to his desk and tried to refocus his thoughts. But no sooner had he sat down, than Forbes came stalking out of his office and called out, 'Detective Inspector McAllister, a word if you please.'

As Tom entered the office he could see the grimace of pleasure on the superintendent's face that told him there was trouble in store.

'Door,' Forbes snapped.

Tom elbowed it shut. 'What is it now? Sir.'

'Quite a creditable performance in front of the media just now,' Forbes said, easing comfortably back in his desk chair with a smile. 'You actually managed to make it sound as though you're getting somewhere with this case. Of course, you and I both know that's a long way from the truth.'

'We have the spent cartridge,' Tom replied. He felt like adding, 'Which, incidentally, was found where Thins Waller and I thought it would be. As opposed to where some gobshite said we'd find it.'

'What's the latest forensic report on that?' Forbes asked.

'Still waiting. It takes time to get a DNA result.'

'Where were you yesterday afternoon? You seemed to be absent from your desk for a considerable length of time.'

Tom could imagine Forbes sitting there staring at a hidden camera monitor, stopwatch in hand, just waiting to catch him AWOL from duty. 'I was talking with Dr Fielding from Metcalfe House, over at Bullingdon. She knew both of the victims.'

'And did anything useful come from that?'

'If she thinks of anything, she's going to call us.'

'Sounds like a lot of ifs and maybes to me,' Forbes retorted.

Tom shrugged. 'I have to follow up all the leads I can.'

'And meanwhile, your killer is liable to strike a third time as the whole world watches.'

Tom frowned. '*My* killer?'

'You're treading water, Inspector. Risking making a laughing stock out of this entire police force. To be quite frank with you, I'm not entirely sure that you were the man for such an important and responsible assignment. And I must tell you that it wasn't my decision.'

Tom said nothing. He was staring dully at Forbes's desk and wondering how hard a punch it would take to crunch the thick wooden top right in half.

'The good news is, that while you've been wasting time, I've cracked the case for you.'

Tom's frown deepened. 'What do you mean, cracked it?'

Forbes pulled open a drawer, yanked out a printed page and waved it like a victory flag. 'I mean, thanks to the fact that at least one officer in this department is on the ball, we now have the first substantial lead in what I'm confident will result in catching our man.'

Tom snatched up the paper.

'While you were running around the county yesterday, I was going through some archives,' Forbes said. 'Eight months ago, a member of the public taking part in a phone-in on Thames Valley Sound, one Terry Brennan, said that he wanted to shoot sex offenders.'

Thames Valley Sound was one of Oxfordshire's biggest and most popular independent radio stations. Forbes went on: 'The phone-in was in response to a panel discussion on the subject of the latest government treatment programme for sex offenders in prisons. Every caller has to log their name and address with the station before going on the air, and every call is recorded. Needless to say, they had no idea that Brennan was going to come out with what he did, and they cut him off.'

Brennan's exact words were quoted on the printed transcript Tom was reading. He'd managed to get as far as 'These men are vile trash and every one of them deserves to die. I'd happily blow their brains out myself, and one day I'm going to!' before the station had hit the mute button.

'Have you seen the comments on the press conference?'

Tom said. 'A lot of people feel that way. Doesn't make them killers.'

Forbes shook his head. 'Read on, Inspector. Terry Brennan just so happens to have had a son named Luke. Does that name ring any bells?'

Tom stared at the sheet. The name did sound familiar, and now it became clear why as his memory twigged it. 'Luke Brennan was one of Rafferty's victims.'

Nigel Rafferty had been an RAF cadet sergeant, convicted a few years earlier of molesting boys at the Air Cadets Witney Squadron HQ in west Oxfordshire. His method had been to befriend youths he'd singled out – all his victims were slender boys with fair hair – and, having gained their trust, to get them alone, sedate and then rape them. By the time he'd been caught in 2016, he'd clocked up nine victims, and gathered a collection of hundreds of indecent images taken while they were unconscious. Rafferty was sentenced to twenty years in prison. After being repeatedly beaten up and moved from one facility to another, he'd finally hanged himself in his cell at HMP Stafford. Predictably, public opinion hadn't expressed a great deal of sympathy for his unhappy end.

Forbes said, 'Luke Brennan was thirteen when he was first assaulted by Rafferty. Up until then he'd been a happy boy, popular at school, a star pupil, talented at sports and dreaming of becoming a fighter pilot. After the abuse he changed radically into a troubled, disenfranchised youth, doing drugs, seeing child psychiatrists, and in scrapes with the law.'

'I remember it,' Tom said. 'He died after inhaling lighter fuel. Sixteen years old.'

'Official verdict, death by misadventure,' Forbes said. 'But it doesn't take much imagination to suppose that the family would blame the abuse for the tragic change in Luke's personality.'

Tom was inclined to agree with that, though he still

couldn't see how Forbes was making the connection with this case. 'So his father, Terry Brennan, had good reason to hate child molesters and paedophiles. I get it. You can't blame him. But he's not the only one. This is a case where half the population wanted the victims dead.'

'I'll grant you that, McAllister. But not everybody is the assistant manager at the Tilsley Park Shooting Centre. Or was. Brennan left there eighteen months ago. He no longer holds a firearm certificate, but as you know the details of former FAC holders remain on our Firearms Department records. He worked at the club for seven years, a qualified range officer and a competitive rifle shot.'

Forbes leaned back in his chair, lacing his fingers behind his head and eyeing Tom with glittering satisfaction.

'So there's your suspect, Inspector. Brennan has both the motive and the skills. He couldn't take his revenge on the man who destroyed his son's life, so instead he takes it out on others who've committed similar crimes. And he'll do it again, unless we get him first. Which, I might add, was never going to happen with you in sole charge of this case.'

'I'll check it out,' Tom said. 'Ask around and see what I can find, starting with the gun club Brennan worked at. But it won't be him.'

The satisfied leer on Forbes's face disappeared and he shot forwards in his chair. 'Oh? And how can you be so sure of that?'

'Too obvious,' Tom said. 'Serious killers don't make idle threats. They just get on with killing. He wants to take out perverts like Nigel Rafferty, why set himself up to be the prime suspect by announcing it to ten thousand listeners of Thames Valley Sound? And just because he used to own a rifle on a firearms licence, it doesn't account for how he could've got hold of an unregistered semiautomatic weapon. They don't exactly grow on trees, do they? Sir.'

'It's a suspect, McAllister,' Forbes growled at him. 'Something that, until this moment, was conspicuous by its absence in your investigation. Now, you've got the eyes of the world on you, and if this killer strikes again you'll have the media howling for blood and accusing this police force of being either too incompetent or too disinterested to do anything about it. Do you want me to remove you from this case and take charge personally?'

'No, sir.'

'Then do your job and keep your mouth shut, Inspector.'

How often had Tom heard those words before? They were still ringing in his ears minutes later as he jumped into the Barracuda and burned rubber out of the city, in the direction of the Tilsley Park Shooting Centre.

CHAPTER ELEVEN

The gun club was a low, long, utilitarian red-brick building situated in the scorched countryside near Abingdon, eight miles south of the city. The centre stood back from the road, with hedged lawns that were freshly mowed and patchy yellow in places from the hot sun. The place had once been a farm, judging from the disused grain silo in the adjoining field that was used for corporate clay pigeon events. Now it was the main hub for Oxfordshire's target shooting fraternity, with indoor and outdoor ranges and its own shop selling firearms and supplies.

Tom pulled up in the car park behind, and the throb of the Barracuda echoed back at him off the red brick wall. As he walked from the car he could hear the sporadic pop-pop of muted gunfire from within. Through an entrance foyer with plastic plants, he was greeted by the welcome blast of air conditioning. Most gun clubs he'd seen were little more than Nissen huts with an earth-banked quarry range out back, but Tilsley Park SC was an upmarket kind of joint with a comfortable lounge area, complete with a coffee bar and a big stone fireplace. Tom sniffed the air and caught the aroma of fresh espresso and pastries. He was getting pecan nuts and maple syrup. The temptation hovered in front of him for a couple of instants before he revisualised himself on the YouTube video and decided he should lay off sugary confections for a while.

One wall of the lounge was a broad window of soundproof glass offering a rear view of the twenty-five-metre indoor range. At one time it had been a pistol club, before law-abiding British shooters had had that freedom taken from them. Now, the shooting that took place there was all done with lever-action carbines, like the Winchesters in every western Tom had ever seen. Four of the six lanes were in use, which accounted for the muffled pops he'd been able to hear from outside. Tom paused a moment to watch the shooters. A couple of them were reinventing the colander, peppering holes all over their circular targets, but one guy was a real crack shot in the process of cutting out the bullseye with deadly precision. Some members of the club were obviously pretty handy at punching paper. Tom wondered about the mental leap a man has to make in order to transition to shooting at the real thing.

Adjoining the lounge area was the gun shop, where racks of target rifles, hunting rifles, airguns and shotguns were on display behind security glass. Some of them were pretty high-ticket items. This was where you'd come if you had twenty-odd grand to spend on an engraved sidelock double twelve-bore to go grouse shooting with at the manor. It wouldn't be the top choice for a criminal wanting to obtain an illegal, unregistered semiautomatic rifle suited for medium-to-long-range assassination.

Tom walked over to the shop counter, where one guy was serving a customer while another was arranging colourful cartons of ammo on a shelf. He discreetly flashed his warrant card, introduced himself and asked if he could speak to the manager.

'I'm John Murray,' the manager said a moment later, emerging from a side office and looking nonplussed at this unexpected police visit. 'Can I help you, Inspector? Is there a problem?'

'No problem,' Tom said. 'But I'd like a word with you in private.'

'Of course.' Murray ushered Tom into the tiny office. 'Excuse the mess. Please, take a seat. Can I offer you some tea, coffee?'

Tom politely declined and explained that he was here regarding the centre's former employee, Terry Brennan.

Murray frowned at the mention of that name. 'Is Terry in trouble?'

'I just have a few questions you might be able to help me clear up,' Tom said. 'Have you heard from Mr Brennan recently?'

'No, not for a long time, not since he stopped working here.'

'He was asked to leave, is that correct?'

'I'm afraid so, yes. Terry was a valued member of the team for a long time, but he became . . . let's say, he became difficult to work with.'

'After his son's death.'

Murray nodded sadly. 'A terrible thing. A real tragedy. Luke was a great kid. But very troubled.'

Tom asked, 'Did Terry talk a lot about the reasons why Luke started having those problems?'

'I've known Terry for a long time,' Murray said. 'He used to be a happy-go-lucky kind of guy, always cheerful. When it came out what that pervert had been doing to Luke, it totally changed him. He never got over it. Did he talk about it? Yes, constantly. He couldn't talk about anything else. He was so filled with hate for that man. I mean, I would be too. Who wouldn't? And then, when the poor boy took his own life that way . . . it just broke him completely.'

'Mr Murray, there's something I'd like you to listen to.' Before leaving the station Tom had got a recording of Terry Brennan's radio phone-in call uploaded to his mobile. He replayed the brief audio clip for Murray. 'Can you confirm that's Terry Brennan's voice?'

'Yes, no question. It doesn't surprise me, what he said.'

'Did he express those kinds of intentions to you?'

'About wanting to kill paedophiles? Christ, yeah, plenty of times. When I heard that pervert Rafferty had hanged himself, I thought Terry might calm down a bit. But it only made him worse. He wanted them *all* dead. He'd get so worked up about it, he'd be literally foaming at the mouth. It scared me, to be honest. He'd been drinking a lot already. At that point it got totally out of control, like he was a different person. Violent, too. That's why Anne kicked him out.'

'His wife?'

Murray nodded. 'She couldn't handle him any more.'

'And he was fired from his job around the same time?'

'We all felt sorry for him, you know? Tried to support him. But it was no use.'

'Before all this happened, Mr Brennan was a keen target shooter, wasn't he?'

'Lived and breathed it,' Murray replied.

'Was he good?'

'He was one of the best I've known. He won our fullbore rifle competition almost every year, out on the thousand metre range at Bisley.'

Good enough for a fatal shot on a human target at a third of that range, Tom thought. Could they really have a suspect here? And could Forbes actually have been right? That was the part that bothered Tom the most. They'd never hear the end of it, if the gobshite cracked the case.

'I don't understand why you're asking me all this,' Murray said. 'Is something wrong? Does this have to do with the shootings that've been on the news?'

'It's just a general inquiry,' Tom said, fudging. 'Tell me, why did Terry give up his guns?'

'Because after his marriage broke up, and Anne kicked him out of the house, he didn't have anywhere to keep them any more. He spent six months living in a camper van, and the police weren't going to let him store firearms in it. He'd pretty much given up shooting already, and so then he just sold up and surrendered his licence. I think he needed the cash, to be honest. The rifles were worth a bob or two.'

'Does he still live in the camper van?'

'Last I heard, he was living in rental digs in Northmoor. Hold on, Josh is around.' Murray went to the door, poked his head out and Tom heard him say, 'Josh, would you step in here a minute?'

Josh was the younger guy who'd been serving the customer earlier. Like everyone else in the world, he went all stiff and nervous on finding himself in the presence of a plainclothes copper. You sometimes had to wonder what they all had to hide.

Murray said to him, 'You bought Terry Brennan's .308 Sako off him, didn't you?'

Josh had indeed purchased the rifle, one of the two bolt-action target weapons Brennan had possessed, and as part of the necessary paperwork for transferring a firearm between license holders he had Brennan's address recorded on his firearms certificate as the seller of the weapon. As Tom noted down the address, he could sense Murray fairly writhing with anxiety next to him. 'Is Terry a suspect?' Murray asked.

'Call it a process of elimination,' Tom replied with a smile.

He thanked them both for their time and help, and left the shooting centre.

His next port of call was going to be the address he'd been given for Terry Brennan. The drive to Northmoor was a dog-leg of about nine miles, heading out to the west of the county. As he returned to the car he considered whether he should run by the station and pick up Billie to bring along as backup, if he intended to visit an actual potential suspect. Forbes might tear another strip off him for not following protocol. Then again, Tom decided Forbes could go hang. In the event Brennan actually turned out to be their guy, he wanted to strike while the iron was hot.

Twenty-five minutes later, the iron was suddenly ice cold again.

Northmoor was a typical kind of semi-rural Oxfordshire village, with labyrinthine narrow lanes and a nice old church and a traditional pub and some fine country properties that were strictly in the millionaire department, while others were emphatically not. Tom wasn't surprised to find that the address he had for Terry Brennan was of the latter type. 'Cottage Mews' sounded romantic and villagey enough on paper, but the reality was a squalid low-rent flat-roofed conversion of an old stable, jutting like an outhouse from the back of a rundown stone cottage that belonged to probably the most ancient, and definitely the deafest, person Tom had ever had to deal with. When his knocking on the mews door didn't produce any results he walked around to the cottage to try his luck there. Mrs Casey had to be a hundred years old and was, or had been, Terry Brennan's landlady – with the emphasis on the past tense, since her tenant had moved out over a year ago, owing two hundred pounds in rent and without leaving a forwarding address, and not been heard from since, the dirty dishonest rascal. It took fifteen minutes of shouted repetitions to get that much information from the old lady, at the end of which Tom felt exhausted and walked back to the car empty-handed.

It was after midday now, and the heat of the sun was giving him a headache. Visions of a pub lunch and a cold beer tormented him like a mirage in a desert. Sitting at the wheel of the Barracuda he reached for his phone to call Billie and see if she could run a trace on a more current address for Brennan. Her number was engaged, so he left a voicemail and was just about to put his phone away when it began to burr in his hand. He thought it was Billie calling back, until he saw the unfamiliar caller ID.

'McAllister.'

'Hello, Tom,' said the voice whose sound instantly cleared away his headache. 'It's Desi Fielding.'

A dozen different responses came to him, like 'I didn't expect to hear from you so soon' or 'I was hoping you'd call' or 'This is a pleasant surprise', all of which were true, but they all rushed into his mind at once with the effect of jamming it up solid, so that he couldn't speak.

His silence didn't seem to faze her. 'I was doing some thinking after we met yesterday,' she said. 'There's something I'd like to show you. I think you'd find it interesting and maybe useful.'

'At the institute?' Tom asked, finding his tongue and trying not to sound too eager. He looked at his watch. He could be in Summertown in half an hour, and to hell with lunch.

'No, I'm working from home today. I have private clients for most of the afternoon, but I'll be free after five. Why don't you come around then?'

CHAPTER TWELVE

The sun wasn't any cooler that afternoon. Tom kept the windows down as the Barracuda rumbled under an unbroken blue sky through the village of Kennington, just south of the city. Following the directions Desi Fielding had given him, he turned off by St Swithun's Church into the narrow, tree-shaded Bagley Wood Road.

He was driving along the winding lane, wondering what she had to show him, when his phone went again. He pulled over to answer it, blocking up the road with the bulk of the car and worrying that it was Desi calling off their meeting.

He was half right. It was a cancellation, but it wasn't her.

Harvey said, 'Listen, so sorry about this, but I've got a problem. There's been a major pipe leak in my building and the landlord's sorting it out, but I'm going to have to cry off our session in the morning.'

'How about tonight instead?' Tom suggested, surprised by his own keenness.

'You'd have to bring a wetsuit and goggles. My place looks like something out of Jacques Cousteau's undersea world.'

'Then we could meet somewhere else. Do you know the Claddagh pub? Just up the road from you.'

'Oh yes, the Claddagh and I are well acquainted,' Harvey said.

'Then I'll meet you there at eight.'

Tom drove on. Bagley Wood was an ancient forest that had belonged to one of the Oxford colleges since sometime in the 1500s. At one time it had been a popular haunt of highwaymen who used to stick up coaches and travellers venturing through the woods. More than a few robbers had ended up hanging from trees. Nowadays it was an affluent area with expensive properties that peeked at Tom through the foliage as he drove by gateposts and ivied stone walls. The kind of houses his mother had always said they'd live in if they ever won the pools.

It was a little after five by the time he found her place. She lived in an impressive modern house shaped in an L, big windows and Cotswold stone, at the end of a long driveway. The lawns were neatly tended but burnt brown and yellow in places by the hot summer. Tom was surprised at the size of her home. This psychology lark must pay pretty damn well, he thought – then the thought struck him that maybe Desi Fielding was married to some rich private consultant or cosmetic dentist. For some reason he'd assumed until now that she lived alone.

He tried to banish that disheartening thought from his mind as he swung the Barracuda off the lane and pulled up next to a gleaming white convertible BMW parked on the drive. He was still wearing the same good suit he'd put on that morning for the press conference. He hoped it wasn't too rumpled from driving around all day. There was a flutter in his stomach as he walked up to the house and rang the bell. What a big eedjit I am, he thought, to be getting all nervous like this.

The door opened. Desi Fielding was taller in high heels, wearing a businesslike linen suit, and her hair was tied in a ponytail. Her welcoming smile was warm, and the entrance hall was cool as she invited him inside. He followed her down a broad passage, unable to help but notice that her legs were long and tanned below the hem of her skirt. When he spotted the little ankle chain she was wearing, his heart skipped a beat. *Get a grip on yourself, man.*

'You certainly have a beautiful house,' he said.

'Thank you,' she replied over her shoulder. 'It's much too big for one person. I kind of rattle around in it, all by my lonesome.'

'Oh,' he said with a smile, letting the image of the rich husband dissolve in his mind. 'I live alone, too.'

'Really?'

Desi paused at a door, and turned to him with an apologetic look. 'My client kept me a little late, so if you don't mind I'd like to change into something more comfortable. You can wait here in the study. I won't be a minute, okay?'

Tom wandered inside the room as she trotted up a staircase. Desi Fielding's study wasn't some poky little home office. It had high bookcases on three sides and a double arched French window, through which the sunlight gleamed on the broad expanse of polished wood floor. The window overlooked a white stone patio and a stepped lawn that sloped off towards the woods. There was a gazebo near the fence at the bottom of the garden.

In front of the window was a broad desk. On it, next to a closed laptop, a large appointments book lay open showing entries and names that Tom assumed were her private therapy clients. He noticed the vintage filing cabinet next to the desk, with little brass plaques on its drawers neatly labelled from A to Z.

Tom ran his hand along the cool back of her leather desk chair and thought about what a contrast the elegant study was with Harvey Pepper's dive of an office in Cowley. A baby grand piano stood glimmering and black in the corner, with BLÜTHNER written in gold. Its lid was raised and a book of Bach three-part inventions rested above the keyboard. Tom had never heard a Bach three-part invention, but the music looked incredibly dense and hard to play. He pressed down a couple of piano keys, drew his hand away quickly at the discordant sound, and glanced nervously towards the door.

Desi Fielding returned a moment later, humming a tune to herself as she trotted back down the stairs and breezed into the study. She'd let her hair down and was wearing tight jeans and a sleeveless tee-shirt, the high heels changed for a pair of open sandals.

'I like your study,' he said. 'You should see my office. I'd love to work in a place like this, so I would. Even your filing cabinet's classy.'

She laughed. 'Thank you. It's not just for style, though. I'm a stickler for paper records, and I keep copies of everything just in case.'

He nodded approvingly. 'It's digital everything now. I don't trust it either.'

'Phew, it's warm in here,' she said, walking over to open the French window. 'I could do with a drink. Would you like some chilled lemon tea?'

He hesitated. 'Is that any better than normal tea?'

'It's tea. Except it's chilled and it has lemon.'

He pulled a face, and she laughed. 'Do you have any coffee?' he asked.

'Of course. How do you like it?'

'Lots of cream, lots of sugar. If it's no trouble.'

She smiled. 'No trouble at all, Inspector.'

Tom strolled up and down, avoided getting too close to the piano and scanned rows of book spines that meant nothing whatsoever to him until she came back a few minutes later carrying a tray with a small continental-style coffee percolator, a cup and saucer and a tall glass of pale liquid that he guessed was her chilled tea.

'Please, do take a seat,' she said, waving him over to a plush sofa with an armchair opposite, separated by a low coffee table on an oriental rug. He sat, and the sofa seemed to swallow him up as he sank into it. She bent down to lay the tray on the coffee table; Tom averted his eyes, but not quite in time to avoid snatching a glimpse of a black bra and tanned, toned flesh. She poured steaming coffee into the cup and handed it to him. Their fingers touched momentarily as he took it.

'Thanks.'

'You're welcome.'

The cup was a tiny little delicate porcelain thing. The mugs Tom was used to slurping out of at work and at home were big, workmanlike and anything but dainty. He couldn't get his fingers through the little handle, so instead he held it in his fist like a gorilla clutching a live robin, feeling stupid and heavy and clumsy. He was terrified of dropping it as he took a sip. The coffee was hot and rich.

'Is this where you do it, then?' he asked, motioning at the sofa he was sitting on. 'The therapy sessions, I mean,' he added, blushing.

'It's good for the clients to feel at their ease. So how's it going?' she added.

'My therapy? I'm seeing him again this evening, as it happens.'

She smiled. 'I meant the case.'

'Oh, that.' Tom shrugged. 'My boss thinks he's cracked it.'

'But you obviously don't agree, or you wouldn't have come

here.' She cocked her head to one side. Doing that psychological mind-reading stuff on him again.

Tom was thinking that he'd have come here anyway, even if Terry Brennan had copped to the shootings and was behind bars. 'I don't know,' he replied. He told her about their potential suspect, the radio phone in, his firearms expertise, his motive. 'It all fits, except for one thing. Our shooter seems to know where he can find these guys. He knows where they live, stuff that's meant to be confidential. He tracks them, follows them, gets to know their movements, and then he hits them in a way that he can get away clean. That takes planning.'

'Which would imply you're looking for someone with inside information,' she said. 'Or someone who knows someone with access to it.'

'Okay, who would that be?'

'Police?'

'Don't be funny.'

'I'm not,' she said. 'You know as well as I do that plenty of law enforcement officers would jump at the chance to carry out that kind of retribution in their spare time, if they thought they could get away with it.'

'I have an alibi,' Tom joked.

'Then there's prison personnel. They're the ones that have to deal with these individuals on a daily basis, and they're often not happy to see them released. In fact there's a long list of people who potentially have access to data files not available to the general public. The Ministry of Justice is a huge, sprawling system, as you know. Information could be leaking out anywhere, especially when you consider the nature of the crimes.'

'Nobody loves a paedophile, that's for damn sure.'

'Oh, no question about that. If you asked a million people to identify the demographic subgroup they hated and feared the most, nine times out of ten it'd be child abusers. Not just among the law-abiding population, either. Some of the people that hate them the most are other sex offenders.'

That didn't make sense to him. Desi saw his look of puzzlement.

'That's why I asked you to come here this afternoon,' she said. 'You see, after we talked I did some checking back through my files. There's a man called Vinnie Sweeney.'

CHAPTER THIRTEEN

'Who is he?' Tom asked.

'Until a couple of months ago, he was a high-security inmate at Reading prison. Early release, eight years into a seventeen-year sentence.'

'Let me guess. He wasn't put there for shoplifting.'

'Vinnie Sweeney is a rapist,' Desi replied. 'He's also one of the most dangerous and violent men I've ever met, and I've met a few. I worked on his case three years ago and videoed a couple of one-to-one sessions with him. He's a religious maniac who believes the Lord has chosen him to do His work.'

'To rape women?'

'There's more to it than that,' she said.

'Tell me.'

'Oh, I could tell you lots. But you can see for yourself.'

Desi got up, went over to her desk and brought back the laptop. Instead of returning to her armchair she came around the edge of the table to sit next to him on the sofa. He felt the cushions give under her weight. He could smell her subtle perfume. He liked being this close to her. She opened the laptop and set it on her knee, angled so that he could see it.

'The video I'm about to show you was recorded in the high security wing at Reading prison,' she explained, tapping in a passcode to unlock the encrypted file. After a few moments the playback started.

Tom frowned and sat forward to peer at the screen. He took another sip of the coffee, cradling the delicate cup in his hand. The scene in the video was a stark white room with a plain table, identical to a million interview rooms Tom had been in, and not unlike the one where Desi had interviewed the prisoner yesterday at Bullingdon. The single camera was focused on the inmate seated across the table from Desi. He was wearing the usual prison-issue T-shirt and jogging bottoms. His hands rested easily on the tabletop and his face wore a smirk. He was about thirty-five, white, brown hair, not big, not small, nothing physically distinctive or remarkable about him except for the gleam in his eyes which Tom noticed immediately. He'd seen eyes like that before. They were sharp and intelligent. But more than that. They were the eyes of a sadist.

The playback started mid-stream, with Vinnie Sweeney talking. He spoke in a soft voice, so that Tom had to listen hard to his words.

'Just an irrational moment,' Sweeney was saying. 'Why should I be banged up in here just because of an irrational little moment?'

Desi's voice, offscreen, said, 'It wasn't just one irrational moment, though, was it, Vincent? It was a whole series of them. That's what makes you a habitual sex offender and not just some man who lost control for a moment.'

Sweeney's face hardened. 'What makes you think I'm a sex offender?'

'When you hold a knife to a woman's throat and force her to strip so that you can rape her,' Desi's voice replied in a matter-of-fact tone, 'that makes you a sex offender.'

'Women are deceitful, sinful bitches,' Sweeney said. 'I give them what's coming to them. That doesn't make me a sex offender.'

'Do you think God approves of what you do to them?'

'Of course He does,' Sweeney said vehemently.

'Did God tell you to rape Nadine Davis?'

'Yes.'

'In what way did God guide you to do that?'

'By speaking to me in my dreams. By watching over me every moment of every day, so that His wisdom influences my actions. The presence of the Lord was with me when I broke into her house. I sneaked up the stairs. I'm very quiet. She was asleep. I shone the torch in her face and that woke her up. She started screaming and crying. I grabbed her by the neck. I said, "I'm going to rape you and nobody will hear you screaming. Nobody's going to save you." She cried louder. Then she said, "My baby. Please don't touch my baby." Sweeney smiled. 'She should have known I would never have harmed her baby. God was speaking to her, too. He speaks to us all. But she wouldn't listen.'

'Tell me why you wouldn't have harmed the baby,' Desi's voice said.

'Because children are pure creatures, free of sin,' Sweeney replied with a look of tenderness. The smirk was gone. He was speaking sincerely. 'God has a plan to protect the innocent.'

'Do you believe you are part of that plan, Vincent?'

Sweeney's face hardened again. 'God tells me I am,' he said. 'It's His purpose for me, as His righteous instrument here on Earth.'

'What does God want you to do?'

'To punish the wicked and the unfaithful,' Sweeney told her. 'And, most especially, to cleanse the world of evil men who harm and defile children. God put me here to punish them for their filthy sins. That's my mission in life.'

Desi paused the playback. 'In prison he attacked four men,' she explained. 'He used his bare hands, no weapons. Two of them were very badly injured.'

'All paedos?' Tom asked.

She nodded. 'It was a few years ago, but you can see the hate is still there. And he was capable of showing extremely violent ideation when his blood was up. Watch.' She resumed the playback, fast-forwarded it for a moment and let it go on.

'The warden tells me you've taken up chess,' her off-camera voice was saying. 'That's a rewarding activity for you.'

Sweeney nodded and his lips broadened into a smile. His teeth were grey, like little fangs. His eyes were gazing steadily at her past the camera. 'But mostly what I do is think about you, Dr Fielding,' he told her. 'I've been thinking about you a lot. I have a new fantasy I've been working on.'

Tom guessed that in those instances the therapist just had to let them talk. She wasn't going to encourage him to describe the fantasy, but she couldn't tell him not to. On the video playback, Desi said nothing. Next to him on the sofa, Tom felt her tense. He could feel his own muscles tightening.

'It's very special,' Sweeney said. 'I'm in this room with you, just like we are now. But the difference is that we're all alone with no guards, and I have my knife. I've been keeping it hidden for the right moment. I hold the knife against your face. Cut you, just a little. I like to see the blood on your lips. You're mine now, and you're quite helpless in my power.'

Tom felt sick. He clutched the cup tightly in his hand.

'It's only a fantasy,' Desi said on the video. 'It's not a real event. It's part of what makes you unhappy.'

Sweeney crawled forwards in his seat, like a snake uncoiling itself. His eyes were fixed hard on her and his teeth were clenched. His arms were flexed on the tabletop, the muscles standing out. 'You love the pain. You want more, and you want me to be the one who gives it to you. I bend you over this table and pull up that skirt you're wearing. You have no underwear on, because you're just another filthy bitch in heat like all the others in need of punishment. You scream while I'm raping you. Then I use the knife to cut away your clothes, one bit at a time. I feel your breasts. They're so full and round. I squeeze harder. I fasten my teeth around one of your nipples. You shriek, because you love it. Then I bite the nipple off.'

There was a crack. Desi turned sharply around on the sofa and looked down at the coffee that was spattered all over the two of them and across the fabric of the cushions. It was dripping down onto the oriental rug that was under the coffee table.

Tom opened his fist and stared in horror at the porcelain fragments on his palm. His hand was cut from the shards of the crushed cup. He'd got blood on the sofa, too. 'Jesus,' he said. 'I'm sorry.' He reached into his pocket with his other hand, took out a crumpled ball of Kleenex and started dabbing at the fabric.

'It's okay,' she said. The video was still playing. She quickly closed the laptop and put it on the table. 'Never mind the furniture,' she said. 'Your hand's bleeding.'

'I'm really sorry,' he said again. He couldn't think what else to say. 'What a nob I am.'

'Come on,' she said, and took his wrist. 'You can trust me, I'm a doctor.'

'I thought you were a clinical psychologist.'

'I am,' she replied with a smile. 'But before I got qualified in that, I trained in medicine.'

'You're a lady of many skills,' he said.

'Aren't you the lucky one?'

'Not sure that's how I feel right now,' he admitted.

'Come with me.'

He followed her meekly across the room, dripping blood on the polished wood. Across the hall was a little downstairs cloakroom. She led him inside to the wash-basin, made him pull up his jacket sleeve and shirt cuff and hold his hand under the cold tap as she gently washed the blood away.

'Hold on. You've got a splinter.'

He winced as she plucked out a shard of the broken cup that had lodged under the skin. He was much taller than her and twice as wide, but he felt like a ten-year-old boy being nursed by his mother. Desi tore a wad of toilet tissue from a roll, dabbed his hand dry and then took a tube of antiseptic salve from a little corner cupboard. 'This will sting a bit.' Holding his hand in hers, she squeezed some into his open palm with her other hand and caressed it gently in with her fingertips. Her forehead was furrowed with concern.

'I can't believe I did that,' he said apologetically. 'I'll pay for the cup, and the cleaning and everything.'

'Don't be daft. I'm the one who should be apologising. The cup must have been cracked.'

'No, it wasn't. It was when he—' Tom started to explain, then said no more.

She'd finished rubbing in the ointment, but she was still lightly clasping his hand. They stood like that for a silent moment, and then he self-consciously drew his hand away.

'I think that's going to need a dressing,' she said.

'It's okay. Thanks. Once again—'

She shushed him. 'Really. Don't worry about it.'

Tom followed her back to the study, still feeling unbearably foolish. He winced at the sight of the coffee stain on the sofa and the dark patch on the rug. His trousers were wet and cold where it had soaked through. He let out a long sigh, thinking with disgust that it looked like he'd pissed in his pants.

'I have an old pair of men's boxer shorts I could lend you,' she said, noticing the stain on his crotch. 'I don't think you'll fit into my jeans.'

'I'll change at home,' he said.

As she dabbed the sofa and rug with foam fabric cleaner, he tried to refocus his thoughts on Vinnie Sweeney. 'You say he came out a couple of months ago?'

'I'd have to check the exact date of his release,' she said. 'But it was around then.'

Which meant Sweeney had been at large for several weeks by the time of the first paedophile shooting. 'Have you seen him since his release?' Tom asked.

'He was scheduled to attend some sessions at Metcalfe House. He showed up for the first one, and told me about trying to get his life back together. The probation service set him up in a little flat in Carterton, near the army base. He was working in a country store or something. But that's the last I saw of him.'

'Did anyone inform the authorities, when he didn't show up for his remaining sessions?'

'Metcalfe House isn't a probation centre,' Desi explained. 'It's not our role to monitor them in the community. If they don't report to their probation officer once a year, we don't even get to hear about it. There, that's got the stain off, no problem.'

'I'm glad,' Tom said. 'So when you saw him again, did he seem any different?'

'Overall, he seemed to have improved a good deal. He'd calmed down quite considerably since our last interview, and it was felt that his behaviour had moderated enough for his medications to be considerably reduced. That was one reason he got the early release. There's a complex approval process involved.'

'Would you have approved?'

'It's outside of my jurisdiction to decide who gets released when. My job's just to report my findings.'

'But you thought the therapy had worked,' Tom said. 'That he was rehabilitated.'

'I thought so, at the time. We talked about the feelings of animosity he used to have toward women, and he said he no longer felt that way and was ashamed of what he'd done to them. I believed him.'

'What about his hatred of child abusers?'

'He told me that God had asked him to forgive them. It was no longer his spiritual mission to punish the wicked.'

'For real?'

'It seemed real at the time,' Desi said.

'But now maybe you have your doubts.'

'I wouldn't have showed you the video otherwise,' she replied. 'What if Vinnie was just telling everyone what they wanted to hear? What if in fact he still hates them as strongly as before?'

What indeed, Tom thought. He asked, 'Did he ever mention an interest in weapons, firearms?'

'Not that I can recall. It's not a subject that generally comes up in discussions, thankfully. I dislike guns extremely and know nothing about them.'

'How about other hobbies and interests, generally?'

'I remember that he lost interest in chess while he was inside,' she said. 'But I know he was very keen on motorbikes. At least, I think it was motorbikes. He said something about it in that one session we had at Metcalfe. He was very passionate about it. He was all pleased that he was reunited with his old friend. Talked about it like a lover. Said something about polishing it while watching television.'

That struck Tom as curious. He had a vision of Sweeney manhandling a motorbike up a flight of stairs to his flat. 'So I'm guessing he must live on the ground floor.'

She shrugged. 'I suppose so. Or maybe he takes the TV outside in the hot weather.'

Tom was thinking about motorcycles. About quick getaways. Heavy jackets like the one the eyewitnesses in

Stanton Harcourt had seen the strange man in the woods wearing, and a helmet to hide your face. Cross-country escapes over the dry, iron-hard summer fields. You could easily carry a rifle concealed in a gun slip across your back, or strapped to the pillion seat. Some varieties of weapon could be taken apart quickly and easily to fit into a bag no larger than a laptop case, making them very easily transportable.

'He didn't happen to say what kind of motorbike it was, did he?'

'It was something a little unusual,' Desi replied. 'Not like Honda or Yamaha or Triumph, or any of those makes that you'd recognise. Letters, not a name. I remember I wrote it down, because of the strange way he talked about it. A little obsessive. We always take note of things like that.'

'Letters, not a name,' Tom said. 'Like BMW?'

She shook her head. 'I think it had a Z in it. Z-something. Or something-Z. I'd have to check my case file.'

'MZ, maybe?'

'Would that make sense, if it were?'

'I had one, way back when I was a junior copper. The letters stood for Motorradwerk Zschopau. Old East German two-stroke. Tough little thing, it was. You could pick them up for a song then.'

And maybe you still could, he thought. Cheap wheels for a broke ex-convict to get around on while rubbing out evil men who harm children. *Hmm.*

Tom always carried a little notepad. He scribbled *Vincent Sweeney MZ motorcycle*, drew a circle around it and slipped it back in his pocket. Then, noticing the time, he said, 'I'd really better get moving. Sorry for the mess.'

'Sure you won't stay for another coffee? I'll make it in a mug this time.'

Tom thanked her, apologised once again, and she walked him to the door.

He paused as he was about to leave, turned to her and heard the words come tumbling, quite unplanned, out of his own mouth: 'Will I see you again?'

She smiled. 'There's always that possibility. Take care, Inspector. I hope you catch your man.'

He drove away from Desi's feeling even more of a big eedjit than before.

CHAPTER FOURTEEN

Battling the clock Tom raced back home, threw off his best suit, now covered in coffee and blood, leaped into the shower and changed into jeans and a comfortable old shirt. He fed Radar, wolfed down a cold meat sandwich, watered his herbs, then raced back into Oxford with the dog riding happily in the back seat. On the way there he called Billie, who was working late at the station, and asked her to grab an address for a Vinnie Sweeney in Carterton. 'Should be on the probation service records.'

'Got it, chief.'

It was ten past eight when Tom screeched up outside the Claddagh on Cowley Road. His rendezvous point with Harvey that evening was the last true Irish pub in Oxford, or maybe in England. In a world of gentrified wine bars it was refreshingly rough around the edges with shabby dark-wood decor; the kind of spit'n'sawdust place that took you back to the good old days, where they served Guinness with a shamrock artfully drawn into the creamy head of your pint and Planxty or the Dubliners were always blaring from the sound system when there wasn't a live band on. Tonight a group of hairy musicians – fiddle, accordion, guitar and bodhrán – had assembled for one of the Claddagh's typical improvised ceilidh sessions in the covered beer garden area outside. Most of the punters had gathered there to hear them and sing and dance and clap along, leaving the pub relatively empty.

Harvey had arrived on time, and was already at work on his first pint of Guinness in a little nook near the bar. The Claddagh was also one of the last pubs on the planet to allow dogs, so Tom brought Radar inside and made him lie under the table as he joined Harvey with a pint of his own and a couple of bags of crisps. It might have been an unconventional setting for a therapy session, but neither man cared.

'Sorry I'm late.'

'No worries. Is he friendly?' Harvey asked, reaching under the table to let Radar sniff his hand.

'He only bites criminals,' Tom said.

'Cheers.'

'Cheers.'

'So how have things been since our first session?' Harvey asked, wiping a creamy Guinness moustache from his upper lip. They talked for a while about Tom's frustration with the case, though there was little he could openly discuss about an ongoing investigation.

'How about those feelings that we talked about?'

'Oh, you know, so far so good.'

Harvey pointed at the big band-aid Tom had slapped across his cut palm. 'What happened to your hand? You haven't thumped anyone else, have you?'

'It's just a scratch,' Tom replied evasively. It made him think of Desi, and he lapsed into a brooding silence for a few moments.

'I sense that something else is on your mind,' Harvey observed. 'You want to talk about it?'

'Not really. It's personal.'

'This is therapy, Tom. We delve into the dark recesses of the human spirit, where only the brave and the bold dare to tread.'

'All right, all right. If you have to know, I'm thinking about a woman.'

'Ah,' Harvey said.

'You know how I told you that I never really get involved . . .'

'Nothing serious, grown-up stuff, you have fun, exactly what you need out of life. I remember.'

'Anyway, this time it's different,' Tom went on with a sigh. 'I don't seem to be able to get her out of my mind. There's something about her, you know? It's stupid but I feel like I want to protect her, take care of her.'

'And is there any reason why she should need your protection? Is she a battered wife? Is she ill? What does she do? How did you meet?'

'Through work. You're going to like this. She's a shrink, too.'

Harvey smiled. 'Are you two-timing me?'

'I wouldn't be her kind of client. Her job's rehabilitating sex offenders. I wish it wasn't.'

'Because you think it's a waste of time?'

'No. Well, maybe. But I just wish she wouldn't do it. You should hear how those bastards talk to her.'

'It makes you angry?'

'Back to that again.'

'Always with the big emotions.'

Tom sighed and took a long swig of his pint. 'Listen, this is going to sound really corny, so it is, but I'm going to say it anyway.'

'You know you can tell me anything,' Harvey said. 'Corny or not.'

Tom looked at him. 'Do you believe in love at first sight?

Because I think I'm falling in love with her. I know that's hard to imagine, coming from a guy like me.'

Harvey asked, 'And what about her, does she feel the same?'

'She probably wouldn't pee on me if I was on fire. When I'm around her I feel tongue-tied like a teenager on his first date. A big clumsy oaf.'

'A goddess to be worshipped from afar,' Harvey mused, raising his glass. 'We pay tribute to thy immortal form.'

'Yeah, well, there's the thing,' Tom said. 'I don't want to worship her from afar.'

'Is there some professional reason why you need to keep a distance here?' Harvey asked, more seriously. 'Given the nature of her work, I mean.'

'Not really. It's not like she's that involved with the case.'

'Then why don't you just ask her out? Seems to me you've nothing to lose.'

Tom chewed on the idea for a while. 'Truth is I'm scared. You know, I'm just a working-class Irish guy from the Falls Road. Semi-educated, not too smart. She's a cultivated, sophisticated lady. You should see where she lives. And she drinks chilled lemon tea out of these dainty wee cups. Which I managed to break. She's out of my league.'

'Your social superior.'

'She's my superior in every way.'

'So much for our brave new classless society.'

'You know that's all bullshit. Anyway what do you think I should do? What would you do?'

'I'd take it one step at a time,' Harvey said. 'Get to know her better. Let her see your charming side.'

'I'm still trying to find it myself,' Tom said. 'Anything more specific?'

'Just go for it,' Harvey said. 'Ask her out.'

Tom pursed his lips and looked grim. 'Might say no.'

'There is that possibility. In which case, you're big enough and ugly enough to cope with it.'

'This is what they teach you at shrink school?'

'Not everything is in the psychology books,' Harvey said. 'Forget about all that guff for a moment. Isn't it better to take the plunge and find out where you stand? To take a risk? To throw caution to the wind and just go with your heart?'

'You're not exactly what they'd call a normal therapist, are you?' Tom said.

Harvey grinned. 'Fancy another pint?'

Tom had kept his phone turned off during their session. When he left the pub he turned it back on to find a message from Billie, who had found Sweeney's address in Carterton. It was an eighteen-mile drive but he thought, why the hell not. 'What do you think?' he asked the dog. Radar didn't seem to care either way.

It was quarter to eleven when Tom took out his phone once more, this time to dial Desi Fielding's number. He hadn't expected that they would speak again so soon. He felt a flutter of nervousness as she answered.

'It's Tom McAllister,' he said. 'Hope I'm not calling at a bad time?'

He could hear the smile in her voice as she replied, 'No, I was just making some cocoa. I've got another hour's work to do tonight. Anything to put it off. It's nice to hear from you.'

'Listen, the thing about Vinnie Sweeney's motorbike. Can you run it by me again?'

'What's the matter?'

'Just a hunch,' he said. 'I've been thinking about it.'

'Hang on,' she said. 'I'm just running over to my study now. Okay, I'm opening the file on Sweeney,' she continued a few moments later. 'Here we are. I did write it down. The bike was something called a CZ. He liked to spend a lot of time with it, watching TV as he cleaned and polished it.'

'CZ, not MZ?'

'Sorry if I got that wrong. Does it make a big difference?'

'That's what he definitely said, polishing and cleaning the CZ in front of the TV?'

'Definitely,' she said. 'Straight from my notes.'

'Okay, because if that's what he said, we might have a little bit of a problem.'

'What kind of a problem?'

'One, Sweeney's flat is on the second floor of the block,' he said. 'And there's no lift. So there's no way he could have got a motorcycle up there, not even a tiny one. So that rules out tinkering with it in front of the TV. And there's no garden, so he couldn't have brought a TV down. All he has is a little balcony.'

'You've already been there?'

'I'm standing outside the building right now,' he said.

'Have you seen him? Spoken to him?'

'That's problem number two. I've just been talking to the neighbours. Nobody's seen him for weeks.'

'Maybe he moved out.'

'If he has, he hasn't notified the probation authorities. Problem three is the CZ bit. Even if he could have got the bike into his flat, it doesn't make sense.'

'Why not?'

'Because men are a funny bunch.'

'Tell me about it.'

'It's the wrong type of bike,' he explained. 'I've known guys who brought their bikes into their kitchens and treated them like royalty. But those were thoroughbred machines like Ducatis and Laverdas and Harleys. This is a CZ.'

'I don't know one end of a motorbike from the other,' Desi said. 'What exactly *is* a CZ?'

'CZs are ratty old commie workhorses that were produced in Czechoslovakia. They smoke, they get covered in oil, they're slow and they're made of crappy metal. You leave one standing out in the rain for ten minutes, next thing there's rust bubbling up through the paintwork. That's why you hardly ever see them any more, because they're all on the scrap heap. The only people who rode them back in the day were broke students, and even they didn't give a damn about them. They're the most neglected and unloved motorbike on the planet. Nobody would polish a CZ.'

'Don't be so sure. Some mental health patients are very obsessive. They can form strong emotional bonds with things that a normal person might just disregard. But I don't understand what point you're making, Tom. Why is this such a big deal?'

'Is there a number after CZ?' he asked. 'You know, the way motorbikes have an engine capacity, like Honda two-fifty?'

'Yes, there is,' she said, after a moment to check her notes again. 'Seventy-five. Does that matter?'

'CZ seventy-five? You're sure?'

'That's what I wrote.'

'You're sure you copied that down right?'

'If it's what I wrote, it's what he said,' she replied, with a touch of irritation.

'I knew it,' he said. 'And I'm getting a warrant to search Sweeney's place.'

'What is it?'

'There were other factories in Eastern Bloc Czechoslovakia making better things than crappy old two-stroke motorbikes,' he said. 'A CZ75 isn't a motorcycle. It's one of the most classic military handguns of all time.'

CHAPTER FIFTEEN

Things began to move quickly after that. Tom hung around outside Vinnie Sweeney's building, ready to intercept him if he happened to come home. Meanwhile, at the station, Billie Flowers jumped on the phone and pulled out all the necessary stops to fast-track a search warrant. Tom didn't have to wait long before the magistrate gave them the green light and three police vehicles hustled to the scene.

'Break it down,' Tom ordered, pointing at the door. With a splintering crash they were inside Sweeney's flat.

The first thing Tom saw when he turned on the lights confirmed what the neighbours had reported: nobody had lived there for weeks. Tom had seen more squalid dwellings, but not often. The place stank like a dustbin and the low hum of buzzing flies filled the air as they walked in.

'Smells like rats have been in the place,' complained one of the constables, grimacing. What the rodents had left of the remains of a fast food meal mouldering on a tray on the floor, next to a grimy sofa that was the only furnishing in the main room, the bluebottles were feasting on. Scummy dishes were piled high in the tiny kitchen, and the bathroom looked like something out of a Third World cell block. Sweeney's bedroom consisted of a piss-stained single mattress with a sleeping bag on it. The one piece of reading material he appeared to possess was a tatty, well-thumbed bible.

But Tom wasn't interested in the man's living arrangements. Off the tiny hallway was another locked door, which offered little resistance to the battering ram. The room was pitch black and the light didn't work. Tom used a torch to peer inside. His beam shone off glinting dull metal. It was a few instants before his brain was able to register what he was looking at.

'Jesus Christ,' said one of the uniforms, standing behind him in the doorway. 'The guy's got a whole bloody arsenal in here.'

The bare, unfurnished room was full of guns. Tom counted at least a dozen rifles propped against the walls, and at least as many pistols and revolvers lying around the floor. He was no expert, but he could generally tell one thing from another. Some of the weapons looked old and antiquated, like relics from World War II, while others were more modern. Sweeney's collection included assault rifles, grenade launchers, and submachine guns. In addition to the weapons, it looked as though he had plenty to feed them with, too. In one corner was a stack of oblong steel boxes with white stencilled writing on them. Ammo crates. In another, more containers filled with dull brass cartridges. Next to those, a beer crate filled with British army hand grenades that looked like little olive-green pineapples. But it was the object in the middle of the floor that made Tom catch his breath. It was a heavy machine gun mounted on a tripod, with snakes of belt ammunition coiled underneath.

'Touch nothing,' Tom ordered the officers. 'Rob, get on the radio. I want a specialist firearms unit, bomb disposal and a forensics team out here within the hour.'

They were there sooner. The entire area around Sweeney's apartment was soon cordoned off and awash with flashing blue light as neighbours were evacuated to a nearby sports hall for their safety, at the insistence of the bomb team. Sniffer dogs and men in full protective armour invaded the building to verify the contents of the boxes and crates, as well as to investigate the potential presence of any explosive booby traps, before anything could be moved. Once they were given the all-clear, the apartment became an ant's nest of activity. A photographer snapped every detail of every room, and officers from the specialist firearms division wearing plastic gloves carefully tagged and bagged each item of Sweeney's weapons cache before loading it into an unmarked van. It took three men to lug the heavy machine gun, wrapped in plastic sheeting, out of the flat and down the stairs. When the arsenal was safely on its way to police HQ for examination, the forensic team began gathering further evidence.

Tom stayed on site for the next hour, talking on the phone to Billie and to Forbes and overseeing the operation. 'Sweeney must've had the guns stashed somewhere while he was in prison,' Billie said, so revved up by this major breakthrough that she was almost breathless with excitement. 'A lock-up storage unit, maybe, or with a mate. Be worth finding out about him, too. This is great, Tom.'

'Be even greater if we knew where Sweeney was,' Tom replied. 'And whether he's got the .300 Blackout and the CZ pistol with him.' As far as he'd been able to make out, they were missing, and that worried him.

Forbes didn't sound so pleased by the news. 'Don't be too sure of yourself, Inspector. The evidence on this suspect is far less substantial than what we have on Brennan.'

Tom got off the phone with him as fast as he could. Soon afterwards, the flat was closed up and the damaged doorway sealed off with police tape. The neighbours, some of them amused by the incident and others bewildered and jittery, were ferried back home in police vans. Two more patrols were assigned to guard duty, in the unlikely event that Sweeney might decide to return home. Meanwhile, a full manhunt was swiftly getting underway.

Tom drove home with Radar, tired and hungry and his mind going in six directions at once, but riding high after a good evening's work. Back at the cottage he pulled the cork on a nice bottle of red, cooked himself a pork loin steak with tomatoes and olives, served it up with rice, and hit the sack in the wee small hours, too exhausted to worry about finding Vinnie Sweeney. Besides, he had other things on his mind.

Tom was awake not long after the golden-red dawn light began filtering through the trees. His last thoughts before falling asleep had been of Desi Fielding, and he was thinking of her again now as he trudged downstairs and let Radar out for his habitual early-morning mad dash and bark at the world, scattering a flock of ducks that had gathered by the riverside. An hour later, feeling slightly more human again after a couple of mugs of coffee, Tom finally plucked up the nerve to pick up the phone and dial her number.

'Me again. I wanted to thank you. Looks like you might have made a good call.'

'I saw it. It's all over the morning news. I'm stunned. Do they have any idea where he went?'

'Not yet. But we'll get him. Thanks to you. Listen . . . uh . . .'

'What?'

He hesitated. What the hell. *Go with your heart*, the man had said. Tom leaped into the abyss and blurted, 'Would you have dinner with me?'

There was an agonising beat's silence on the line. Tom didn't breathe. Hoping that the thudding inside his chest couldn't be heard on the phone.

Then Desi replied warmly, 'Yes, I'd like that very much, Tom.'

He felt suddenly all gushy and jelly-kneed. 'Jeez, I'm awful pleased to hear you say that. How about tonight?'

'Tonight would be lovely. Where are we going?'

'To the very finest restaurant in Oxfordshire.'

'The Four Seasons?'

'Oh, much better than that.'

'Wow, must be pretty swanky,' she said. 'Don't you need to make a reservation?'

'Not this place,' he said. 'Not when you have the right connections.'

'I'm duly impressed. What's it called?'

'The Three Bay Leaves.'

'I've never heard of it.'

'That's because it's so exclusive, hardly anyone even knows about it,' Tom replied. 'Meet you there at eight?'

'It's a date,' she said. 'How do I get there?'

He was bursting with elation as he rumbled off to work some time later. She'd said yes! Every time he replayed the magic moment in his head he couldn't repress a big cheesy grin that spread all across his face and made him want to thump the steering wheel for joy. Right then, Vinnie Sweeney was the very last thing on his mind.

It was as he was hacking through the traffic choking the Botley Road end of town that Tom's phone rang, and reality came flooding back like a bucket of cold water.

'Good morning, dear boy. Waller here.'

Tom felt a jolt. He'd been waiting for Thins to call with that much-anticipated DNA analysis report. 'Did you get the trace off the cartridge? Is it Sweeney?'

'I wasn't calling about that,' Thins replied, dashing Tom's hopes. 'Can you scoot over to the lab? There's something I'd like to show you.'

Tom arrived at Thins Waller's domain in the basement of the police HQ hoping that what he was about to be shown wasn't of the lying-cold-on-a-slab variety. Not that Tom was squeamish, particularly, but the sight of a mottled corpse wasn't his ideal way to start the morning. To his relief, Thins, holding a clipboard and looking quite preoccupied, ushered him away from the morgue and autopsy lab and down a corridor to the evidence room.

It was a veritable grotto down there, albeit a well-organised one, though Tom couldn't remember the last time he'd seen it so cluttered. The bounty from the raid on Sweeney's flat filled every corner. Dull black angular shapes were dimly visible through thick polythene. Here and there Tom could see a barrel or a magazine or the grain of a wooden stock pressed up against the plastic, leaving streaks of gun oil and grease. Some of the objects were small and lay stacked in shallow trays. Some were long and sat propped up against the wall. The middle of the floor was taken up with the huge, squat shape of the heavy machine gun, too bulky for an evidence bag and instead covered with a polythene sheet.

Thins Waller tapped a bony finger on the clipboard he was holding. 'Okay, here we go,' he said laconically. 'You've got a fair list of stuff here. Pistols: nine-millimetre Browning, Colt Government automatic, couple of Lugers, three Smith & Wesson .357 Magnum revolvers, a Ruger single action, two thirty-eight Webleys. Moving on to rifles, we've got an old British army SMLE .303, a German Wehrmacht Mauser K98 from about the same time. A much older Martini Henry. An M1 carbine, US army issue, dated 1943. A Kropatchek Steyr bolt-action.' Waller looked up. 'Rare one, that. Then we have a variety of modern assault weapons, including one Soviet Kalashnikov and one Chinese copy. Couple of pump-action shotguns. Five submachine guns: an Uzi, two old Berettas, a Sten Mark Two and a Russian Kiparis. Real collector, your man. The big one,' he said, motioning without looking at the massive gun on the floor, 'is a Vickers heavy machine gun. Then we've got assorted odds and sods, like the Vickers ammunition cans, machine gun belts, assorted magazines and about nine hundred rounds of ammo in various calibres. Not to mention eighteen fragmentation grenades, all of your regular Mills Bomb variety.' He flipped the clipboard and shrugged. 'That's the lot. I've been through them all with a fine-tooth comb. The few prints I could find match samples gathered elsewhere in that grot-hole of a flat of his, which in turn match up to his records on the IDENT1 database. There aren't many of them, because he keeps his collection pretty clean and oiled. Nobody else appears to have touched them, not without gloves on anyway.'

Tom ran his eye around the room. 'Yer man's got enough hardware to start a war, so he does.'

Thins raised a grizzled eyebrow. 'Except that if you did try to start a war with this little lot, it would be a very quiet war indeed, and it'd be over pretty damn quick.'

Tom felt a leaden weight sink to the pit of his belly. 'Don't tell me.'

Waller nodded. "Fraid so, Tom. They're deacts. Every one of these weapons has been decommissioned in accordance with the current regs. Must have cost him a packet to put a collection like this together, but it's completely kosher. Anyone could buy guns like these by mail order, no licence required. He's even got the proof house certificates.' Thins reached over to a desk, snatched up a transparent plastic folder and waved it under Tom's nose. Inside it was a sheaf of documents. The top one was aged and yellowed, and Tom could see the letterhead of the government firearms proof house in Birmingham. 'All present and accounted for. Everything's in order, serial numbers match, and so on,' Thins said.

'What about a CZ75 pistol?' Tom asked.

Thins shook his head. 'Not on the list.'

'So that one could still be out there. Along with the .300 Blackout rifle.'

'The *hypothetical* .300 Blackout rifle,' Thins reminded him. 'At this point you've got no evidence that it's his. In fact I'm sorry to say that you have no evidence of anything at all, other than the fact that our dear Mr Sweeney belongs to a peculiar subculture that's a trifle fixated on inert weaponry. For all we know, he might have been buying and selling them to make some extra cash. Which would be perfectly legitimate. And as for the alleged CZ pistol, if it's a deact like the rest of them, it's just another gun-nut's paperweight. The only way to kill someone with it would be to club them over the head. You'd do a better job with a hammer.'

'Could he have reactivated one? And the rifle too, maybe?'

Thins looked doubtful. 'Bit of a media myth, that. I'd like to see someone try to get one of these up and running again, after the mutilation they've been subjected to. Breech blocks milled out, barrels welded up solid, actions frozen, firing pins removed. There isn't one of them that will ever go bang again.' He paused. 'However, that doesn't exclude the possibility that Sweeney could have obtained the real, unadulterated thing from somewhere. You never know what kinds of contacts he might have made while he was shopping around for this lot. Of course, then we'd be talking real money. Especially for a modern, silenced semiautomatic rifle. More the province of a professional soldier of fortune than a nutty ex-jailbird. I'm sorry, Tom. I know it's disappointing.'

It was, and not least because Tom was now going to have to account to his superiors for having launched a full-scale raid on the home of a man who might well turn out to be perfectly innocent, for once in his life. But at this moment it would have taken much worse news to bring down Tom's spirits.

'We won't know for sure until we find him,' he said, smiling.

'Or he finds us, with a solicitor threatening to sue our arses off for smashing down his client's door.'

'You seem to be taking this very well,' Thins observed wryly. 'Someone's in a cheery mood this morning.'

Tom felt his smile spread into a grin. 'I'm meeting someone tonight.'

'I see. Hot date?'

'Just dinner, that's all.'

'That doesn't sound like the Tom McAllister I know. You're not getting all soft and gooey, are you?'

'This one's special, Thins.'

Gordy Nash looked at the date on the calendar. In just a few more short weeks he'd be free. He'd known about it for the last three months, and he'd been counting the days ever since.

He smiled to himself as he thought how easy it had been to fool them all, the do-gooder therapists and social workers, the shit-for-brains probation officials, the whole stupid lot of them. He'd sat in front of them and told them how sorry he was for what he'd done. He'd even started frequenting the prison chapel.

And it had worked beautifully. Because three months ago, the panel had reconvened to announce their decision that, after serving only fifteen years of his sentence with another eight to go, Gordy was cured.

Hallelujah. Bingo. His prison time slashed by more than a third. Which was what he'd have liked to do to the face of the one sour old battleaxe on the parole board who'd given his application the thumbs down.

Well ha ha ha to you, witch bitch. Nice try, but I'm getting out of here.

He was still a young man in his prime. He was fitter and tougher than he'd been when they caught him, and he'd had a lot of time to think about what he'd done wrong: about the boy, and his feelings for him. That had been Gordy's downfall. When you start to feel something for your victims, you make mistakes. You make mistakes, you get caught.

Next time, Gordy would make no mistakes.

He thought about what he'd do when he got out. He thought of the gunman who was in all the newspapers. No way was he going to hang around Oxford waiting to be shot down like a dog. He thought of Scotland. That's where he would head for, as far north as you could go without getting your feet wet. Nobody would ever find him there. There were lots of little communities a man could lose himself in. The kind of work he could do would pay in cash, so no names. He could start all over again, mow lawns, wash cars, do shopping for old folks, volunteer at the church, put his friendly face about and gain people's trust.

And the trust of their kids. That was how Gordy planned on getting in.

And next time, he wouldn't get caught.

CHAPTER SIXTEEN

For the moment, there was little more to be done. Tom's investigation was juggling two different suspects, the whereabouts of both of whom were unknown. On his return to St Aldate's he found himself being summoned to Forbes's office and the two of them argued over the conflicting directions in which the case seemed to be going – but it was an impasse. In the meantime, the troops on the ground were scouring the county for any trace of either Vinnie Sweeney or Terry Brennan, spurred by DS Flowers who could be anything but sweet and honey-toned when placed second-in-command of a major murder enquiry that was whipping up more media frenzy with every passing day.

Tom grabbed some hours out of his schedule and rushed home earlier than usual that day to prepare for dinner. He was frantically busy for the next few hours, wearing his chef's apron, fully in his element. Dead paedophiles were pushed to the extreme back of his mind and his sense of anticipation was building as the time for Desi's arrival ticked closer. He was in the kitchen putting the finishing touches to the dessert when, right on the stroke of eight, her white BMW appeared at the top of the lane and came rolling up to the cottage.

Tom stripped off his apron and went out to meet her, his stomach full of butterflies. She was wearing a light summery dress and her hair was loose and shining in the evening sun.

'Good to see you, Desi. I'm glad you could make it.'

'I wasn't sure if I was in the right place,' she said, looking around her, a little baffled.

'We certainly are,' he replied. 'Home sweet home.'

She smiled. 'It's a lovely spot. But I thought you said we were going out to the best restaurant in the county.'

'We are,' he said.

'Shall we go in your car, or do you want me to follow you?'

'Neither,' he said, enjoying her confusion. 'It's just a few steps away. Come on, let's take a dander down to the river and I'll show you.'

The weather was perfect; warm and balmy with just the lightest breeze. The sunlight filtered golden through the trees and sparkled across the water. A procession of swans had chosen the perfect moment to come sailing past like stately galleons, right on cue as though Tom had hired them for the job.

'And there it is,' he said as the roofless structure of the old stone watermill came into view through the riverside foliage. 'The Three Bay Leaves. Or it will be, when I finish restoring it.'

'This is *your* restaurant?'

'That's the plan,' he said. 'One day, diners from all over the county will be lining up to eat here. But for the moment, we have it all to ourselves, so we do.'

He led her down to the mill and through its craggy stone archway, to where he'd set a table for two. 'Best seats in the house.' Nearby was a wooden trestle on which he'd laid out the dishes and an ice bucket. Their main course was being kept warm on a slow-burning wood stove. The birds were starting their evening chorus, over the gentle burble of the river and the soft creak of the waterwheel.

'This place is magical,' Desi said, gazing around her. 'I had no idea.'

'Champagne?'

'This is too much.'

'I hope you like fish.'

'Love it.'

Just then, the dog came tearing out of the trees where he'd been foraging and ran over to join them.

'He's beautiful,' Desi said, petting him. 'Such intelligent eyes. What's his name?'

'This is Radar. He's more a housemate than a pet.'

'How long have you lived here?'

'About sixteen years. Longer than I've ever lived anywhere.'

'It's so peaceful.'

They clinked glasses. The champagne was chilled to perfection. Tom rubbed his hands together and said, 'Hungry? Let's eat.'

Their entrée course was a chicken liver pâté in a stone dish garnished with three bay leaves, which they ate served on little toasted triangles of Tom's home-baked bread. Desi's eyes opened wide at the first taste. 'Oh my God. Did you make this?'

'Just this afternoon. It's better the second day, but I didn't have time yesterday.'

'This is amazing. I'm seeing a whole new side of you here. You're a real dark horse, Inspector McAllister.'

'More like a black sheep,' he said.

She smiled. 'So what's happening with Vinnie Sweeney?'

'Let's not talk about all that.'

'You're right. This is too nice. Then let's talk about your

111

fabulous restaurant. Does this mean you're planning on quitting the police one day?'

'That's the idea,' he said, nodding. 'If I live that long. Every year that passes, the Three Bay Leaves seems to get three years further away from ever happening.'

'You're doing all the restoration yourself?'

'Mostly. Me and Sparrowhawk. He's an odd-bod who lives on a barge and comes upriver to lend me a hand from time to time. I'm hoping to get the roof on this summer.'

'I like it like this,' she said, gazing up at the sky and the trees.

'Aye, until it starts pissing down.'

After another glass of champagne, Tom lifted the platter from the wood stove and revealed their main course. 'Side of salmon poached in fino sherry, with lemon and butter,' he said.

'Unbelievable. I don't cook at home. I reheat.'

Tom served the salmon with crispy sautéed potatoes and leaves of curly red lollo rosso lettuce from his vegetable garden, for which he'd made a vinaigrette dressing with virgin olive oil. 'Ach, it's just simple stuff,' he protested modestly as she gushed with praise at how delicious it all tasted.

'You're a magician.'

'Wait until you see me do my Liam Neeson impression.'

They lingered over the main course, talking about their lives, their hopes, their dreams, anything and everything other than their work. Tom had never really heard her laugh before. It was more intoxicating than the champagne.

Dessert, which he went up to the cottage to fetch from the fridge, was one of his speciality puddings. 'Mango and lime syllabub. I hope you like it.'

'It's beautiful.'

'A dash of gin, that's what gives it that extra something. But don't tell anyone. Trade secret.'

'I knew you had a secret.'

'Plenty of them,' he said. 'What's yours?'

'Wouldn't be a secret then, would it?' she replied with a smile.

As their dinner wound to an end, the sun set over the river in a blaze of colours. The night birds settled down and stillness descended.

'Thank you for this. I've had a wonderful time,' she said.

'Me too,' he replied, and felt the blush on his cheeks.

'Whoops. Think I drank a little too much champagne, though.'

'Are you okay to drive?'

'I don't really know,' she laughed.

'Let me take you home.'

'What about my car?'

'I'll have the police bring it round to you in the morning. Seriously, it'd be my pleasure.'

The evening had become a beautiful starry night as they set off in the Barracuda, winding through the lanes with the summer breeze wafting in through the open windows. 'Look,' she said, pointing. 'Stop a moment.'

Tom pulled up. In a wildflower meadow bright with milky moonlight, some horses were playing and gambolling as though they were savouring the magic of the night. Desi stepped out of the car and leaned on a fence, watching them. Tom joined her. He didn't feel like he had to speak. She was someone he could share a comfortable silence with. As if he'd known her all his life.

They stood and drank in the scene, and then he said, 'Come on, let's get you home.'

But as he turned the key to restart the car, to his mortification nothing happened.

'Dead. I don't frigging believe it. It's never let me down before.'

'Is it the battery?' she asked.

'I don't think so. The ignition's coming on and the lights are working.'

'Could be a fuse is blown somewhere?'

'I have no idea,' Tom grumbled. 'I'm not a mechanic.' He felt like thumping his head on the steering wheel. For this to happen, now!

'Don't worry about it,' Desi reassured him. 'We'll just call a breakdown service.'

He sighed heavily, ripped his phone from his pocket and climbed out of the car to make the call. After ten minutes of wrangling with the recovery company, he stalked back to the car with a face like thunder.

'Well? What did they say?'

'They said they'll get here as quick as they can. Whatever that means.'

'Then we'll wait,' Desi said. 'What choice do we have?'

Tom was all flustered apologies, until she laid a hand on his arm. 'Hey. It's okay. It's a beautiful evening and we're not in a rush, are we? How about some music?' She peered at the car radio. 'What is that thing?'

'It's the original 1970 eight-track cassette player. I never had the heart to replace it.'

'I've never seen one before. Got any tapes for it?'

He leaned across to rummage in the junk-filled glove compartment and found one. 'How about this?' he said, slotting it in.

'Old house, old car, old songs,' Desi commented as the music began to play. It was *Blueberry Hill*, the Elvis Presley cover that Tom preferred to the Fats Domino version. 'You're a man of particular tastes, Inspector McAllister.'

He shrugged. 'Out of step with the modern world. Living in the past. Whatever you call it. They don't make things like they used to.'

'I love the old things too. This one takes me back. My

mother was a big Elvis fan.' Desi leaned back and closed her eyes, then rocked suddenly forward in her seat and turned to him with a smile that gleamed in the darkness of the car. 'Makes me want to dance.'

'Dance?'

'Yeah. Come on. The perfect end to the perfect evening.'

'It's not over yet.'

Desi jumped out of the car. 'Come on,' she repeated, motioning for him to join her. 'Are you afraid to dance with a girl?'

Tom hesitated, then clambered back out and stepped over to her in the moonlight. They clasped hands and he placed a nervous hand behind her waist. She felt trim and strong.

'I haven't danced in years,' she chuckled, as they slowly moved to the music. She moved nicely. All he could do was sort of shuffle along with her.

'At least you remember the last time,' he said.

'You dance okay.'

'For a fat guy.'

'You're not fat.'

'Sure, I'm a fifteen-stone Nureyev.'

She laughed. *Blueberry Hill* was coming to an end. The next track on the album was *True Love*, an old Cole Porter song. 'I didn't know Elvis recorded this one,' Desi said.

'I think he recorded everything there was.'

'It was in the movie *High Society*. Frank Sinatra and Grace Kelly sang it as a duet.'

'It was Bing Crosby and Grace Kelly,' Tom corrected her. 'The scene on the yacht. Great scene. Makes me tear up like a big Jessie every time I see it.' He couldn't believe he'd admitted that.

She looked up at him. Her eyes were shining in the moonlight. 'Are you a romantic, Tom McAllister?'

'I've been called a lot of things. Never that.'

'But you are.' She fell silent for a drawn-out moment as they danced some more. 'I like you, Tom,' she said very softly.

'I like you, too,' he replied.

'I . . . I haven't been in a relationship for a long time.'

'Is that what this is, a relationship?'

'I don't know. Would you like it to be?'

He felt such a jolt of schoolboy trepidation that he couldn't reply to the question, as obvious as the answer was to him. 'I'd have thought guys would be queuing up,' he said. 'How come there isn't anyone in your life?'

Her hand was warm in his. He could feel her very close. 'Career,' she replied. 'Priorities. Plans. Always looking ahead. That's what I like about you. You live for the moment.'

'Do I?' Tom had never realised that about himself before.

She nodded. 'I can never do that. At least, not yet. Too much to do first. I'm very ambitious, you know. That's my middle-class upbringing, I suppose.' She hesitated. 'Sorry. I'm talking too much.'

'I like the way you talk.'

She looked up at him. 'I don't want to talk.'

'What do you want to do?' he asked. His heart was thudding like a drum.

'Something like this.' She moved closer.

Then, just as they were about to kiss, they were suddenly bathed in dazzling light. The recovery truck had arrived.

CHAPTER SEVENTEEN

Fifty-year-old American muscle cars were beyond the powers of the recovery guy to fix at the roadside, and their only option was to be towed home. Tom should have been angry about the car and embarrassed about showing himself up in front of Desi, but he found it impossible to be anything other than giddy with excitement as they rode back to the cottage in the breakdown truck. Desi didn't seem to mind, either. In the darkness of the cab she clasped his hand and kept smiling at him.

But by the time they'd returned to the cottage the romantic mood had fizzled out and the two of them were as awkward and self-conscious as teenagers on a first date. Desi still felt unsure about driving, so he offered to run her home in her BMW and she agreed.

It was after midnight by the time they got to her place in Bagley Wood. 'Would you like to come in for a coffee?' she asked in the front doorway.

'It's late. I should go.'

'Well, thank you for a lovely evening.'

'Ha, ha.'

'I'm serious. It was great. Really.'

He hesitated a beat and then asked, 'Will I see you again?'

'Of course you will,' she replied warmly.

'I'll give you a call sometime, then.'

'No. You give me a call soon, Tom McAllister. All right?'

She touched his arm, then raised herself up on tiptoe and kissed him on the cheek. The touch of her lips sent tingles all through him.

'Good night, Desi.'

'Good night, Tom.'

With a last smile she stepped inside her house, and was gone. He stood there for a moment, still basking in the glow. He murmured to himself, 'Wow.'

He couldn't remember a fresher and more beautiful summer's night. Or maybe it was just him. Taking out his phone as he walked away from the house, he was about to dial up the number of a local taxi firm he knew when the phone starting burring in his hand and Billie Flowers' call ID appeared on the screen.

'Where are you?' she asked. She must have tried his home line first.

'I'm over at Dr Fielding's place.'

'Oh, I see,' Billie said knowingly. 'Well, I hate to break in on your fun, sir. But there's been a development.'

'What kind of development?'

'We've found Terry Brennan.'

* * *

By the time Billie had sped over to pick him up in an unmarked squad car, Tom had walked down to the bottom of Bagley Wood Road and was waiting outside St Swithun's Church.

'Don't worry, I'm not even going to ask about you and Dr Fielding,' Billie said as she took off.

'I'm pleased to hear it. Where is he?'

'An address in Whitlington. Units are in position, ready to move.'

Whitlington was a small village to the east of the city. 'Who found him?'

'Oh, just the most brilliant detective in the Thames Valley force,' Billie replied nonchalantly.

'Second best,' Tom corrected her.

'I've been doing a little digging. Turns out Terry Brennan came from a dysfunctional family and was taken into care when he was nine, then adopted. When he was eighteen he found out about his real parents and tried to get in touch with them. They didn't want to know, but he went back to using the family name anyway. Meanwhile it seems that he stayed close to his adoptive brother, Mike Horton, who runs a contracting business in Stratford. Nine months ago, Horton took out a lease on a little semi in Whitlington. Why would he do that? Well off, lives thirty miles away in a nice big house with his wife and three kids. So I looked into it. Guess whose name the phone and electric bills are paid in?'

'So Brennan's adoptive brother rented a place for him when he fell on hard times,' Tom said. 'Maybe you are the best detective in Thames Valley, after all.'

Billie's discovery that night had triggered a chain of response. On the assumption that their suspect could be armed and likely dangerous if cornered, a tactical firearms unit were on standby down the street from Brennan's house, while a police entry team were waiting for the green light to invade. Tom was anxious to get there fast, though he didn't need to tell Billie to step on it. 'Last thing we need is for one of those cowboys to get twitchy and start blasting, so it is.'

'You still don't believe Brennan is our shooter, do you?'

'I'd let Forbsie make that bet,' Tom replied.

It was after twelve-thirty when they reached Whitlington. The village was mostly in darkness but the blueish light of televisions flickered behind the curtains of some downstairs windows. Brennan's place, on a narrow street close to the village square, was one of them. Billie parked a distance from the house, behind the plain black panel van in which the firearms team were preparing for war.

Tom and Billie stepped from the car. Whitlington was known for its proximity to a big sewage works, making it perhaps not the most desirable place to reside within the county. Maybe Brennan and his adoptive brother weren't so close after all. 'They should call this place Shitlington,' Tom commented, sniffing the air.

'That's really not very funny,' Billie said.

'Neither would be living here. Jesus.'

Taking charge of the scene, Tom spoke to the firearms team commander, a squat, buzz-cut character called Dalrymple, who looked like he was itching to lead his men into battle. Last time they'd been out was to shoot a mad bull that had been running loose, and now they were anxious to use their toys on a real person again. Tom nixed any notion of an armed assault on the house and made it clear he intended to go in first. 'Understand? I see a gun on the street without my green light, and there'll be hell to pay.'

Tom and Billie left Dalrymple's boys hopping and frowning in frustration and walked up to the house. As they got closer they could hear the sound of the TV coming from the living room. Tom tried to peer through a chink in the curtains, but could see nothing. He stepped up to the front door and knocked three times, hard and loud.

No response. Nothing moved inside the house and the TV went on blaring. After twenty seconds, Tom knocked again, then bent down so he could speak through the letterbox. 'Mr

Brennan? Police officers. We'd like to have a word. Please open the door.'

Still nothing. Tom signalled to Billie that they should go around the back. A narrow path led down the side of the house to a rear porch. Tom tried the door and found it open. He glanced back at Billie, then led the way inside. The porch adjoined a small kitchen, from which a passage led towards the living room where the sound was coming from. It was a movie playing. Tom could hear the *peeow-peeow* of gunshots, followed by the unmistakable drawling voice of John Wayne. The film was either *El Dorado* or *Rio Bravo*; Tom couldn't be sure. Terry Brennan was obviously a western fan, and he had the volume turned up high enough that it had probably drowned out Tom's knocks at the front door.

They moved closer towards the living room. Tom pictured Brennan sitting there, maybe relaxing with a beer, chomping a late-night snack, completely unaware of their presence in the house. Or maybe he was lurking behind the living room door with a loaded rifle, getting ready to pepper the hated pigs with bullets the instant they appeared. Tom saw the gleam of nervousness in Billie's eyes and felt his own slight pang of doubt, wondering briefly whether he'd made a mistake telling the tactical response boys to hold back.

'Hello? Mr Brennan? Detective Inspector McAllister, Thames Valley Police. We need to talk to you, please. The back door was open.'

No response from the living room.

This same scenario had happened to Tom once before, years earlier, back when he was in uniform. On that occasion he'd entered the room to find the guy hanging from a beam, dead for several days: the stuff of nightmares for a long time afterwards. Tom swallowed. His mouth was dry. He reached the living room door. It was open a crack. He gripped the handle and swung the door wide.

And there, alone in the room, was Terry Brennan.

Brennan wasn't dead, and nor was he lying in wait with a semiautomatic weapon. He was sitting immobile in a big chintzy armchair facing the TV screen. His eyes rolled a few degrees sideways to watch Tom and Billie walk into the room, but he didn't get up from his chair, or show any reaction. His only noticeable movement was a peculiar convulsive tremor of his right hand where it lay in his lap, as though it was fluttering about with a life of its own. He looked shrunken and collapsed. A small table by his elbow was covered in medication bottles.

And that was when Tom knew that he'd been right, and that Forbes couldn't have been more wrong.

As a kid in Belfast, Tom had had a beloved Aunt Flora who'd become afflicted with a vicious little neurodegenerative condition called Huntingdon's disease. Nobody in the family had ever heard of it before, but they'd soon become all too familiar with the symptoms: a paralysing, crippling shutdown of the body's motor systems until it effectively ceased to function. The onset had been sudden, and there was no cure; all the drugs in the world could only palliate the worst of the suffering. The young Tom had watched helplessly as his aunt's health deteriorated so fast that, within a year of her diagnosis, she no longer had the ability to walk, talk or swallow.

And the sight of Terry Brennan was bringing back all those memories. Though Tom was no doctor he'd have put money on it that he was seeing the same thing. Huntingdon's could affect your quality of life in all kinds of devastating ways. Some victims might be luckier than others. But if there was one physical motor function the disease was one hundred percent cast-iron guaranteed to rob you of, it was the ability to execute a medium-range rifle shot over challenging terrain with the skill and accuracy of a trained sniper.

There was no way on God's earth that the miserable,

broken-down shadow of a man sitting in that chair could be the shooter.

Tom looked at Billie and saw she was thinking the same. He said to Brennan, 'I'm very sorry to have disturbed you, sir. We'll lock the door on our way out.' On the police radio he reported to the teams outside, 'Stand down. This was a bad call.'

'The super's not going to like it,' Billie said as they left the house. 'Not even a search for weapons?'

'That's his tough shit. If Forbsie wants to believe this poor bastard's armed and dangerous he can come and search the house himself.'

But Forbes wasn't the only problem. Tom and Billie walked around to the front of the house to find that Dalrymple had disregarded his order and the tactical squad had come strutting up the street to gather at the gate, guns at the ready, as though the battle was about to erupt. Worse, the scene had now drawn the attention of several neighbours, who were emerging from their houses to investigate. One of them was videoing it on his phone. A large, angry woman in curlers and a dressing gown had planted herself in front of Dalrymple with her hands on her hips and was shouting hoarsely, 'What the hell do you people think you're doing here? You should be bloody ashamed of yourselves!'

'Excuse me, Madam. Pull back,' Tom told Dalrymple with a cold glare. 'We're getting out.'

It was a long night, and things had only got worse by the morning. Terry Brennan's outraged neighbours had wasted little time posting the video footage of the abortive police raid online, and the social media were already awash with the cringe-making spectacle of the armoured, goggled warriors of Thames Valley Police deploying in a sleepy Oxfordshire village like some kind of Special Forces ninjas. Worst of all, the video featured a couple of momentary shots of Tom himself emerging from Brennan's house, and as the negative comments piled up online a number of eagle-eyed viewers had identified him from his earlier, much-publicised, appearance at the press conference. Accusations of harassment and heavy-handedness were flooding in from all quarters.

Superintendent Forbes was at his desk by eight, huffy and peevish and uncharacteristically reluctant to look Tom in the eye, which was fine by Tom. By nine, Terry Brennan's wealthy adoptive brother Mike Horton had waded into the fray. It now appeared that Horton had been paying for a professional carer to come in and attend to Brennan's needs twice daily as the illness worsened; a more recent hire of his was a belligerent-sounding solicitor named Fenwick who was threatening all kinds of litigation against the force for what he called its 'bullying police-state tactics, appalling incompetence, blithe disregard for human dignity and disgraceful persecution of a critically ill innocent member of the public'.

Things weren't going Tom's way, at least not until Thins Waller called with the news that the DNA result from the Stanton Harcourt cartridge case had finally come through late yesterday evening.

'You'll be pleased to know that it correlates with samples the forensics team took from Sweeney's flat,' Waller said. 'As pretty a match as I ever did see.'

'So it *was* him,' Tom said.

'Don't sound so surprised. Congratulations, Inspector. Looks like you nailed your man.'

'Great. Now all we've got to do is find the frigger.'

Saturday, warm and bright, and the mid-morning sun was shining out of a perfect blue sky over Port Meadow, a large tract of land that stretched from Jericho to Wolvercote around the northern and western edges of Oxford. The meadow's many winding footpaths were busy that day with cyclists, joggers and walkers; horses were grazing on the open pasture land. Over to the eastern side, swimmers were diving off the footbridge at Fiddler's Island, where the Thames met Castle Mill Stream. Across to the west, a small group of kids had got together to kick a football around on a patch of scrub grass, close to the narrow strip of woods that fringed the Burgess Field nature reserve.

The kids had ridden their bikes over from Jericho, down Walton Well Road and over the cattle grid into the meadow. There were nine of them; the oldest was fifteen, the owner of the football, and the youngest was a twelve-year-old boy named Toby Friar, whose elder brother Kev was among the gang. Toby wasn't a sporty child and hadn't really wanted to come along. He would sooner have stayed at home reading but Kev had dragged him into it to make up the numbers for their kick about.

The main reason why Toby hated sports so much wasn't that he was unsocial – in fact like all boys his age he craved the approval of his peers – but that he was quite overweight and too unfit to do much more than lumber breathlessly around, never able to keep up with the others, let alone get to kick the ball. Kev's secret plan, of course, was to make sure that Toby was on the opposing team so as to hamper their chances of winning. But after just a few minutes, red-faced and feeling humiliated and upset, Toby had had enough and shuffled off to the sidelines to sit against a tree and watch. The others' mocking laughter and calls of 'you're useless, fatty' brought salty tears of indignation and shame to his eyes. He should never have let himself be persuaded to come along.

Toby was soon completely forgotten by the rest of the gang as they raced around the grass belting the ball back and forth. He was wiping his red eyes and wondering if they'd even notice if he just got on his bike and went home, when he saw the man appear from the trees and walk towards him.

Toby had no idea how old the stranger was, because when you're twelve all grown-ups seem ancient. He looked friendly, and was smiling as he approached. He was wearing shorts and flip-flops and a loose flowery shirt that Toby thought looked kinda cool.

The man came right over and squatted in the long grass next to Toby, still smiling. He said, 'You all right there, bud?'

Toby nodded, and sniffed. He was self-conscious about crying in front of a stranger, but the man's reassuring way put him at his ease.

'I saw what happened,' the man said, nodding over at the football game. 'People can say cruel things sometimes. You shouldn't listen to them. Hey, my name's Stuart, but you can call me Stu. All my friends call me Stu.'

'My name's Toby,' said the boy.

'It's good to meet you, Toby. You want a bit of fudge?' He produced a packet from his shorts and offered it.

Toby knew he wasn't supposed to take anything from strangers, but Stu seemed really nice. Toby hesitated, then reached out and took a piece. Stu had one, too. It was vanilla, Toby's favourite.

'You know,' Stu said, leaning closer and speaking in a confidential kind of tone, 'when I was your age they used to call me names, too.'

'Really?'

Stu grinned. 'Oh, yeah. Really horrible. Jelly belly, lunch bucket, Jabba the Hutt, all that. Used to upset me, same as you.'

'But you're not fat.'

'That's 'cause I made myself really fit and strong,' Stu explained. 'I wanted to show them. And I did, too.'

Toby gazed across at his brother and the rest of them, still playing. The game had moved a little further away now. Nobody was paying a blind bit of notice to him any longer. 'I'd like to show them,' Toby muttered bitterly.

'And you could, easily,' Stu said.

'Really?'

'No sweat. Absolutely.' Stu ran his eyes appreciatively up and down Toby's podgy body. 'I mean, you're actually in really good shape. I don't think it would take you long at all. You want to know how I did it?'

'How?' Toby asked, accepting another bit of fudge and keen to hear Stu's amazing secret.

'I learned how to do karate,' Stu told him. 'And when I used my moves on them, it gave them such a fright that nobody ever teased me ever again. You should have seen their faces! How'd you like to teach those guys over there the same lesson?'

Toby nodded, his eyes brightening. He'd known that Stu was cool. But this was cooler still. 'Okay. That'd be awesome.'

Stu laughed and offered Toby a high-five. Toby laughed, too. Stu said, 'You know, if you wanted to get started right now, I could show you some really great moves. They're not hard to learn.'

'Okay.'

Stu glanced back at the trees, and pointed. 'It's nice and peaceful over there, behind those trees. There's a hut. The perfect place where I could give you your first lesson.'

'Seriously? Like, for free?'

'Come on, we'll have fun. You'll love it.' Stu was so full of enthusiasm that Toby felt himself being swept along. Stu jumped up and started heading towards the trees, beckoning for Toby to follow. Toby scrambled awkwardly to his feet. With a last glance at the gang, he followed Stu. Soon they were deep in the trees, and the foliage was so thick you couldn't see the meadow behind them. Stu was pushing through the branches ahead. He turned and smiled and said, 'Come on, Tobe. It's just up here.'

They reached the hut. It was a tumbledown old thing that looked like a lot of older kids came here to smoke and drink beer. The door was open. Stu was motioning for him to go in.

Toby hesitated. 'Are you sure?'

'Yeah, yeah, of course. It'll be great!' But Toby thought there was something different about Stu's smile, and his voice sounded a little weird. He stopped and took a step back.

'What are you worried about?'

'I think I should go,' Toby said. 'I don't like this.'

'Don't be stupid. Come here!' Stu had stopped smiling. He reached out and grabbed Toby's arm. He moved really fast and his grip was so hard that it hurt. Toby let out a yelp. 'Agh! Let go!'

But Stu didn't let go. Toby felt himself being pulled off his feet. He fell into the dirt. Stu's hand was suddenly clamping tight over his mouth and a voice was rasping in his ear, 'I told you this would be fun, didn't I?'

Toby wanted to cry out, but he couldn't. He was pinned, helpless. Stu's weight was crushing him.

And then Toby heard the strangest noise. A funny sort of pop, a bit like the cork coming out of a bottle of fizzy wine the grown-ups had at Christmas, but louder. Then he heard it again. Pop. Stu's weight suddenly wasn't crushing him any more, and the voice in his ear had stopped because now Stu was rolling over in the dirt, clutching at his chest and making a terrible wet grunting sound like 'Hyuk, hyuk.'

As Toby looked up through his veil of tears he realised that they weren't alone any more. There was a man all dressed in black standing there, where before there had been only branches and leaves. He seemed to have come out of thin air. You couldn't see the man's face, because it was hidden behind a black mask that covered everything except his eyes and mouth. He had something in his hand. Something he was pointing at Stu. It went pop-pop twice more.

Toby had never seen a real gun before, but in that moment of surreal horror he suddenly realised what was happening. He stared at the masked man in black, then at Stu's body in the dirt. Stu wasn't grunting or moving any longer. Four new flowers had appeared on his flowery shirt. Big red ones. They were growing. Spreading. Turning darker.

That was when Toby finally found his voice again, and screamed.

But when the boy turned back towards the man in black, he was gone.

CHAPTER EIGHTEEN

Within minutes of the shooting, Tom's task force had been alerted and he was en route to the location in his newly fixed Barracuda, courtesy of Ken Sparrowhawk. The man was a genius. So, apparently, was the masked shooter who'd once again managed to slip away from the scene of the crime and vanish without a trace.

Despite having reportedly introduced himself as 'Stu' to his intended victim, the dead man was identified from a bloodstained driving licence found in his wallet as Ewan Moss. Moss was twenty-nine, unemployed, and lived in a shared house in the Headington area of the city. He was also a convicted paedophile who'd been sentenced to four years for possessing thousands of images of child pornography and attempting to sexually assault a ten-year-old boy in Oxford's Angel Meadow. It was standard practice for relatively minor sex offenders to serve only half their jail sentences; in Moss's case, citing mental health problems, he'd been able to finagle his way to early release after just over a year and had been walking free for the last five months. His spell in prison evidently hadn't done much to cure him of his child-molesting impulses. Now the shooter had put an end to them, permanently.

As Tom arrived at Port Meadow the police were in the process of closing the place off to the public and interviewing possible witnesses who might have seen a man in black entering or leaving the meadow that morning. That was the only detail they had to go on, based on what the boy, now being treated for shock, had told his elder brother. Toby Friar's parents had been called and were now with him at the hospital. Meanwhile, officers were on red alert hunting for a suspect fitting Vinnie Sweeney's description through this whole area of the city.

Tom parked the Barracuda at the entrance and was taken in a police Land Rover down the bumpy track into the meadow. From the grassy patch near the edge of Burgess Field nature reserve he threaded his way through the trees to where the killing had taken place. The busy crime scene was already cordoned off and Tom recognised the familiar figure of Thins Waller finishing off his preliminary work before the body was removed.

'Morning, Inspector,' he said laconically. 'No rest for the wicked, eh? Just as I was looking forward to watching the cricket this afternoon.'

'What've we got?'

'An interesting change of modus operandi, for one thing,' Thins said. 'No rifle this time. The gentleman died from four gunshots, fired at close range from a handgun, possibly a nine-millimetre though it's hard to say until I yank the bullets out of him.' He motioned at the body. 'See? No exit wounds, which tells me the rounds were possibly subsonic, with expanding hollowpoint bullets. Lots of damage. There probably won't be much left of his heart and lungs, once we open him up. I'm guessing the weapon was fitted with a sound suppressor, as well as a case catcher because we haven't been able to locate any brass.'

Tom nodded. If Thins was right, the switch from a rifle to a handgun fitted with the theory that Sweeney was armed with a CZ auto pistol in addition to his sniper weapon. He was versatile. And showing a considerable level of proficiency with different types of firearm. Tom could see that the bullet holes in the victim's chest were tightly grouped together. Even at close range, it took skill to plant your shots so fast and accurately. Not to mention the almost uncanny ability he had to disappear into thin air. The kid had said he was there one second, gone the next. So far, not a single person had reported seeing a man in black leaving the meadow in a hurry. It was early days; but still, Tom wasn't optimistic.

Such hopes as he had only faded away as the day dragged on. Every available officer had been deployed across Oxford, surveillance camera footage scrutinised, dozens of people interviewed, without a ghost of a sighting of their suspect. He spent a while at his desk, slurping coffee and chasing shadows, then wandered through into the staff lounge where a number of officers, including Billie Flowers, were watching a BBC Oxford news update on the big screen. The breaking story of the third killing was whipping the frenzy up to a whole new level and the media hadn't hung around in grabbing young Toby Friar's parents for their first television interview. Tom had a feeling it wouldn't be their last.

John and Maureen Friar were standing outside the hospital, surrounded by a jostling crowd as they spoke to the news reporter. He was tall and gaunt, and she was short and round. While his wife was visibly emotional, John Friar's face was tight with fury and he looked ready to eat the camera alive.

'As far as I'm concerned, the police should call off the hunt for this hero who's cleaning up our streets and ridding the world of this trash. If it wasn't for him, I don't even want to think about what might have happened to our boy.'

The news reporter started gamely trying to say something about the dangers of supporting vigilantism, but Mrs Friar interrupted, in a voice hoarse from crying, 'How can the authorities allow these monsters to roam our towns, our parks where our children play? It's disgusting. Something should be done about it!'

'Something *is* being done,' seethed her husband, not letting the reporter get a word in. 'And the police want to stop it! Maybe they should try doing their real job, protecting innocent people from sick predators. Maybe if the courts didn't let these animals walk free with no more than a slap on the wrist, then we'd have some proper justice. Well, I say justice has been done.' Turning to look directly into the camera, he added, 'Whoever you are, sir, I want to thank you for saving my boy.'

The reporter struggled for words, then put on a frozen smile and closed off with, 'And there you have it. Jan Pilling, BBC news.'

'Before you know it, they'll be nominating Sweeney for mayor,' Tom muttered, having seen enough and going off to get more coffee. He was back at his desk with a fresh cup in his hand when his phone rang.

'I've just heard,' Desi said.

'I was about to call you.'

'About Ewan Moss?' she asked.

'Was he one of yours?'

'He did go through Metcalfe House after he was released. But no, he wasn't one of mine. Meaning I never had any dealings with him personally.'

Tom had in fact been about to call her, but not really to talk about Moss. He'd been unable to get Desi Fielding out of his head since their evening together, and had slept very little the night before. 'When can I see you?' He blurted out the words in an undertone, worried someone might overhear. 'I have something after work but I could come over later.' Tom and Harvey had arranged another therapy session for seven that evening, if that was what their meetings could still be called, now that the Claddagh pub had become their regular venue and the topic of discussion seldom focused on Tom's original reason for seeing him.

There was a hesitation in her voice before she replied, 'I'm sorry, I've got private clients lined up bumper to bumper until late this evening. By the time I'm finished I'll be so knackered I'll want an early night.'

Tom had a mental flash of the appointments diary he'd seen on the desk in her study, crammed with entries. 'Seeing clients on a Saturday?'

'What can I say? I'm so much in demand, I have to fit them in where I can.'

'You work too hard, so you do.'

'I'm not the only one. You sound super-stressed out.' She paused. 'What about tomorrow night? You could come over to the house and we could watch a movie or something. Help you relax.'

'Tomorrow, then,' he agreed.

'You look super-stressed out,' were Harvey's first words when Tom walked into the back bar of the Claddagh at seven that evening.

'That's what everyone says. Get you a pint?'

Harvey was already halfway through his first. 'Why not?' Then, as Tom returned to their corner table a few moments later, Harvey said, 'I think I have an idea why you look so worn out. This investigation of yours is leading you a merry dance, isn't it?'

Tom took a very long and very welcome pull at the creamy top of his Guinness. 'And then there were three,' he said with a dark chuckle.

'Think he'll ever stop?'

'He'll stop,' Tom said, 'the day I throw his arse in a cell.'

'Maybe you won't catch him,' Harvey said. 'Maybe it'd be better if you never did.'

Tom looked sharply at him. 'How's that?'

'I was thinking about what the boy's father said on television. It was brave of him to make an admission like that. Then again, I'm sure he's not alone. A lot of people, including some within your own profession I'm sure, could be excused for secretly wanting things to take their natural course. Who knows,' Harvey pondered, 'maybe if I had kids, I'd be the first in line to cheer this killer on. It's not as though he's harming the innocent, is he? And yet, can a civilised society condone the actions of a lone executioner who takes the law into his own hands?' Harvey finished his first pint with relish and attacked the second. 'Exploring the dark borderlands between legality and ethics. Dangerous ground for a man of your calling to venture onto, and no mistake. It's quite a philosophical conundrum, isn't it?'

Tom grumped and said, 'Aye, well, it's not the only conundrum in this case. And I wouldn't say it's the one that's bugging me the most, either.'

'If you'd care to share your worries with me, I'm only too happy to offer my advice. Strictly on a therapeutic basis, of course.'

'It's Sweeney,' Tom said after another long draught of his pint. 'Nothing about him seems to fit.'

'Such as?'

'Think about who this shooter is,' Tom said. 'This guy is clever, he's efficient, he's capable. He knows his way around the system well enough to get inside knowledge of where these released paedos live. He picks his targets, then he watches them, probably for days, even weeks, following them around and getting to know their movements and their routines without ever being noticed, holding back from making his move. Then when it's time to strike, he chooses the perfect spot and just the right time to do the job quick and clean and then disappear into thin air like a spook. What I can't figure out is how a nutjob lowlife maniac loser like Vinnie Sweeney could pull even half of that off without getting caught. How's he getting the inside track on where to find them? And where'd he ever learn to shoot so well?'

'That part's explainable,' Harvey said. 'I thought you said he was heavily into guns.'

'Deacts,' Tom said. 'You know who spends all their cash on a pile of useless metal like that? The kind of wankers who stand in front of the mirror and do the whole Travis Bickle thing.'

'*Taxi Driver*,' Harvey said. 'I remember that one. Robert de Niro, right?' He screwed his face into a mean-looking scowl and made a pistol with his fingers. '"You talkin' to me? You talkin' to me?"'

'Yeah, exactly. That kind.'

Harvey considered for a moment, then said, 'So you're concerned that the emerging profile of this skilled, efficient assassin doesn't fit with what we know about the suspect. I have to admit, based on what little you've told me, I have a hard time reconciling in my own mind how an impulsive, violent lunatic like Sweeney, a loose cannon you might say, could have the patience and discipline, not to mention the intelligence, required to plan and carry out these near-perfect crimes.'

135

'You put it better than I can,' Tom said. 'But that's pretty much the size of it.'

'But what about the DNA evidence? I thought that was absolutely conclusive proof?'

'It is. Or it ought to be, in theory. The empty cartridge came from him. He touched it. He carried it in his pocket. It must have been his.'

'You're right,' Harvey said. 'It is a conundrum.'

They sat in silence for a moment, both thinking. 'I'm getting another drink,' Tom said.

When Tom returned from the bar with two fresh pints, Harvey said, 'I've figured out how it could work. To use another fiction analogy, consider that Sweeney is Renfield to a hypothetical Dracula.'

'Renfield, the fella that ate the flies? I saw that fillum.'

Harvey nodded. 'That's the one, although I'm not suggesting that this particular person eats flies.'

'There were enough of them in his flat to have fed him for a month, that's for sure,' Tom said.

'The point being, the same way Renfield acted as his master's servant in the story, doing his bidding, helping him to carry out all these nefarious deeds, perhaps Sweeney was in cahoots with someone else, someone more talented, the real brains behind the operation, who's got the inside track as you say and is picking the targets, perhaps also doing the actual killing. Or maybe, just maybe, Sweeney has some contacts from prison that enable him to locate where these released offenders live. Either way he's involved somehow. That could explain how his DNA came to be on the cartridge case. No?' Harvey looked expectantly at Tom. 'What do you think? Personally, I think it's brilliant.'

'Maybe,' Tom replied doubtfully. 'Maybe not. Still doesn't feel right.'

'That was my best shot. I give up. So what are you going to do?'

'Go on hunting for Sweeney. What else can I do? But at the same time I'm going to keep digging. There's something more to this than meets the eye, and I'm damned if I won't find it.'

The concept of time was just a faded memory now. Day and night were merged into the same endless pitch blackness; the outside world seemed to belong to another reality, one that only existed in the man's feverish dreams. A place where the faces and names of people he'd known all seemed to float about in a jumbled confusion. Some of them were people he'd hurt, but he could no longer recall who, or why. Voices, talking to him but their words unclear. Calling his name. A pretty woman in a red dress, smiling at him. Who was she? Had he known her? Was she one of the people he'd hurt, too?

Other times, he dreamed of escaping from this place. Running, running, feeling clean air rushing over his face. The dreams were so vivid sometimes that they jolted him awake, disorientated and blinking in the dark. Then as consciousness slowly returned, he would realise with a sense of sickening dread that nothing had changed and he was still a prisoner behind these grimy steel bars. Knowing that sooner or later his captor would always return, and that perhaps the next visit was when he'd carry out his threat of torture.

Slowly, slowly, the man had come to understand that his captor was drugging him – that the nausea, the drowsiness, the fog that seemed to envelop his mind and befuddle his thoughts, were caused by something that was being put in his food. Often he awoke with that bitter aftertaste of whatever it was still on his tongue.

In one of his more lucid moments, the man had decided that he would no longer eat what he was brought. He'd rather starve to death than go on like this, an animal in a cage. His intention wasn't to take a stand against his captor by going on hunger strike. He didn't want his captor to know, because the plan he'd formed in his mind needed the bastard to be off his guard.

So, since three feeding times ago, the man had been tossing the contents of his dish out of the cage by the fistful, forcing his arm painfully between the bars in order to throw it as far away as he could. He'd listened to the squeaking and scraping noises as the cellar rats ventured out of their holes to eat it. Sometimes he could hear the tortured squeals of a rat that had eaten too much of the drugged food and was unable to move as its peers set upon it and tore it apart. It made the man think about what he would do to his captor, when the moment came.

The man was weak with hunger now, and the lightheadedness caused by his starvation was almost as debilitating as the effects of the tranquilliser. But not quite. His hatred and burning desire to escape kept his mind sharp as he lay there working over and over his plan.

He'd been working over it yet again, lying curled up beneath his thin blanket, when he heard the familiar rattle of keys, followed by the soft pad of descending footsteps. The dim light came on. The man in the cage lay very still and kept his eyes firmly closed. His heart was pounding so loudly he was afraid the captor might hear it.

Satisfied that his prisoner was soundly unconscious, the captor drew open the spring latch on the cage's mesh door. The door swung open with a groan of rusty hinges. The man remained perfectly inert as the captor stepped inside the cage. He could feel, almost touch, the presence of his hated enemy close by, but he lay there breathlessly waiting for just the right moment. He knew his window of opportunity would last just a few seconds while the captor replaced his slop bucket and refilled his empty food dish.

Then the man gathered all his energy like a coiled spring and lashed out with a savage kick that caught his enemy in the back of the legs and sent him sprawling against the far side of the cage. The man sprang to his feet. His heart was bursting with fierce energy, his hunger and weakness all forgotten, as the black-clad figure of his captor lay face down across the floor of the cage, one foot sticking out of the open door. His head had hit the bars hard enough to stun him. He was groaning and trying to get up.

Rage burned through the man's veins like fire as he stood over him. Now the tables were turned. Now he was the strong one, and his enemy was weak and vulnerable. Now he was going to destroy him.

Smash his brains to a pulp. Stamp his bones into pieces. Break him apart.

But the man was too slow. Regaining his senses, the captor twisted up on one elbow. The gunshot exploded like a bomb. The man felt the searing heat of the flash on the side of his face and the shock as the bullet ploughed past his cheek and took off part of his left ear, before it shattered the hanging light bulb and plunged the cellar into pitch darkness. He staggered back, tripped against the bottom of the open door and fell out of the cage. The captor fired again, a halo of orange-white flame spitting from its muzzle. The man clambered desperately to his feet and kicked the cage door shut. The spring latch went home. The captor was trapped inside.

The pistol boomed a third time. The man felt the path of the bullet scorching through the air just inches from him. He ran, stumbling, blind, wildly groping his way towards the cellar steps. Tripping over the first and barking his shin to the bone against the second. Scrambling up the steps on all fours like an animal. Making it to the top of the steps and crashing through the door.

The man found himself in a dimly lit passage. He had no memory of this place, because he'd been drugged unconscious when he was brought here. Plaster hung off the walls as though nobody had lived here for years. Dizzy from weakness and pain and shock, pouring blood from his torn ear but every nerve in his body alive with exhilaration, he staggered along the passage to another door, pushed it open and tasted fresh air for the first time in how many days, he didn't know.

The man stood swaying on his feet and gazed around him. It was night. He could see no lights of neighbouring houses, because there weren't any. This was some kind of farm, or had been. Now it was just a rundown wreck of a place, with broken windows and rotting woodwork. He wanted to set fire to the house with his captor trapped down there in the cellar, bury him under fifty tons of burning wreckage. But more than anything, he just wanted to get away from here. His captor would die a lingering death from starvation anyway. Let him rot down there.

Parked around the side of the rundown farmhouse, the man found a car. It was an old banger of a thing, half eaten away with rust, but the key was in the ignition and when he twisted it the engine coughed into life. He crunched the stick into gear and took off down a rutted track. He was in no fit state to drive. The blood was leaking all over him and his vision was kind of cloudy. The car skidded and slewed from side to side and almost ran off the edge of the track, but he made it to the bottom and surged out of the gate, finding himself on a winding narrow country road. Hedges zipped by in the dim headlights as he sped wildly along.

Now he was approaching a junction, marked with signposts that his brain was too fuddled to read. He skidded out into the middle of the junction without slowing down, saw the lights of the car coming the other way and heard the squeal of brakes, but too late to react even if his reactions had been good. The collision spun the banger around in the road and shattered the passenger side windows. Through his mental haze he saw the other car roll off the verge and into the ditch.

The man didn't care. He laughed. He was free. Nothing else mattered. He restarted his stalled engine and kept going, veering all over the road. On and on, the white line streaking towards him and starbursts of light making him squint, the scream of horns blaring as they shot past on both sides. He felt floaty, quite disconnected from reality. Everything was like a dream, like being back in the cage where he'd had no concept of time going by, except different. The road became much wider now, and there were lights coming at him from all directions, dazzling and confusing him.

The man barely registered the oncoming articulated lorry or heard the blare of its airhorns until its headlights were filling the whole inside of the car, and by then the head-on collision was inevitable. As though in slow motion the front wings folded like paper and the man felt the forces of sudden, extreme deceleration lift his body out of the driver's seat and catapult him through the windscreen. For a hundredth of a second his world flashed blinding white, and then went black.

CHAPTER NINETEEN

The major road smash that took place at 10.06 p.m. on the A34 dual carriageway sixteen miles from Oxford that Saturday night involved several vehicles. Five people were injured, three of them seriously, in addition to the single fatality who had been the lone occupant of a 2002 Honda Stream that caused the accident.

Several alarmed motorists had called in to report the Honda driving erratically at high speed the wrong way down the dual carriageway just moments before the crash. The car had already been involved in a separate incident a few miles away, in which another vehicle had been forced off the road. Its driver had luckily escaped unhurt, but the trucker at the wheel of the articulated lorry into which the Honda subsequently ploughed headlong at a combined speed of over 120 miles an hour had been much less fortunate, needing to be cut from the wreckage of his cab and airlifted to the John Radcliffe Emergency Department with a ruptured spleen, broken back and compound fractures of both legs.

Meanwhile, first responders were setting about the grim task of recovering the corpse of the Honda's driver, which was removed from the scene in three separate body bags. He hadn't been wearing a seatbelt and the car's airbag system appeared to have malfunctioned. The least mangled body part they found was an intact left arm, severed above the elbow, which had been thrown over forty feet from the crash site.

Beyond the fact that he was a white male possibly in his mid-thirties, identifying the body proved unusually difficult, as the driver had been carrying no ID and the car had not been registered to him or anyone else. A DVLA search quickly revealed that its number plates were taken from a scrapyard; an examination of the twisted wreckage would later show that identifying numbers had been removed from the engine and chassis. Nor had anyone called in to report the mystery man missing, even after breaking news of the smash appeared on local TV. Running out of options, pathologists had resorted to taking fingerprint samples from the recovered left arm and running them through the police database in hope of a match.

They'd got one.

Tom McAllister's phone rang at twenty past midnight, just as he was winding down after his solitary evening meal. He'd been feeling too restless and agitated to cook anything fancy that night, and had settled for a frozen pizza instead, washed down with a single bottle of Langtree Hundred.

He snatched up the phone on the second ring. 'McAllister.'

It was Thins Waller, calling from the forensic lab. 'Sorry to bother you so late, Inspector. But I thought you might be interested to know that I'm sitting looking at the remains of one Vincent F. Sweeney on my slab. Or should I say, the bits of him that were scraped off the fast lane of the A34 just over two hours ago.'

And with that, the hunt for Sweeney had come to a grinding halt. Tom was suddenly sitting bolt upright on the sofa. 'You're sure?'

'Would I lie to you?'

Tom looked at his watch. 'Can I come over?'

'I'll be here for about another hour.'

Tom jumped in the Barracuda with Radar and raced over to the lab, where Thins was the only person working late. He led the way to Tom's favourite place, the morgue area. Disinfectant fumes were so thick in the air they stung Tom's eyes. Thins gave him an overall and a surgical mask to wear. 'Doesn't it freak you out, being here alone at night with all the deaders?' Tom asked.

'Poh, you soon get used to it, dear boy. Besides, I find that the dead make for more congenial company than their living, breathing counterparts. Present company excepted, of course.'

'Best compliment I've had all week,' Tom said. 'Is this him?' Pointing at an amorphous shape under a sheet on the autopsy slab. 'Show me.'

'Are you sure? He's not a pretty picture.'

Thins pulled on a pair of latex gloves and drew back part of the sheet, revealing the body but keeping the head covered. He'd been right. To even call the collection of grisly parts a body would have been a misnomer. Tom swallowed, and was glad he hadn't eaten a rich meal that night.

'You're lucky we were able to identify him at all,' Thins said. 'Dental records aren't often much use when the subject has gone head-first into the grille of a Scania eighteen-wheeler at a hundred miles an hour.' He pointed at the disembodied arm on the slab. 'But we got a nice set of prints from that. Sweeney having been in the prison system, it was an instant match. Now, there are a couple of interesting anomalies here that I thought you should know about. First is the presence of a fairly high level of Phenobarbital in Mr Sweeney's system. The blood pathology results could have taken days, but I have a friend at the hospital who was able to run a test in a couple of hours. I'd just got them back when I called you.'

'Phenobarbital?'

'It's a barbiturate drug used to treat seizures, but also as a powerful sedative. The after-effects can linger in the system for days. Our boy had enough in him to dope a horse. He could have been prescribed it, but I'd doubt that as phenobarb is less often used these days. More likely it came from some illicit source. Plenty of those around.'

'Might account for why he crashed the car?' Tom asked.

'In large part, for sure. But he's also showing signs of anaemia, low sodium and dehydration, due to starvation. That in itself could have caused faintness and disorientation.'

'He's been starving himself?'

'Either that, or someone else has been doing it to him. You tell me. He also has some ligature marks on his wrists, or at any rate, the one wrist that's still intact enough to tell. Looks like he's been tethered up with something like steel handcuffs, not too long ago. Then there's this.'

Thins yanked back the rest of the sheet, revealing the crushed head underneath.

'Jesus.' Tom tried not to return the china marble gaze of the single remaining eyeball, flattened out of shape and loosely held in the mangled socket. This was going to put him off hard-boiled eggs for a long time.

'Massive trauma to the skull, as you can see. Most of his face was sheared off when he went through the windscreen, along with much of the hair and scalp. But look at this here.'

Tom peered where Thins was pointing with his gloved finger. 'All I see is minced beef.'

'His left ear. See the way the bottom part of the lobe has been clipped off? Could be a glass injury, but look at the way the flesh is cauterised along the edge of the lesion. To my eye that looks like a bullet wound. Furthermore, this remaining part of his cheek has tiny traces of GSR embedded in the skin.'

GSR was gunshot residue. Thins said, 'Suggesting that your boy could have been on the receiving end of a firearm discharge, from close range, no more than about five feet away, and quite recently.'

'Someone shot him?'

'Don't quote me on that,' Thins replied. 'I certainly wouldn't stand up in court and stake my reputation on it. A positive GSR test can mean all kinds of things. Anyone who's been in proximity to a recently fired weapon could get residue on them, just by handling it and then touching their face. It's something of an inexact science. Even suicide victims can test negative for GSR.'

'But if you were right,' Tom said, 'and if we put it all together, it'd look like someone kept him prisoner until very recently, starved and doped up, then maybe tried to blow his brains out when he escaped?'

'It's a rather tenuous hypothesis. But plausible enough, I suppose.'

'In which case, how's he going around taking out paedophiles all this time?'

'As to that, I couldn't even begin to take the wildest of guesses,' Thins said. 'Not my job, Inspector.'

It was after two by the time Tom got home, feeling baffled, frustrated and irritable and still unable to forget the sight of Sweeney's staring eyeball. He barely slept that night and was back in the office before eight, fuelled with enough black coffee to keep him wired for the rest of the day. His first email of the morning was from the SCIU, Serious Collision Investigation Unit, confirming that the 2002 Honda Stream was an unregistered vehicle with VIN numbers removed and fake plates. Was it Sweeney's? Could it have belonged to an accomplice? Or, if the nagging doubts that Thins Waller had planted in Tom's head and kept him awake through the small hours were right, could the car's owner be the person who had been keeping Sweeney prisoner?

But none of these concerns seemed to affect

Superintendent Forbes, who appeared to have recovered from his embarrassment over the Terry Brennan matter. 'This crosses off the only name on our suspect list,' he told Tom in his office. 'Shut down the investigation,. Case closed. We're done and dusted here, effective as of last night.'

'Could that not be acting a wee bit prematurely?' Tom said. 'Sir.'

'I understand you have certain reservations, Inspector,' Forbes replied, motioning at Tom's report on his desk. 'I don't happen to share them. There's no compelling evidence whatsoever to contradict the fact that Sweeney killed these people. The DNA evidence speaks for itself. It's time to move on. I'm reassigning you to the Jonathan Baxter case.'

'The Baxter case?'

'Mr Baxter is a very important man,' Forbes said, peering down his nose at Tom. 'I'm getting pressure from on high to resolve this issue as a matter of urgency.'

Jonathan Baxter was a high-up and little-liked official of Oxford City Council who'd been suspected of corrupt dealings in the past, and lately had drawn controversy over his push to close and sell a popular sports and recreation centre in Temple Cowley. Public outcry against him had become so fierce that he'd received anonymous death threats. Tom happened to know that Forbes belonged to the same golf club as the Very Important Man and a number of his council cronies.

'Seriously? Like I've got nothing better to do?'

'Let's have a little less lip and a little more action from you, Inspector. Now, if you don't mind, I have some important phone calls to make. Close the door on your way out.'

* * *

'I can't stand that gobshite. If only the good fairy could stick a roof on the watermill for me, I'd have the restaurant open in a fortnight and sod the whole force.'

It was Sunday evening, and Tom and Desi were sitting together in her comfortable living room, having a glass of wine while waiting for the meal she was cooking to be ready. She'd asked him over the phone earlier whether he liked Italian, and said she'd do a pasta bake. The way she described the recipe, Tom wasn't sure if he had much confidence in her culinary skills. But when you're in love you'll eat anything. Just being in her presence was exhilarating. He so much wanted to lean over and kiss her, the way they'd been about to do the other night when the breakdown truck interrupted them. One step at a time, Tom told himself.

Desi had said Radar could come too. The big shepherd was stretched happily out on the living room rug at their feet, making himself very much at home. The living room had the same view as her study, and the sun had set over the trees of Bagley Wood. It was another warm night. Every window was open and a fresh summery breeze circulated about the house.

Tom hadn't wanted to get into discussing work, but the conversation had inevitably drifted that way and he told her the whole story of Sweeney's death, his dialogue with Thins Waller and the way Forbes had shut the case down and put him on another he considered a waste of his abilities. Almost like Forbes was slyly looking for some way to punish him for having shown him up with the Brennan affair. Tom was aware that he was probably talking too much. Desi was saying little in reply, and seemed subdued.

'That's enough about my troubles,' he said, changing the subject. 'Are you okay? You look a little out of sorts.'

She sighed, 'Sorry. I'm just tired, and a bit preoccupied. One of my private clients is going through a really bad time and I keep thinking about her. I know we're supposed not to get emotionally involved. But sometimes it's difficult to stay objective.'

'Police work isn't much different. We're dealing with people's lives. And I told you, you work too hard.' Tom was about to say more, but then, catching a smell in the air, he broke off and sniffed. 'Something's burning.'

'Shit! The bake!' Desi leapt off the sofa and ran towards the kitchen. Tom got to his feet and ambled after her, drink in hand. Sure enough, smoke was pouring from the oven door. Desi blinked and coughed as she opened it, put on a pair of oven gloves and lifted out the baking dish with its blackened, incinerated contents. She laid it on top of the cooker hob and stared at it disconsolately. 'It's ruined. I must have turned the heat up too high.'

Tom came over and peered at the carbonised mess. Privately, he was thinking that Desi's pasta bake was only slightly less edible now than when it had gone into the oven, and she'd done the poor thing a favour by cremating it like that. But putting on a show of sympathy he touched her shoulder and said, 'Oh, what a pity. I was looking forward to it.'

'I've nothing else in the house that I could offer you instead. What a disaster. What an idiot I am.' She looked almost ready to cry.

'Don't worry,' he said cheerfully. 'Listen, I passed a fish and chip shop in Kennington on my way over. What do you say to a takeaway?'

'I so wanted to make something nice, to thank you for the other evening. Not that I could ever hope to live up to your standard in a million years.'

'Fish and chips is nice too,' Tom said. 'It's one of the grandest old traditions in British food culture, so it is. You sit tight. Stick that Chablis back in the fridge. Be a shame to let it go warm. I'll be there and back in ten minutes flat.'

He was, clutching two paper packages that he put into the still-warm oven while he took charge of things. Tom

McAllister, to the rescue. There was a sea salt grinder, a fresh lemon, some mayonnaise and a bottle of cider vinegar in her kitchen. Perfect. He sliced neat wedges of lemon for the fish, then quickly devilled the mayo with just a pinch of cayenne pepper and a little mustard, dolloped tastefully on a side dish and served up with the impromptu meal at her small kitchen table. 'There. This is cosy,' he commented, smiling.

'It's not the Three Bay Leaves.'

'It's good enough for me,' he said. 'Cheers.' They clinked glasses.

Desi's mood improved as they ate, helped by the wine, and the pasta bake soon became a memory. Tom hadn't laid out knives or forks and she followed his example, eating with her fingers and dipping chips in the devilled mayo.

'It's delicious. And so simple.'

'Simple is good.'

'You're amazing.'

'That's what everyone says.'

There was no more shop talk, and before long they were relaxed and laughing and conversing like two people who'd known one another all their lives. He felt good with her. She seemed to feel good with him, too. It felt right, as right as it had that night under the stars in their own private open-topped restaurant. No, he thought. It felt even better than that first night.

After dinner they returned to the living room with more wine, and sat together on the sofa to watch a movie, something silly and fun. It didn't matter. They laughed at the daft jokes and the slapstick routines, and snuggled gradually closer.

Then it was late and time for him to go. He said, 'I should be getting back.'

But Desi laid a hand on his and looked at him and said softly, 'No. I want you to stay with me.'

CHAPTER TWENTY

'So it's over, then, is it?' Harvey said.

Eleven days had gone by since the demise of Vinnie Sweeney, and there had been no more shootings. Every successive day that passed appeared to confirm more and more definitively that the paedophile killer was finished and gone.

Tom and Harvey Pepper were ensconced in their usual corner of the Claddagh, working through another of their therapy sessions. The pub was quiet that evening and the back bar room was almost empty apart from themselves. Speaking in low voices under the raucous fiddles and flutes of the Dubliners, they could talk quite freely about the things that Tom, not always strictly in accordance with police non-disclosure regulations, had confided in his friend.

'Maybe,' Tom replied.

'Hmm. Is that a degree of ambivalence that's shared in common with many of your fellow officers?'

'No. And I don't share it with them, either,' Tom replied. When a case was solved he always felt some instinctual sense of closure, but not this time. There were still too many things that didn't make sense to him. Sweeney's ligature marks, the suspected gunshot injury, the drug residue in his system, the signs of recent starvation . . . night after night they preyed on his mind as he lay there unable to sleep.

But hey, Thames Valley Police had nabbed their man thanks to the wizardry of DNA forensic science, and done their bit to protect the public (not that the public had been much concerned); and if that was good enough for Forbes and the top brass, who the hell was he to argue?

Being the perceptive individual he was, arguably even more perceptive when he had a couple of pints inside him, Harvey Pepper could read all those thoughts on Tom's face as clearly as if they'd been printed there. He paused, nodding reflectively as he composed his own thoughts on the matter. 'For my part, I'm still betting on my own little hypothesis, the one I told you about that Saturday night before Sweeney was killed.'

'Dracula and Renfield.'

'That's the one. I'd say that the more mysterious elements of this case, these incongruous little details that give you so much grief while your superiors conveniently choose to ignore them, only serve to strengthen the slave and master theory.'

'Then again, it's been eleven days,' Tom said, not really listening. How many times had he gone back and forth on this? It was driving him nuts. 'Who knows. Maybe they're right.'

'Or else maybe Dracula is still out there. Doing what a good vampire does, after he's lost his ghoulish little helper.'

Tom looked at him. 'Which is what?'

'Which is to seek out a replacement,' Harvey said.

Tom gave a grunt. 'Aye, right. I can just see myself strolling into Forbsie's office and trying to sell him on that one.'

'You'd become a hero. They'd have to promote you to . . . what's the next rank up from you?'

'Detective Chief Inspector.'

' . . . for calling it so accurately. Because if I'm right, it's only a matter of time before our serial-killer mastermind finds himself a new Renfield, some willing lackey who loathes paedophiles just as much as he does, and can help in his quest to eliminate every last one of them. Then bingo, he'll be back in action. Just remember, you heard it here first.'

'All right, smarty-pants. Seeing as you're so hot on this theory of yours, explain to me how come Dracula turned on his own guy and tried to rub him out.'

'Maybe he decided he couldn't trust Renfield any longer,' Harvey said. 'Perhaps Sweeney had outlived his usefulness. Vampires are fickle like that. He'll always be able to find another.'

'Can we not talk about this any more?' Tom groaned. 'It's beginning to bore the hole off me, so it is.'

'Sorry. But you *are* my most interesting client. So tell me instead, how are you getting on with unravelling the plot against our illustrious city councillor?'

'Made some progress. I found out who wanted to kill the guy.'

'Really? Who?'

'Me,' Tom said. 'I swear, if I have to spend another day on that frigging case—'

'And yet, you don't look totally unhappy, for a chap who's got so many troubles at work.'

'You're the shrink. Take a wild guess why that might be.' Tom couldn't quite repress the involuntary grin that took control of his face.

'I wouldn't pry into a man's love life.'

'Is that a fact?'

'Well, maybe just a little,' Harvey admitted.

'No complaints in that department,' Tom said. 'Things are great between us. I'm on cloud nine, Harvey.'

'I'll drink to that sentiment.' Harvey raised his glass.

'Tell you what, though. I never realised what a workaholic she is. We've been seeing each other whenever we can, but her schedule's so full it's like you have to book her a week in advance. I keep telling her she should slow down a wee bit. I'd love to be able to spend some proper time with her, you know?'

'Maybe if you were to offer her a real treat. Like a trip somewhere.'

'You must've read my mind again,' Tom said. 'I've got a free long weekend coming up next month and I asked if she'd come away with me, maybe book into a nice hotel together for a couple of nights, check out a couple of really top-notch restaurants while we're at it. Might be able to steal a menu idea or two.'

'And were you able to persuade her?'

Tom shook his head. 'Not a chance. This time it wasn't because of her work, though. She's got this uncle Hugh who lives in a village called Hurley, in Berkshire. She visits now and then, and she'd already arranged to go and see him on those dates. So there goes my romantic weekend.'

'You couldn't have found some way to combine the two? Surely there must be some decent enough hotels and restaurants in Berkshire.'

'I had the same idea,' Tom said. 'No go. Apparently old uncle Hugh's a bit of a curmudgeon. Likes to have her all to himself.'

'Ah, the possessive type.'

'They're very close. She told me he was like a father to her, growing up, taught her all kinds of stuff.'

'Looks like you have some stiff competition there, Tom.'

Tom sat frowning for a moment, but then the beaming smile returned to his face. 'She's worth the effort, though, Harvey. She's worth every bit of it, and more.'

'I'm happy for you, buddy,' Harvey said. 'Really I am.' Then he looked down at the table for a moment, and Tom noticed a flash of pain and sadness pass through his expression, like a cloud scudding across the face of the sun.

'All this talk about me and my life,' Tom said. 'What about you? You okay?'

'I'm fine. It's nothing.'

'Sure?'

Harvey put on a smile, but there was something strained about it. 'Sure. Thanks for asking.'

Three more weeks went by, with the usual tally of assaults and robberies and assorted petty crime that was Thames Valley Police's stock in trade but not a single gunshot fired in anger and, more importantly, not a single child molester dead from unnatural causes. Although there were those who lamented the end of the paedo killer's career, whether privately or publicly, for most people across the county Sweeney's murderous little spree was all but forgotten and life was moving on.

Meanwhile, Tom had found out the identity of the person who'd made the threat against the city councillor and smashed his windows. The culprit was Graham North, an assistant manager at the health centre under threat of closure, who risked defaulting on his mortgage if he lost his job. North was duly brought to justice. Tom was the arresting officer but he felt for the guy. Shouldn't have let himself get caught so easily: the moral of the story was, don't go bragging to your mates what you've done, because you never know when one of them might repeat the tale of your exploits on their social media page.

Tom and Desi had been spending more time together whenever they could, going on country rambles and long walks down by the riverside, spending nights at the cottage, nights at her place. He was getting to feel more and more at home there. It was too modern for his tastes, and some of the art on her walls was a bit weird, and she couldn't cook to save her life, but none of it meant a thing to him. He'd never known such a fulfilling relationship, nor one that had felt so stable and, if he dared to even think about it, permanent. This is the one for me, he'd said to himself a thousand times. Life was a dream. He wanted this long, hot, perfect, magical summer to go on forever.

The weekend Desi was away at her uncle's place in Berkshire, Tom spent with his helper Ken Sparrowhawk working on the mill restoration. He'd managed to source some reclaimed oak roof beams from a local salvage company, and hired a two-ton flatbed truck to deliver them to the cottage. Negotiating the track was an adventure in itself, while the task of manhauling the huge, enormously heavy beams down the riverbank to the mill and hoisting the first of them into place with block and tackle was a labour of Hercules that left the two of them, plus two more guys from the force drafted in as extra muscle, exhausted and flat out on the grass, gulping pitchers of Langtree Hundred under the hot sun as though it was water.

The following night, Desi phoned him to say she was back home. Something in her tone told Tom all wasn't right. It was like when she'd been preoccupied about her client, but more so.

'It's my uncle,' she admitted. 'He's seventy-six and his health hasn't been too good lately. He was trying to keep it from me so I wouldn't worry.'

'Shit. I hope it's nothing serious?'

'I don't think so, but all the same . . .'

'Want me to come over?'

She said she would, and within five minutes Tom was jumping in the car.

When he arrived at her place, he found her up a stepladder dusting the tall bookshelves in her study. She greeted him with a huge smile and hurried down the ladder to embrace him.

'Sorry if I seemed upset before. It's just that my uncle's pretty much my only family.'

'I'm sure he's going to be fine,' he reassured her.

She'd taken scores of books of all shapes and sizes down from the shelves and stacked them high on a table, on the floor, on armchairs, everywhere. Tom asked, 'What's with the housekeeping?'

'Just dusting these shelves. They were thick with it. I don't know where it all comes from.'

'Want a hand?'

'I was nearly finished.'

'Don't mind me,' he said.

As she returned up the ladder, he noticed the opened bottle of cold white wine and a half-empty glass on the piano. 'Mind if I have a sip? I'm parched.'

'Be my guest,' she replied, and went on dusting. Tom sipped the wine and went over to examine a stack of books. He picked one up, turned it over in his hands like a foreign object, laid it down and picked up another. He'd never seen so many books in one place, outside of a library.

'Have you actually read all these?'

'Yeah, most of them,' she replied without looking down. 'Some of them are reference books, but all the fiction stuff I've probably read more than once.'

Tom shook his head ruefully. 'I was never much of a reader. At school I hated English class even more than I hated maths. Wish I'd paid more attention. Then maybe I wouldn't be such a big ignoramus.'

'You're hardly an ignoramus, Tom.'

'Sometimes I think I should give it a go again. Reading, I mean.'

'I think that's a great idea.'

He went on browsing for a moment or two, then saw one that appealed to him. It was *The Master of Ballantrae*, by Robert

Louis Stevenson. A grand old swashbuckling adventure story – Tom had first seen the 1950's movie adaptation as a boy, then caught up with it again a few years ago. Errol Flynn: you couldn't ask for more. And his leading lady had been Beatrice Campbell, a compatriot of Tom's from Ulster. If the film was good, maybe the book would be even better.

He asked, 'Would you mind if I borrowed a couple of these? I'll look after them, I promise.'

'Of course,' she replied absently, without looking down from the ladder. 'Help yourself.'

Tom slipped the Robert Louis Stevenson into one jacket pocket and something by Thomas Hardy in the other, picked up the wineglass and stood at the window gazing out as she finished her cleaning.

'Fancy some dinner?' she asked.

He'd already pre-empted another attempt at her pasta bake. 'I brought homemade pesto sauce, tagliatelle, some parmesan cheese, the good stuff, and more champagne.'

'You spoil me horribly, Tom McAllister. What are we celebrating this time?'

'I feel like I have a lot to celebrate right now,' he said, kissing her.

It was another enchanting evening. Desi's anxiety about her uncle had relaxed. Afterwards, walking under the starlight, Tom stopped and turned towards her, clasped both her hands in his, plucked up his courage and said croakily, 'Desi, I'm in love with you. I've never said those words to anyone before.'

'Oh, Tom.'

She pressed herself against him and they held one another tight for the longest time.

'Let's get back to the house,' she whispered.

CHAPTER TWENTY-ONE

As the month of August rolled on peacefully by, even Tom began to let go of his doubts about the Sweeney case and accept the official version. Life seemed quieter now, though with Desi he had a great deal to occupy him, as well as the disappearance of an eighteen-year-old girl who'd last been seen leaving a nightclub in Oxpens Road. Tom hated working those kinds of cases because they nearly always ended up tragically with the discovery of a stripped body half-buried under a pile of leaves in the woods. But for once, that wasn't to be. After two solid weeks of searching, he and Billie had found the girl alive and well and living with her boyfriend: it turned out that the parents disapproved of him, and the young lovers had decided to run away together. Tom was there at the tearful family reunion. A happy ending, for a change.

Tom had been seeing less of Harvey Pepper over these last weeks, and had the feeling that his friend was dealing with some personal troubles. In the meantime the watermill's last roof beam, a real bastard of a thing, two centuries old, iron-hard and impossibly heavy, was now up in place. Tom and

Sparrowhawk marked the occasion by getting drunk and vowing they'd never risk crippling themselves like that again.

Over dinner at the cottage one evening, Desi announced that her birthday was approaching, and declared her intention to hold a big party at her house. 'I'm going to invite lots of people and make a real day of it.'

'Can I come?' Tom asked.

'What a thing to even ask. Of course I want you there. You're guest of honour.'

'I like birthdays,' he said, smiling. 'I have so few of them myself, so I do. I might throw a party too, when it's my tenth.'

Desi stared at him. 'Your tenth?'

'My tenth birthday.'

'Have you gone mad? How can you be nine years old?'

'I didn't say I was nine years old,' he replied. 'But because my birthday only happens every four years, technically speaking I've only had nine of them in my life. Born on February twenty-ninth, see? Leap year.'

They joked about it for a while, her calling him her little boy. Then as they'd finished up their main course and Tom was returning from the kitchen with their dessert she said, 'Oh, I have to tell you something that happened today. I met a friend for lunch at that nice little place near the city centre, and afterwards I had an hour to kill before running back up to Summertown, so I decided to take a walk in the botanical gardens. It's so lovely there. Anyhow, quite by chance, I happened to run into this really interesting guy.'

'Uh-huh?' Tom said, serving their dessert. He was trying out a new tiramisu recipe and was keen to get her reaction to it.

'His name's Julian, Julian Kendrick. He's a New Zealander. I think you'd like him.'

'How did you meet? Tell me what you think of that.'

'Oh, wow. This is delicious. Well, it's funny, really. He was there to meet a prospective client but she never showed up. At first he thought I was her. Came up and introduced himself. Then we just got talking.'

'Oh, aye? What kind of client? What does this guy do?'

'He's a photographer.'

Tom thought his improved new recipe was pretty good, too, but now he'd suddenly lost all interest in it. 'Honestly, people can be so naive. Even smart people like you.'

Desi paused with a spoonful of tiramisu halfway to her mouth. Her brow creased with irritation. 'What do you mean? Naive how?'

'I mean, do you really believe some cock-and-bull story like that, the client not turning up? Give me a break. It's obvious this Kendrick character was hitting on you.'

'He was *not* hitting on me. How can you assert that, when you weren't even there?'

Tom gave a loud snort. 'Who the hell meets clients in the botanical gardens anyway? I'll bet he's not even a real photographer.'

'He is, for your information. I looked him up.'

'Oh yeah? And what does he take pictures of?'

'Portraits, mostly. Said he'd like to do one of me, too. Apparently I'm very photogenic.'

Tom wasn't about to disagree with the guy there, but it didn't do much to soften his attitude. 'Wants to take your picture, does he? I'll bet he does.'

'You don't need to get all touchy and sceptical about it.'

'I'm a cop. Sceptical is what I do. Wise up, for Christ's sake.'

'Don't be ridiculous. It's nothing dodgy, if that's what you're thinking.'

'No?'

'Not in the least. There's a whole gallery of images on his website. He's worked with a few celebs, one or two faces I recognised although you probably wouldn't, unless they were Hollywood stars of yesteryear. And he does a lot of wildlife photography, too. Been to all kinds of places around the world. A real nature kind of guy.'

'Hey, I'm a nature kind of guy too,' Tom said. 'Look around you. Isn't this a nature kind of place?'

'Listen to you. So defensive. Anyhow, I have no intention of letting him or anyone else photograph me. I hate having my picture taken.'

Tom stabbed his spoon into his dessert, shovelled in a mouthful and said nothing.

She shrugged. 'Well, you can act all surly and grumpy if you want. I thought you'd be pleased that I met someone who might turn out to be an interesting friend. I happen to think you'd like him. He's very charming and well informed. But I thought he seemed sort of lonely, too. I'm wondering if I should invite him to my party. What do you think?'

'Hey, it's your party. Go and ahead and invite the bodie, if it pleases you.'

'Bodie? What does *that* mean?'

'It's just what we say back home.'

'Is it an insult? Sounds like one.'

'Not all Irish expressions are insults.'

'That's settled then,' she said. 'I *will* invite the bodie. You and he will get on like a house on fire.'

'I bet we will.'

* * *

The day of the party was fine and sunny, as all days had become. It also coincided with one of those bureaucratic boardroom meetings that were an unavoidable part of modern policing, for an officer of Tom's rank. This one was even more infinitely tedious than usual, dragging on late into the afternoon as Tom kept glancing at his watch and tried to contain his mounting desperation to get away. Free at last, he rushed from the station, fairly sprinted to his car, sped home as though he was competing in the Daytona 500, fed the dog, watered his thirsty herbs, showered and changed and raced back across the county to Kennington.

Desi hadn't been kidding when she'd said she intended to invite a lot of guests. She seemed to be friends with more people than Tom had ever known in his life. Her yard was crammed with parked cars and more of them lined the sides of Bagley Wood Road for fifty yards in both directions.

The house was crowded with strangers and filled with laughter and music. As he moved through the throng he heard Desi's cry, and she rushed across to kiss him. 'Tom! There you are – I was going to call to see where you'd got to.'

'Sorry I'm late. I got held up at work. Happy Birthday.' He patted his pockets, searching for the present he'd so painstakingly packaged up neat the previous evening, fussing over the gift-wrap like a bear trying to do origami. It wasn't there. A hot flush of realisation flooded through him. In all his racing around he'd left the cottage without it. 'Oh no. Shit! What a—'

Desi laughed. 'What does it matter? As long as you've brought yourself, that's all I care about. 'Here, let me introduce you to some of my friends. Sandra, Millie, Roy; this is Tom.'

He was introduced to this one, and that one, smiling and shaking hands and doing the small talk. As more people arrived, Desi excused herself to run off and play the hostess, a role she acted to perfection. Tom grabbed a drink and circulated without her. He didn't consider himself much of a socialite, but when he met new people he generally expected to like them, and to be liked in return. Desi's friends seemed to be a pleasant enough bunch, many of them colleagues from work, others perhaps present or former private clients, although one didn't inquire. There was a gay couple called Frankie and Freddie, who were both exactly the same height and wore summery shirts with different-coloured hibiscuses. During a gap in conversations, Tom wandered out to the garden where lively chattering groups had gathered on the lawn. Desi had brought in a catering firm and the aroma of barbecue scented the warm evening air. He leaned against the stone patio balustrade and was thinking he should go and refresh his drink when a voice behind him said, 'I'm so pleased that Desi has found someone.'

He turned: Pamela, one of Desi's colleagues from Metcalfe House, to whom he'd been introduced minutes earlier. Frizzed mousy hair, makeup plastered on with a trowel; and as she tottered over to lean against the balustrade next to him it was clear that she'd consumed a couple too many glasses of the bubbly she was clasping. 'I've never seen her so relaxed and happy,' Pamela cooed. 'You're good for her.'

'She's good for me,' Tom answered, for want of anything better to say.

'So you're in the police?'

'For my sins.'

'I love the way you speak. I think the Northern Irish accent is so strong and manly, don't you?'

Tom was searching for a reply when Pamela's attention suddenly drifted and she gazed bright-eyed past his shoulder to gasp, 'Oh my God. Is that Brad Pitt's younger brother that's just turned up?'

Tom turned to look. He and Pamela weren't the only ones to have noticed the entrance of the new arrival. A few female heads turned to admire him; he didn't escape the attention of Frankie and Freddie, either, as he walked coolly and confidently up towards the house clutching an extravagant bouquet of red and yellow roses, a tastefully wrapped gift package and a bottle bearing the distinctive label of Dom

Pérignon. Desi appeared from the house to greet him. Tom watched as she received her birthday gifts with a squeal of joy, pecked him on both cheeks and seized his arm to bring him inside.

'Mr Charm, all right,' Tom muttered, too low for Pamela to hear.

Moments later, Tom found himself being introduced. Julian Kendrick was about the same height as him, six-one, but a good few pounds lighter, a few years younger and unquestionably far better looking, the bastard. 'It's a pleasure to meet you,' he said to Tom, as though he actually meant it.

'So you're the famous photographer,' Tom said.

Mr Charm was as studiously modest as he was handsome. 'Oh, hardly famous.'

'Well, you should be,' Desi said. Clutching the gift he'd brought her, she asked, 'Can I open it?'

'Please do. I hope you like it.' As the wrapping came off, Kendrick said, 'It's the Tarkovsky films I was telling you about. Special Blu-ray collector's set.'

Desi thanked him and reached up to kiss him again on the cheek. Three kisses in as many minutes, Tom observed. Was it his imagination, or did the embrace linger just a moment longer than it needed to?

'This is fantastic,' Desi said. 'My favourite director.'

'So are you staying here long?' Tom asked, looking Julian Kendrick in the eye.

'I'm sorry, I don't—'

'You're a New Zealander, aren't you? So when are you going back home?'

'I live here now. I've got a place in Buckinghamshire.'

'I see.'

Desi laughed uncomfortably. 'Don't mind Tom, he always asks direct questions. He's a policeman.'

A small, older lady belonging to the group of Desi's friends who'd gathered around them piped up, 'Is it true that you were the officer who arrested that awful murderer?'

'Nobody arrested him,' Tom explained to her. 'He died in a car accident.'

'Well, good riddance anyway.'

'Some would say the same about his victims,' said another man, to whom Tom hadn't been introduced. 'What's your opinion, Mr Kendrick?'

Kendrick smiled, looking at Desi as though they were the only people in the room. 'My opinion is that this is the best party and the finest home I've been to in the three years since I arrived in England. Not to mention its hostess. A lady of rare beauty and taste.'

'You're too kind,' Desi said, blushing. 'Beauty, I don't think. Taste, even less.'

'I've not seen a Paula Rego painting on anyone else's wall,' Kendrick said.

'The one at the top of the stairs? That's only a print.'

'*The Firemen of Alijo*. I saw the original at the Tate Modern. Masterful. Just exquisite.'

Tom must have passed that painting a hundred times. He'd thought it pretty odd at first sight, and hadn't given it another glance since. He asked, 'What's the Tate Modern?'

Desi laughed and slipped an arm affectionately around his middle. 'It's an art gallery in London, silly.'

'Actually I believe the exhibition's still on for another couple of weeks,' Kendrick said. 'Well worth a visit.'

'I'd love to see that.'

'I wouldn't mind seeing it again myself. How'd you like to take a trip up to London? There's a great little restaurant at the gallery. We could do lunch.' Kendrick beamed at Desi, then turned a more aloof gaze in Tom's direction. 'I can't believe you've never heard of the Tate Gallery.'

'Is there any particular reason why I should?' Tom said, bristling.

'I suppose not. It wouldn't be quite your sort of thing, would it?'

'What the hell's that supposed to mean?'

'Isn't this weather wonderful?' another of Desi's friends cut in. 'They say it's going to last until late September.'

Tom and Kendrick stared at each other for a few seconds. Desi frowned at Tom. Tom put down his empty glass and said, 'I'm going to the loo.'

On his way back from the bathroom he got waylaid by Pamela, who was three glasses of bubbly further down the hole and felt compelled to tell him all about her brother in Northampton who used to be a police constable before he had to have a knee operation. It seemed to be a matter of life or death for Pamela to remember which knee it was. After several agonising minutes of forced politeness Tom finally detached himself from her clutches and returned to the living room, to find that the groups had all reshuffled themselves, as they generally did at parties. He looked around the room for Desi, but couldn't see her. 'Think she went out to the garden,' someone told him.

As he headed outside he ran into Frankie and Freddie. 'Looking for Desi?' Frankie asked. Or maybe it was Freddie. Tom couldn't be sure.

'Yes. Did she go this way?'

'Yeah, she and that guy . . . what's his name?'

'Kendrick,' Tom said. His jaw felt tight.

'Wanted to show him the new summer house, I think.'

Tom strode off in that direction, not wanting to get worked up about it but unable to stave off the uncomfortable feeling that welled up inside him. Someone spoke to him as he crossed the lawn, but he didn't register them and brushed by. Skirting the corner of the hedge he came into view of the elegant summerhouse, which was situated at the far end of the long garden close to the trees, some forty yards away.

Tom stopped. Desi and Kendrick were down there, all right. She was on the wooden steps with the summerhouse door open behind her, and he was standing half-turned away from her as if he'd been walking away and paused in his stride to reply to something she was saying. Even at this distance the tension in their body language was obvious, all the more so to Tom's seasoned eye. She was fiddling with her hair. Kendrick had lost some of that cool composure of his.

They were too preoccupied by whatever they were talking about to notice his approach, until he was just a few steps away. 'Desi, everything okay?' he asked.

'Everything's fine,' Kendrick said.

Tom fixed him with the cold, hard, withering glare that had intimidated many a cocky little yob in its time. 'Listen, pal. Do you mind? I want to talk to her for a minute.'

Kendrick seemed about to reply, but the expression on Tom's face cut him off dead and he withdrew sullenly, heading back up the garden towards the house.

'What was that all about?' Tom asked her.

'Nothing.'

He pointed at the summerhouse. 'What were you doing in there?'

'I was looking for something,' Desi said. 'Please. I don't have time for this. I have to get back to my guests.' She went to walk away. Tom caught her by the arm.

'You weren't looking for anything. He was in there with you, wasn't he?'

'I'm not going to answer that, Tom. Let me go.'

He released her instantly, feeling bad that he'd grabbed her like that but too riled to back off. 'Wasn't he?' he repeated more loudly.

'Keep your voice down. People are looking at us.'

'I don't give a shit if they are. What were you doing in there with him?'

'It's none of your damn business,' she snapped. 'I don't have to justify myself to anyone. I have nothing to hide.'

'If you have nothing to hide then why can't you just tell me?'

'Okay,' she admitted. 'He was in there with me. We were talking about something.'

'About what?'

She heaved a sigh. 'It's what I told you about before. He's pushing for me to let him take my photo. I refused. He didn't like having to take no for an answer. That's all. Happy now?'

Tom hadn't even realised that his fists were clenched tight enough to crack walnuts. 'What's his frigging problem? I'll give him no for an answer, so I will.'

'Let it go, Tom. Julian's just very intense, that all. He's an artist.'

'Oh, an artist. I get it now. That makes everything all right. I'm going up there to paint your arty little friend a picture that he'll understand.'

Tom turned towards the house. Desi planted herself in front of him, with a look in her eyes that he'd never seen before. 'This is my house, and you'll do no such thing.'

'What's the matter with you?' he demanded. 'Letting this pumped-up wee skitter treat you this way?'

'No, Tom, what's the matter with *you*?'

'Nothing's the matter with me.'

'Of course not. You know what you're beginning to sound like?'

'What?'

'Like someone who's got a great big chip on his shoulder.'

'What's this, a psychology lecture now?'

She snapped back, 'It doesn't take a psychologist to realise that you took a dislike to Julian the instant you met him.

Before that, even. How could you be so rude to the man? If you'd bothered to get to know him better instead of judging him, you'd know that he and you actually have much more in common than you think.'

'Yeah? Like what?'

'He hates paedophiles even more than you do, for one thing.'

'Get in line,' Tom said. 'If I decided that everyone who hates paedophiles was my best buddy I'd have enough of them to fill Wembley Stadium.'

'And he loves dogs. He's really a sweet guy. And he's so unhappy. He suffers from depression. Takes medication for it.'

'Watch out. Some of those pills can make people act nuts.'

'Look who's talking.'

'What's he got to be depressed about?'

'People do get depressed, you know.'

'Not where I come from,' he said. 'Everybody was too busy being miserable.'

'So you think depression's just for the self-indulgent middle classes.'

'This guy's not depressed. He's just self-absorbed.'

'He had a traumatic childhood.'

'Who didn't? I suppose he's told you his whole life story.'

'Oh, for God's sake, Tom.'

'Really getting to know one another pretty well, aren't you? Like two old friends, all kissy-kissy and going off to do lunch at the art gallery.'

'I can't believe this. Are you jealous?'

'Of course I'm jealous. And you're damn right. I don't like this guy one little bit.'

CHAPTER TWENTY-TWO

'And on it went like that,' Tom said to Harvey three days later, over their usual pints, in their usual corner of the Claddagh. 'Hell of an argument.'

Tom had raced across town after another frenetic day at work and was still wearing his dark suit, reasonably presentable and uncrumpled; while Harvey looked as though he'd only recently dragged himself out of bed. His hair was unkempt, even by his carefree standards, he was wearing odd socks again and he hadn't shaved in a few days. But his eyes were bright and attentive as he listened carefully to Tom's account of the party.

'I know I shouldn't have lost it like that,' Tom said glumly, 'but I couldn't help myself. Not after seeing them together like that. And the way she was acting with me. She was like a totally different person.'

'In fairness, Tom, you haven't known Desi long enough to have seen her in that kind of social situation before. The human character is a complex thing and people act differently in different situations.'

'Yeah, like sneaking off down the garden with one of your guests for a quick snog.'

Harvey raised an eyebrow. 'You don't actually know that for sure. You didn't accuse her of it, did you?'

'Not in so many words.'

'So how did you leave it?'

'By putting my fist through the wall of the summerhouse,' Tom replied, with a wistful glance at his bruised knuckles. 'Tell the truth, it didn't quite go all the way through. Just splintered a couple of planks. Nothing a carpenter couldn't put right.'

'Not good.'

Tom heaved a sigh. 'I know. So much for anger management. I've regressed, haven't I?'

'It's partly my fault for having become a bit lax with your therapy of late,' Harvey admitted. 'I suppose it was better than putting your fist through the guy's face.'

'I'm not proud of what I did. It was pathetic. Have I got no willpower at all?'

'Then again, speaking as your friend and not your counsellor, I can't blame you for feeling threatened by this Kendrick character's appearance on the scene.'

'I'm not threatened, Harve, I'm scared.'

'That she'll leave you?'

'I've no illusions. He's better looking than me, he's fitter than me, and he's more cultivated than me. He can talk about the Tate Gallery, and all that. He even knew what arty foreign fillums to get her for her birthday. Meanwhile, there's yours truly turning up at her party with my two arms the one length like a big eedjit.'

Harvey looked blank. 'Your two arms the one length?'

'Honestly, you English. Can't you speak your own language? It means I went there empty-handed, because in all my rushing around I'd left her present at home.'

'I'm sure it was a very nice present,' Harvey said, helpfully.

'A bottle of perfume. Mr frigging Original, that's me.'

Harvey asked, 'So what happened afterwards?'

'You mean after I totally ruined her birthday? I went home and drank beer and tried to calm down. That night and all the next day I wanted to call her but I couldn't bring myself to pick up the phone. Finally, I plucked up the courage and went round there with a big bunch of flowers. First thing I see is the yellow Porsche parked outside the house, next to her car. The same yellow Porsche I'd seen parked on the lane as I was leaving her party.'

'Kendrick's?'

Tom nodded. 'I couldn't know it for sure at that moment, but I had such a bad feeling about it that I almost turned around right then, and drove off. But instead I forced myself to walk up to the front door.'

'So you do have willpower, see?'

'Anyhow, it was him, all right. He was just leaving, but who knows how long he'd been there for? There were two empty wine glasses on the table.'

Harvey drummed his fingers as he mulled it over. 'Okay, maybe that looks bad. And yet, for all you know, he could have been there for some innocent reason.'

'Aye, well, that's what he said. Apparently he'd left his sunglasses and was only coming over to collect them. Might be true, might be bullshit.'

'Did you notice anything odd about their behaviour?'

'Desi was surprised to see me, and I suppose she was a bit on edge with me, seeing as we hadn't spoken since the row. As for yer man, no, he was looking just as full of himself as he was at the party. Acting all friendly like nothing had happened.'

'Then maybe it's nothing to worry about,' Harvey said.

'You know what really gets my goat? I had the dog with me, and Radar's usually diffident with strangers. Especially strangers that he can sense I don't like. But he sat there like a puppy and let the bastard pet him.'

Tom went silent as he replayed the scene in his head: Julian Kendrick all smiles and kneeling down to stroke Radar's head and mane, in spite of Tom's warning not to get too close. 'It's all right. Dogs like me. What's this handsome fellow's name?' Desi replying, 'He's called Radar.' The dog slobbering all over Kendrick's hand, that Judas.

Back in the present moment, Harvey asked, 'So, then he left, and what happened after that?'

'She invited me inside. I was as nervous as hell. I could tell she was, too. But I couldn't stop wondering whether she was looking guilty, too. Like she'd been caught in the act.'

'It's not like you found the two of them in bed together, Tom. Under the circumstances, it's understandable that she was a bit nervous. You hadn't seen each other since the argument.'

Tom shrugged. 'And then I gave her the flowers, and I said I was sorry for what happened, and she accepted my apology, and we made up.'

'There you are, then. All's well that ends well. Maybe it's true that love conquers all,' Harvey added in a different tone, and took a glug of his pint.

'So now we're back together again. But it's not like before, Harvey. Something's changed. I can feel it. Christ, I can't stand the thought of losing her.'

Back home later that evening, Tom drowned his sorrows in a grilled ribeye steak and some red wine, and went to bed still full of nagging doubts and fears. *Maybe it's true that love conquers all*, Harvey's voice echoed in his mind. And maybe it was, too. But had the romantic prat who came up with that old line in the first place ever lain there alone at night feeling like his heart had been trampled by a herd of elephants? Tom tossed and turned and tried to relax, to little avail. It was after 1 a.m.

by the time tiredness finally overwhelmed him and he sank into oblivion.

But his restful state wasn't fated to continue for long. Shortly before two in the morning, his phone on the bedside table jolted him brutally, instantly wide awake. He reached out and snatched it up.

'McAllister.'

'Sorry to wake you, Chief,' said Billie Flowers, 'but you need to get over to Bicester as fast as you can.'

From Tom's place to the Oxfordshire town of Bicester was a twenty-mile journey that he covered in just over seventeen minutes. The address Billie directed him to was a red-brick block of apartments on Heron Drive in the Langford Village development on the edge of town. When he got there, the building and the street were awash with the swirling blue light that signalled something terrible had happened.

Billie was waiting outside the apartment block to meet him, her face anxious. He strode through the milling chaos of police vehicles and uniforms and crackling radios and joined her. An ambulance was waiting to take away the deceased. The elderly woman who'd reported the crime was now being attended to by the paramedics for acute shock.

'None of the neighbours heard any commotion,' Billie said, filling him in. 'Mrs Higgins lives on the first floor, directly below the victim's flat. She went to bed sometime after eleven o'clock and woke up at 1.35 a.m. with something dripping on her face from the ceiling. She thought it was a leaky pipe at first. When she turned the light on, she realised it was blood. She's lucky she didn't die of shock. The emergency call handler could hardly understand a word.'

'What do we have on the victim?'

'Right now, no more than what I told you on the phone. He's Adrian Gibson, thirty-one years of age, a former school caretaker from Coventry who spent four years in prison for grooming a thirteen-year-old girl on the internet while posing as a teenager, and was caught in the act of attempting to abduct her. He got out seven months ago, and relocated from Coventry to Bicester where he was set up with a job stacking shelves in a local supermarket.'

As Billie talked, she was leading Tom up the stairs to the second floor where the murder had taken place. They pushed through the hubbub into Gibson's small, cheaply furnished apartment. Tom wasn't surprised to see Thins Waller there, surrounded by members of his team as he went about his grim work with the usual good cheer. The murder scene was in the bedroom, directly above where the downstairs neighbour had been fast asleep when Gibson was butchered. So much blood had soaked into the carpet that it had turned almost black, spread through the pile in a circular patch four feet across. At the centre of the patch lay the twisted carcass of the late Mr Gibson, eyes wide open staring upwards at nothing and wearing one of the most tortured and terrified expressions Tom had ever seen on a murder victim.

'This one's been shot *and* stabbed, curiously enough,' Thins said, looking up at Tom from where he knelt by the body. He pointed at the gunshot wounds in the dead man's legs. 'One in each, about four inches above the knee, quite symmetrically placed. Looks to me like the same calibre bullet as we dug out of the Port Meadow victim. But it was the knifing that killed him. We've got two extremely deep penetrating wounds to the heart and aorta.'

Tom didn't have to be a forensics expert to see that for himself. Gibson's body had probably been all but drained of blood. As for the gunshot wounds, he'd been preparing himself for this news since Billie had called.

'Shot twice in the legs and then stabbed twice in the chest,' Waller mused. 'Methodical. And a little puzzling, too. If you were going to stab someone, why shoot them first? It doesn't seem to make sense to use both kinds of weapon. Unless your gun jammed or you'd only loaded it with two rounds. But this seems highly deliberate.'

'That's not all that's puzzling,' Tom said. 'Now it looks like we were on the wrong track with Vinnie Sweeney after all.'

'Don't jump to that conclusion just yet, Tom,' Waller replied, shaking his head. 'Not until I get those bullets out of his legs and we can verify whether they match with the ones we extracted from Ewan Moss's body.'

'They'll match,' Tom said. And he was certain he was right.

Just as Harvey Pepper had predicted, the paedo killer was back in business.

CHAPTER TWENTY-THREE

'Nonsense,' Forbes yelled from behind his desk at the team of detectives summoned to his office the next morning. The Chief Super had been dragged out of bed at 3 a.m. and was not having a good day. 'Any beat copper worth his salt would tell you that the MO here is completely different. Sweeney never used a knife. It's obvious that this is a copycat killer. Plenty of people were quietly cheering him on while he was alive, and were disappointed to see him gone. Someone else has decided to carry on his work.'

And to some minds within the Thames Valley force, Forbes's theory wasn't completely implausible. The DNA evidence unquestionably linking Sweeney to the earlier killings was hard to surmount. To Tom McAllister's mind, though he stood there listening to this tirade tight-lipped and silent, the superintendent's protests only showed him up all the more as a sore loser.

Within hours, the call from the forensics lab settled the argument.

'I've recovered both bullets from the body,' Thins Waller said. 'One of them is badly deformed from where it hit bone, but the other's undamaged and I was able to run a close comparison test against the ones we took from the Port Meadow victim.'

'And?' Tom asked tersely. Billie was standing beside him, searching his face with wide eyes.

'My first impression was right.' Waller said. 'No question about it, Tom. Rifling grooves left by the gun barrel match perfectly under the microscope. Even the bullets themselves are the exact same 124-grain hollowpoint, manufactured by the Prvi Partizan ammunition factory in Serbia. They use a distinctive kind of copper jacket, as opposed to other brands like Norma or Fiocchi—'

Waller could have gone on like that for hours, but Tom cut him short. 'So you're saying that Adam Gibson and Ewan Moss were shot using the same handgun.'

'That's exactly what I'm saying. Both victims were murdered by a single killer.'

Tom heaved a deep sigh. 'All right. Let me know if you find anything else.'

* * *

It wasn't long before the news hit. And after all these weeks of silence, now the inevitable media furore started all over again. Local television and radio were on fire with the news that the vigilante assassin had returned. Some voices were raised in condemnation, but as the story gained traction on social media just as many were turned against the authorities.

'"Disgusted that these filthy perverts are being brought into our communities and given jobs while honest people are out of work and living on benefits,"' Billie read out loud from her phone while Tom sat at his desk the next morning, swilling coffee. 'There are hundreds more comments pouring in all the time. Listen to this one: "He's back. He's bad. He's beautiful. Keep up the good work, PK!"'

'Is that what they're calling him, PK?'

'Catchy, isn't it? Here's another: "Kill 'em all, PK. Let God sort 'em out."' Billie rolled her eyes. 'Sounds like something Vinnie Sweeney would have said.'

'They're turning him into a bloody folk hero.'

'Don't you just love the internet. Want to hear more?'

'No, I don't,' Tom grumbled. 'What I want is to catch this guy.'

'We don't have a single thing to go on.'

'Tell me about it.'

A thorough search of Gibson's apartment had produced zero in terms of forensic clues. Meanwhile, teams of officers had interviewed the residents of the Langford Village estate and gone knocking on doors all over the surrounding area in search of a witness who might have spotted the killer entering or leaving the scene of the crime. So far, they were coming away empty-handed. It seemed impossible that nobody at all could have seen him – lots of them might have – but then, as Tom knew perfectly well, he could be anybody. There wasn't even a vague description they could offer the public in the hopes of jogging someone's memory.

Tom was still sitting there wracking his brains and feeling oddly paralysed by a kind of helpless inertia when his desk phone rang.

'How come you never call me any more?'

Tom tried not to actually gnash his teeth at the sound of Suzie Green's voice. 'I'm busy.'

'Come on, McAllister, you have to give me something. I haven't forgotten the way you gave me the brush-off at the press conference. And I also haven't forgotten where you live.'

'I've moved.'

'No you haven't. I won't leave you alone, you know.'

'Good-bye, Suzie.'

But it was going to be impossible to stave off the baying hounds for too much longer. Later that morning, Tom found himself being wheeled out in front of the cameras for another live-streamed press conference, which he intended to make as brief as he could get away with. He confirmed the burning news rumours that forensic evidence had now firmly tied the latest murder to the previous incident several weeks ago. 'We are still investigating the possibility of a copycat crime, but this now seems unlikely.'

Then came the really lame part, begging for help while trying to remain authoritative and outwardly self-assured at the same time. He was cringing inside as he said to the cameras, 'On behalf of Thames Valley Police, I would appeal to the public for anyone with information to come forward. If you were in the vicinity of Langford Village Estate and Heron Drive between approximately eleven p.m. and one-thirty a.m. that night, we urgently need to hear from you.' He repeated the helpline number for them to call. 'That's all for now.'

'Christ,' he muttered as he escaped from the conference room. 'I'm sick of having a camera pointed at me.'

'Better get used to it, Inspector,' said a familiar voice behind him. Tom turned. Forbes had that creepy way of catching you unawares.

'What do you mean, get used to it?'

Forbes's moustache twitched like a hairy caterpillar crawling along a twig. He was almost smiling with pleasure at delivering more bad tidings to Tom. 'I mean that eight hours from now, you're scheduled to appear on tonight's special extended edition of *South Today* for BBC One Oxfordshire. It's a panel discussion show focusing on public attitudes to sex offenders, rehabilitation and the justice system, how modern policing tackles the problem, and so on. You'll be one of five panellists, including the governor of Bullingdon Prison, an eminent author called Dr Maggie Epperson, and a Professor Andrew Ferguson, head of Sociology and Gender Studies at Exeter University.'

Tom stared at Forbes. He felt his jaw hinge open in stupefaction and had to make a conscious effort to close it. 'Why do I have to do this?'

Forbes explained, like a not especially kindly teacher speaking to a particularly stupid child, 'Because, McAllister, in the interests of public trust, at a time like this it's essential for the force to put out positive signals, to get the message across that everything is being done that can be done to uphold law and order.'

'Hold on a minute,' Tom protested. 'I'm a detective, not a PR person.'

'You're a representative of Thames Valley Police,' Forbes said. 'Certainly not the representative *I* would have chosen, as I've said to you before. But there it is. Your job as a senior officer on this force is to assure the citizens over whose safety we watch that they can go about their daily lives in the knowledge that this man will be apprehended.'

It sounded too polished, coming from his lips. Tom was certain that the superintendent had been working on those lines all morning.

'While I ought to be out there catching the bastard.'

'No more arguments. Comb your hair and put on a better suit. I'll be watching.' And with that, Forbes walked away down the corridor.

Eight hours. No way out. *Shit.* As Tom wandered back to his desk, feeling somewhat bewildered, he suddenly remembered that he and Desi had planned to go out tonight. He'd managed to get a table at the Manoir aux Quat'Saisons and had been hearing great things about their new sous-chef and a sensational fish soup recently added to their menu.

Tom bypassed the open-plan space where his desk was, and

headed instead for the fire escape stairway that he often used as a refuge for making phone calls of a more private nature. Standing at a grimy window overlooking the city skyline and the back end of Christ Church, he punched in Desi's number. 'It's me. Can you talk?'

'I'm at work, but I have a minute.'

Something in her voice. Tom noticed it, but he was more focused on what he had to tell her. 'Listen, about tonight. Something's come up and I can't get out of it. They want me to go on TV. Some panel discussion thing for the BBC.' He paused, waiting for her reaction, but she was silent. 'I wish I didn't have to do it,' he went on. I don't know what to say. I'm not an expert, like you. Why couldn't you be there? I could do with the backup.'

'I couldn't even if I wanted to, Tom. The show's producer did approach Metcalfe House, but our director declined the invitation. It's because we keep a low profile. Very few people know what it is we really do here.'

'So it looks like that's put paid to our evening out. I was looking forward to it, too, so I was.'

There was another silence on the line. When she spoke again, he could sense that odd tone in her voice all the more strongly. A distance, a coldness, a restraint that sent a faint chill through him and set off an alarm bell in his heart.

'Tom . . .'

'What? Is something wrong?'

'I was actually going to call you anyway. I . . . there's something I need to say. At first I thought about telling you at dinner, but then I decided we should just get it over with.'

'Say what? Get what over with?' The alarm bell had become a thudding drumbeat that spread up to his throat.

'Tom, I . . . I just don't think things are going to work out between us.'

'What are you talking about? Why?'

'I'm sorry. I just feel that it's best that we don't see each other any more.'

He gripped the phone tightly against his ear. This couldn't be happening, could it? 'Desi, no. No. Listen—'

'Please don't make this harder than it needs to be, for both of us.'

Now the chill was turning into a well of molten lava that coursed up from somewhere deep inside and started bringing him out in a sweat. 'It's him, isn't it? You're dumping me for that Kendrick.'

'It's not what you think. It's got nothing to do with him.'

'Then what's it to do with?' he asked. He could hear the edge of desperation in his voice. 'Look, if this is about the argument, I know you think I was acting jealous and possessive. I already said I was sorry. And I am, because I was out of line that day. If I acted that way, it's only because I love you. Because I couldn't stand the idea of . . . of him and you. I thought you understood that. I thought we'd made it up. That everything was okay again between us.'

'It was,' she said. 'Or I thought it was. I've been doing a lot of thinking, Tom. And I just don't think it's going to work. We've had some lovely times together. But this relationship just isn't what I need.'

'So you're going off with Kendrick instead.'

'You don't own me,' she said angrily. 'If I want to spend time with Julian, then I will.'

Tom gave a bitter laugh. 'I knew there was something going on. The other day at your place, when he was there "to pick up his sunglasses". Oh, of course he was.'

'I'm not going to have this conversation with you, Tom.'

'But you're the one who started it. Everything was fine until then.'

'You can't understand. You'll never understand.'

'Then help me to understand.'

'I have to get back to work.'

'I'll call you later.'

'No, Tom. Don't call me, because there's nothing more to say. It's over between us.'

'Desi, wait. Don't hang up. Please. You can't do this. Not like this, over the phone.'

'I'm sorry. Take care of yourself. Kiss Radar for me. Goodbye.'

And then she was gone, and Tom was left standing there alone on the stairway like a man perched at the edge of a windy cliff, facing the abyss below.

CHAPTER TWENTY-FOUR

The broadcast studio was situated in Summertown, not far from Metcalfe House. That knowledge only deepened the numbing ache that seemed to fill Tom's entire being as he trudged from the car.

The live show was due to go on air at seven, an hour from now. Tom was met by a bubbly producer called Rona or Rhonda, who talked too fast and smiled too much, offered him tea or coffee, which he declined, and led him, morose and taciturn, to a room where they made him sit in a chair in front of a mirror while they made him up for the cameras. Ordinarily he'd have been joking with them that it'd take more than an hour to make him look halfway presentable. But he didn't have the heart to speak, and just sat there slumped and silent as they dolled him up as best they could, like undertakers tarting up a body ready for display in its open casket.

He briefly met his fellow panellists before the show began. He'd figured out that, for the sake of good television, the guest speakers would have been selected to reflect differing views on the topic of paedophilia. Dr Maggie Epperson was a retired lecturer from Georgia, USA, who'd earned her PhD in

Psychology and written a bestseller called *Stolen Innocence: Inside the Mind of a Child Abuser*. Which gave Tom a pretty good idea of where she stood on the spectrum. Right across the other side of it was Professor Ferguson, to whom Tom took an instant dislike. The guy was so smarmy, he made Julian Kendrick look good.

Or maybe not.

Then there was the prison governor, a woman whom Tom had met before on a couple of occasions; a stuffed shirt named Rosser who was something high up in Social Services and very possibly a council pal of Jonathan Baxter; and a couple of others whose names and job titles Tom forgot instants after they were introduced. He didn't want to be here, and was having a hard time remaining in the moment. Twice he drifted off into a kind of daze while the producer was talking to them, and was asked if he was okay.

'I'm fine,' he replied. 'Never better.'

With a few minutes to spare, the panellists were ushered onto the set, where the camera operators and the sound and lighting technicians were gearing up for action. The host and moderator of the panel was a brassy and attractive blond-haired BBC local news anchor named Lucy Tanner, whom Tom vaguely recalled seeing on the box once or twice, not that he ever watched it much. A curved podium had been set up on a low stage, in front of which was an auditorium for the small studio audience who filtered in from a separate entrance as the panellists took their seats. Tom found himself seated near the middle of the row, where he could breathe Lucy Tanner's perfume to his right and listen to the smooth talk of Professor Ferguson to his left. Why'd he have to be seated next to that guy? He squirmed in his chair, trying to get comfortable. Every camera in the room seemed to be pointed directly and exclusively at him, like rifles in a firing squad. His palms were moist, his throat was dry and his shoes felt too tight.

What was he even doing here? He stared into space, losing focus, seeing nothing any longer. His surroundings, the studio, the panel, the audience, all seemed to melt away into oblivion.

'Tom, I . . . I just don't think things are going to work out between us.'

'What are you talking about? Why?'

'I'm sorry. I just feel that it's best that we don't see each other any more.'

'Desi, no. No. Listen—'

'Please don't make this harder than it needs to be, for both of us.'

Some time went by before he realised with a jolt of panic that he'd been drifting off again, and that the show was now live on air. Lucy Tanner was in the middle of her introductory spiel to the audience:

'. . . It's a delicate subject, given who the victims are. Normally the public are on the side of the law when there's a killer on the loose, but because of the nature of the crimes for which these victims were convicted in the past, a large proportion of the public seems to be in favour of a tough new kind of vigilante justice. What social dynamics have given rise to this phenomenon? How do we explain them? And most importantly of all, how does a modern, progressive and diverse society find the answers to these challenging questions? Tonight our panel of experts will explore this controversial and difficult topic that's recently been brought so much to the forefront of our attention.'

In her slick style and flashing white teeth all over the place, Lucy Tanner introduced each panellist in turn. As Tom heard his name mentioned, he shot a startled look at the camera and uttered a sort of Neanderthal grunt. To his left, the smooth professor offered a courteous nod and a beaming smile to the audience.

Tom wanted to bolt. His guts were churning and he was

certain that his face must be the colour of cooked beetroot. *Jesus, get me out of here.*

The thoughts spun and spiralled wildly inside his head. How could you dump me like that? Why him? Did you ever love me at all? He blinked. His eyes burned.

When he regained his focus, Maggie Epperson, seated over at the far right-hand end of the panel, was already replying to her first question. Speaking in a rich Georgia drawl she said, 'Well, Lucy, I'm afraid that all my research shows that these people cannot be cured, for the fundamental reason that their deviant behaviour patterns are so deeply ingrained. When they're in prison they spend all their time fantasising and planning what they're going to do when they get out. Prison may very well stop them from molesting, but it does nothing about the fantasising and the planning. I'm frankly not at all surprised that people are rooting for this guy, because the simple truth is that our current justice system does not provide the answers we're looking for.'

'In my opinion, that's because we're looking in the wrong place,' said the voice on Tom's left.

'Professor Ferguson?' Lucy Tanner handed him the floor.

Ferguson stretched comfortably in his seat and smiled engagingly at his audience, visibly in his element as all eyes and ears turned his way. 'Well, you see, from a scientific viewpoint the fact of the matter is that most males are attracted to young adolescent girls – or for that matter boys – all of which is quite normal despite appearing to fly in the face of our traditional taboos. Such behaviour can't accurately be described as "deviant", and hence it's not rational to single out innocent individuals, who for whatever reason may be more prone to it than others, for barbaric forms of punishment at the hands of the mob. That is counter to all the ethical principles of a truly civilised society.'

'Excuse me,' Dr Epperson cut in. 'I hardly think it's

appropriate to describe a convicted child abuser as "innocent". They've already provided ample evidence to the contrary.'

Lucy Tanner waved her down. 'Please, Dr Epperson, you'll have plenty of time to respond once Professor Ferguson has had his say.'

'Thank you, Lucy,' Ferguson said with a glowing smile. 'As I was saying, in fact it's only in quite recent times that we've started to form these arbitrary notions of what is ethically acceptable within human behaviour. Historically, it was considered quite normal and permissible for an adult man to marry, and to enjoy marital relations with, a girl young enough to be classed as a child by our modern standards. For instance, Henry VII's mother married Edmund Tudor when she was only twelve, and gave birth to our future king at the age of thirteen.'

'Aye, and we used to hang, draw and quarter folks back then too. Are we taking that up again?' Tom thought and felt like saying, but didn't.

Ferguson was just getting warmed up. 'And there are many other examples from history that show this was common practice. It may seem shocking to us now, but that's only because our perspective has altered. You can't call it abuse if the so-called child consented.'

'I don't think we're talking here about consenting partners,' Maggie Epperson retorted. 'You're obfuscating the issue.'

'Dr Epperson, please.' Lucy again, doing her bit as moderator. It was starting to look like Epperson versus Ferguson. None of the other panellists seemed too keen to dive into the fray. The prison governor appeared to have developed an intense interest in her fingernails.

'Not in all cases, perhaps,' Ferguson replied airily. 'But whatever the case may be, what we're looking at here is a wake-up call telling us that we, as a modern society, need to radically redefine our whole outdated and functionally useless concept of what constitutes a 'paedophile'. Like incest, these behaviours are simply a manifestation of perfectly normal, adaptive biological drives hard-wired into our brains through millions of years of evolution.'

Tom leaned forward in his seat and laid his palms flat on the podium surface. He frowned and jutted his jaw and licked his lips and went to say something, but couldn't find the words.

'Detective Inspector McAllister, you seem to want to weigh in on that point,' Lucy Tanner said, noticing the shift in Tom's posture and obviously eager to broaden the discussion beyond the two warring academics who'd grabbed the stage.

Ignoring her, Tom turned around to his left so he could look Ferguson in the eye. His head was aching. The grin plastered all over the guy's face looked like a simpering smirk. Tom stared at it. The audience were all watching and waiting, along with countless viewers catching the live show at home. The moderator repeated, 'Detective Inspector McAllister?'

Tom stared at Ferguson for several more seconds. It seemed to him as though the two of them were completely alone in the room. Nobody was watching. The outside world no longer existed. *Just you and me, pal.*

Tom said to Ferguson, 'I'm sorry, I don't speak your kind of mumbo-jumbo. Could you repeat that last part again, in plain English?'

The audience laughed.

Rattled for only a brief moment, Ferguson quickly regathered his wits and replied urbanely, for the benefit of this semi-educated Ulsterman who seemed to think he belonged on the same panel as a celebrated professor, 'Why, of course, Inspector. Forgive me, and please allow me to rephrase. My point was that what we call "paedophilia", among other supposedly aberrant forms of behaviour, are really just *natural human impulses*.' He laid extra emphasis on those last three words, just in case Tom hadn't understood.

191

'That's what I thought you said,' Tom told him.

The audience laughed again. Though as some of them were beginning to notice the look in the police detective's eyes as he kept on staring at the professor, this time a certain nervousness had crept into their laughter. Tom didn't even hear it.

'Would you like to see another natural human impulse?' he asked Ferguson. His voice sounded calm, but inside him the rising volcanic rage was a force beyond all controlling.

'No, Tom. Don't call me because there's nothing more to say. It's over between us. Goodbye.'

Ferguson's eyes opened wide. 'I—I beg your pardon? What?'

'This,' Tom said. And he swung a fast right hook that even Liam Neeson, in his boxing championship days, wouldn't have seen coming. Professor Ferguson didn't stand a chance.

With a resounding fleshy SMACK that the television microphones picked up with crystal clarity and delivered live into tens of thousands of living rooms across southern England, Tom's fist connected squarely with the middle of Ferguson's face and sent him tumbling out of his chair.

Utter silence; then a shocked gasp, and maybe one or two cries of delight, erupted from the studio audience. Lucy Tanner screamed, 'Inspector McAllister!'

Ferguson lay writhing on the floor with his hands cupped over his nose and mouth, blood leaking out from between his fingers as he bellowed at Tom, 'God damn you! You're fucking insane!'

'I'm done listening to this shite,' Tom muttered. He rose up from his chair, flexed his tingling right hand, and walked off the set.

CHAPTER TWENTY-FIVE

'He was lucky,' Tom said to Forbes the next morning, duly summoned to the superintendent's office. 'If I hadn't been on an anger management course I might actually have hit him.'

Forbes had begun this conversation livid with outraged indignation but obviously expecting that his overwhelming moral superiority would force Tom to get down on his knees, blubber his apologies and beg for mercy. As it became clear that the offender was prepared to do none of these things and instead stood planted squarely opposite the desk returning his superior's gaze with no sign whatsoever of contrition in his eyes – no expression at all – Forbes's anger had mounted into a state of white-faced near-apoplexy that left him choking on his words. With an effort he said, 'If that is an attempt at humour, Inspector, it's incredibly poorly judged. Rest assured that nobody is laughing.'

'No humour intended, sir,' Tom replied. 'I wasn't joking.' The door was firmly closed behind him but he knew full well that half his colleagues were skulking outside it in a breathless hush, trying to catch as much of the conversation through the flimsy office walls as possible.

Forbes shook his head. 'It beggars belief. Never, even once, in all my twenty-eight years on the force, have I come across, or even heard of, a level of misconduct that comes anywhere close.'

Tom might have mentioned Norrie Palmer, Forbes's chief inspector and mentor back when he'd been in uniform, who'd been summarily canned for accepting a hundred-thousand-pound bribe to turn a blind eye to a money laundering operation that'd been going on in the back room of an antiquarian bookshop in Woodstock Road. But he said nothing as Forbes went on:

'The thousands of people who watched you violently assault Professor Ferguson on live television have now grown into an audience of millions as your escapade continues to go viral across the internet. Tell me, did you actually think you could get away with it? Or are you simply psychopathic?'

'Neither,' Tom answered. 'The guy shouldn't have said what he said. It annoyed me.'

'Oh, it annoyed you, did it?'

'Yes. And as for getting away with it, the fact is, Superintendent Forbes, that right now I really don't give a crap what anyone thinks, or what happens next.'

'Well, then, I'm sure you won't be too upset to hear that Professor Ferguson fully intends to press charges against you. Meanwhile, it comes as no surprise to me, either, that our mutual superiors have unanimously decided this morning that you should be suspended from duty with immediate effect, pending an official review. A decision that I wholeheartedly support, coming as it does after repeated warnings over exactly this kind of behaviour in the past, and which I happen to think should have been made a long time ago.' Forbes's voice rose in pitch and volume as he neared the end of his tirade, and there was no question that the listening ears on the other side of the door were catching every word. 'This was simply the last straw, and you've nobody to blame but yourself. You're a disgrace to the force, McAllister!'

'Fine,' Tom said. 'Can I go now?'

'Please do. And I for one won't be sorry if you never come back!'

There was a scuffling of fast-retreating footsteps from outside as Tom turned and headed for the door. He shoved through it and left it open on his way out, getting some kind of fierce satisfaction from Forbes's yell of 'Door!'

Tom walked away. The corridor was filled with an unusually high number of his colleagues all innocently going about their business and appearing not to notice him. He felt nothing as he made his way back through the open-plan area to his desk, closed down his computer terminal, gathered a few personal items and then headed for the stairs leading down to the back exit. A community support officer he knew, called Dave Rundle, popped his head out of a doorway as he passed by, and gave him a big cheesy grin.

'Saw you on the TV,' Rundle said. 'Oh, man, that has to be the best thing I've ever seen in my life.' He punched his fist into his palm. 'Smackdown! Just plain awesome.'

Tom suddenly felt so dejected and weighed down with tiredness that he almost just trudged by Rundle without a word. 'Go and tell that to the disciplinary hearing,' he answered.

Rundle's smile dropped. 'Shit. They're not—I mean, are they?'

'What did you think they'd do? See you around, Dave.'

Billie was waiting for Tom outside the back exit. Her eyes were red and the instant he appeared she stepped up to give him a hug. 'Come here, you stupid idiot.'

'At least you don't have to call me "Sir" any more,' he said, trying to joke.

'I never really did.'

Tom stood there with a lump in his throat and let himself be hugged. His head sank down and rested on Billie's shoulder.

'I don't know what to say to you,' she said, when she let him go at last and stepped back to peer up at him with a look of consternation.

'You don't have to say anything.'

She sighed. 'Well, if it's any consolation, the several million people on the internet who thought you were a scumbag before for going after the paedo killer now all think you're a hero. Seems the professor's comments didn't go down too well with a lot of folks.'

Tom couldn't care less. 'She dumped me, Billie,' he muttered, and now the lump in his throat felt ready to burst with sadness at the thought of her.

'I thought something must have happened. I'm so sorry, Tom.' Billie reached out tenderly to clasp his hand. His knuckles were swollen and tender from thumping Ferguson.

'I don't know what I'm going to do without her.'

'It gets easier,' Billie said. 'I know.'

He nodded. He was deeply touched and grateful to her, but didn't want to talk any more. 'I just want to go home now.'

'I'll call you. Take care.'

When he got back to the cottage he was barely aware of having driven there. As Radar appeared and came running up to greet him, Tom cuddled him and ran his fingers through the dog's coarse fur. 'It's just you and me now, buddy,' he said. That sense of companionship meant a lot to him. But how do you explain the depth of heartbreak, that bleak feeling of total emptiness, to an animal? Not even the comfort of Radar's devotion was going to fill the void that had opened up inside Tom with Desi's phone call.

That was how it was for the next two days. He ate very little, and slept even less. There was enough booze in the house to spend a fortnight roaring drunk if he'd chosen to, but that had no appeal. Even his beloved Langtree Hundred tasted like ditchwater to him. He spent hours just driving aimlessly around, stopping to stare at countryside scenery that normally filled his heart with satisfaction at being alive, but which now looked as bleak to him as a post-apocalyptic wasteland. The rest of the time there was nothing much to do but fret and brood and shamble along the river with the dog, and sometimes go through the desultory motions of tending to his culinary garden with half a view to the day he might feel like cooking again. Even that meant little. The tall, bushy basil plant in his conservatory that he religiously watered each day became parched and droopy, and he didn't care.

As the bitter reality of his breakup with Desi took hold, so did the realisation of how stupid he'd been. On the morning of the third day since his suspension a letter arrived, the envelope printed with the name of a law firm. Ferguson's solicitors, rattling sabres. He tossed it in the cold fireplace, unopened. He was sure they'd send more. Let 'em.

Billie called twice that day, asking anxiously how he was, but he was reluctant to talk even to her, let alone to see anybody. He had a session with Harvey lined up for tomorrow and didn't want to go, but was too despondent to pick up the phone and in any case too ashamed to talk to his friend, who was bound to be one of the millions to have watched his brilliant performance on TV or streamed online. What must he think?

Tom procrastinated over it for a while, but in the end it was Harvey who called him, late that evening as a heavy summer rain was running down the cottage windows. The moment he answered the phone, it was clear something was wrong. The slurred words and the agonised tone in Harvey's voice cut instantly through Tom's sense of self-pity and jerked him to his senses with the realisation that his friend was in even worse emotional shape than he was. He'd obviously been hitting the bottle pretty damned hard, too.

'I can't do tomorrow,' Harvey mumbled incoherently. 'Calling to cancel. Sorry.'

'You sound terrible. What's the matter?'

'Nothing's the matter,' Harvey replied, breaking into a demented kind of cackle. 'Or at least it won't be, after I've finished this bottle. And the next, and maybe the next one after that if I'm still conscious. That's the problem, see. How's a man supposed to drink himself to death if he can't bloody stay awake to do it?'

'Has something happened?'

'Only the end of the world, Tom. Only the end of the world. Or mine, at any rate. How's yours doing? Ha, ha!'

Harvey had called on his landline, which meant he was at home. Tom said, 'Stay right where you are. I'm coming over.'

'No, no. Leave me alone to die in peace.'

'I'll be there in thirty minutes.'

Twenty-eight minutes later, Tom screeched up outside Harvey's building on Cowley Road and hurried up the stairs to his flat. The door was open. Tom stepped inside to see the place a mess and Harvey sitting semi-inebriated in the middle of the wreckage, nursing a litre of cheap scotch and gazing disconsolately at some documents scattered on the floor at his feet. Stepping closer, Tom saw to his surprise that they were divorce papers.

'I knew it was coming,' Harvey croaked. 'There never seemed to be much hope, but I kept hoping. You do, don't you? And now it's all gone. It's over.' He went to take another slurp of whisky, but Tom gently reached out and took it from his hand.

'You can't stay here on your own, Harve. Come and crash at my place.'

Harvey was too miserable to protest as Tom helped him

downstairs and outside to the car. If Harvey hadn't been too preoccupied with his own troubles the last few days to be aware of his friend's spectacular fall from grace, he made no mention of it as they drove back to the cottage in silence. Once they were inside out of the rain, Tom sat him down on the old sofa in the living room, brewed a pot of coffee and served it strong and black in two earthenware mugs. The wet night had made the cottage feel cold, so he lit a fire and tossed on kindling and split logs until he had a warming blaze going.

'You want to talk about it?'

'I'm completely in the shit, Tom,' Harvey replied in a flat tone, gazing at the flames. 'Up to here in debt, savings gone, had to sell my car, don't know where next month's rent is coming from. And then this had to happen. I've been sitting staring at those divorce papers for days, trying to will them not to exist.'

'You never said anything to me about being married.'

Harvey told the story, and Tom listened, now and then tossing another log on the fire. Gillian was a psychotherapist, too; they'd first met at a seminar, hit it off, fallen in love, moved in together and set up a private practice in London. Things had gone well for the first several years. They had a nice office each with their own therapy rooms, lots of clients, a growing reputation and a bright future. 'Then this plastic surgeon started coming for therapy,' Harvey explained. 'Guy's name is Brett Wilson. Can you believe that anyone's really called Brett? Anyway, he's rich of course, with his own clinic in some part of London where I couldn't have afforded a broom cupboard, and making megabucks gluing fake noses on footballers' wives or whatever it is he does. Gillian's already got a perfectly nice nose, but that didn't stop her going off with the bastard.'

'She shacked up with her own client? I thought there were rules about stuff like that.'

'Huh. She got around that one by passing him onto me, saying she was too busy. So there I was trying to help the guy, while the whole time she was seeing him behind my back. Six months later she announces to me over breakfast that they're moving in together.'

'Welcome to Heartbreak Hotel, pal. You and me both. What a pair we are, eh?'

Harvey was still fairly far gone from all the whisky he'd poured down his throat earlier, but he had sobered up enough to catch the hint. 'What? You mean—?'

Tom nodded sadly. 'Yeah. Dumped for Mr Perfect, just like you. Happened three days ago.'

'But I thought you and she had made up.'

'So did I.'

Tom retold the story in all its painful detail, starting with the devastating phone call and finishing with his admission of how he'd rather too publicly taken out his negative emotions afterwards. His guess had been right: Harvey had been too wrapped up with his own problems to have been paying much attention to the news lately.

'You *socked* him?'

'For all the world to see, right there on live TV. So there goes my job, apart from everything else. Forbsie didn't waste any time slinging my arse out of the station, pending an official misconduct hearing.'

Harvey looked aghast. 'What about the case?'

'Oh, that's someone else's problem now,' Tom said. 'They'll probably put some gobshite crony of Forbsie's on the job of tracking down the paedo killer. And good luck to him.' He could see the look in Harvey's eyes. 'I know. I know what you're thinking, so go right ahead and give me a hard time, why don't you. God knows I deserve it.'

'No, I'm the one who should take the blame for this,' Harvey said, shaking his head in self-disgust. 'You came to me for help, and I let you down. Worst psychologist in the world, most probably. If I can't even sort my own stupid problems, why should anyone trust me to fix theirs?' He sank his face into his hands. 'You should have got yourself someone decent, not a burned-out useless quack of a head-shrinker like me. No wonder Gillian walked out.'

Harvey was taking the news so bitterly that Tom felt he had to try to cheer him up. 'Hey. Hey. Give yourself a break, Harvey. You're the smartest man I know. You got it right about Dracula and Renfield, didn't you? Everybody else but you was on the wrong track, so they were.'

Harvey spat out a laugh. 'A lot of good it did. Give me a medal. No, on second thoughts, give me another drink instead. Don't you have anything stronger than coffee in this place?'

'I think you've had plenty enough of the hard stuff already tonight,' Tom said firmly. He looked at his watch and saw how late into the night they'd sat up talking.

'You're right,' Harvey said ruefully, clutching his guts. 'I feel terrible.'

'Now this sofa may look old and knackered but it's built for comfort, not for looks. You can crash here for as many nights as you want.' Tom went up to the bedroom, fetched a spare sheet and a pillow and an old duvet, and ten minutes later a subdued and bleary-eyed Harvey Pepper was crawling under the covers. Five minutes after that, he was fast asleep, curled up on his side and snoring loudly.

Everybody's got problems, Tom thought as he clambered into his own comfortable bed some time afterwards. *What the hell makes you think yours are so special? Get over yourself, man.*

But as comfortable as the bed might have been, sleep didn't come until dawn was creeping through the trees. The whole night he lay there, tossing and turning. It wasn't the sound of Harvey snoring away downstairs that kept him awake – in fact he found it oddly soothing, like the creaking of ship's timbers –

and nor was it the steady drumming of the rain on the roof over his head. As the first rays of sunlight filtered through his curtains and a distant cockerel crowed from somewhere across the fields, his mind was made up and he said out loud, 'Today I'm going to go and talk to her.'

CHAPTER TWENTY-SIX

Harvey was still fast asleep on the sofa when Tom quietly slipped out of the cottage and drove off, leaving the dog behind to look after things in his absence. The heavy overnight rain had finally stopped, and the greenery of the scorched Oxfordshire countryside appeared revitalised, rich and verdant under a clear blue sky. Tom felt anything but revitalised himself, and last night's talk with Harvey had left a cloud of gloom hanging over him – but he was determined to see through his plan and talk to Desi, in the hope that maybe they could straighten things out. He bought a bunch of yellow roses from a florist's in Eynsham, then sped west and south for Kennington and Bagley Wood Road.

That was where his determination began to flag. Too nervous to enter her driveway, he parked up on the opposite side of the lane where he could see the house without – fat chance of that – being too conspicuous.

He sat there for a long time, trying to pluck up the courage to get out of the car and walk up to the door. He didn't know exactly what he'd say to her: if he had any kind of strategy worked out at all, it was just to be humble and forthright, lay himself bare in front of her, tell her he loved her and couldn't be without her, and beg to be given another chance.

How could a guy fail, with such a brilliant plan?

'Don't answer that,' he muttered to himself in reply.

He could see no movement from within the house. From where he was parked, he couldn't see her car, either. Maybe she wasn't in, he thought. Maybe he should just go home, accept it was over and stop tormenting himself. Or maybe he was really just looking for a way out, because he was too much of a big scaredy-cat to see it through.

He was still trying to summon up his courage when the approaching sound of a rumbly diesel engine caught his ear and he looked down the lane to see a big green Land Rover Defender heading towards him. Or, more accurately, heading towards Desi's place. The Landy turned into her driveway, knobbly off-road tyres crunching on the gravel. It was an ex-military vehicle: matt green paintwork, canvas top, spare wheel mounted on the bonnet. Sunlight flashed on the driver's window as it swung into the driveway, so that Tom was unable to see the figure at the wheel.

But he saw him soon enough, when the Landy had parked outside Desi's front door and the driver got out.

Julian Kendrick.

Of course.

But then again, not of course. Because this was a quite different Julian Kendrick from the one Tom had met at the party. In fact he was strikingly different from everything Tom knew about him, from the whole way that Desi had ever described him. The Kendrick Tom knew and detested was stylish, trendy-looking verging on foppish, to his eye at least, with that whole smirking, smarmy debonair self-conscious attitude about him that seemed contrived to convey the outward impression that it concealed some inner vulnerability, the sensitive, complex soul of the creative artist. Basically, it made you want to slap the fucker.

By contrast, the man Tom now watched climb down from the cab of the ex-army Land Rover and walk up towards her house was a square-shouldered and purposeful individual whose whole bearing screamed out the same kind of uncompromising message as the no-bullshit vehicle he'd just rolled up in.

A totally different Kendrick, now that he didn't know anyone was watching. Yet he had the same face. No twin brother could be this identical. He was the same man.

Tom was pretty darn good at sizing people up. When something about a guy was all wrong, he reacted like the world's most sensitive barometer when a squally storm was blowing in.

And something about Julian Kendrick was *wrong*.

'It's not just me,' Tom muttered out loud. 'I'm not imagining it.'

He felt his hackles go up as he watched Kendrick approach Desi's house. Kendrick knocked. Knocked again. No reply. He paced up and down, then tapped on a front window. Still getting no response, Kendrick disappeared around the back for a minute or two before coming back into sight looking even more disgruntled. He looked at his watch, took out his phone and made a short call as though he was leaving a message. He was much too far away from Tom to lip-read, but it could easily have been *'It's me. Where are you? Call me when you get this.'*

After leaving the message Kendrick started walking back towards the Land Rover, then stopped halfway and returned to the house. For an unsettling instant Tom thought the front door was about to open; but it was just Kendrick trying one last time before giving up. He strode back to the Landy, fired it up and pulled aggressively out of the driveway without noticing the big black Barracuda parked across the lane. Tom watched as Kendrick stormed away out of sight.

For a few instants, Tom just sat there behind the wheel as thoughts burned through his mind. Who really was this guy? *Sweet, sad, artistic, sensitive Julian, my arse*, he thought. *This frigger isn't who she thinks he is.*

In the wake of the Ferguson incident, Tom might have thought more carefully about his impulses before acting on them. But he didn't. Five seconds after Kendrick had disappeared through the bends of Bagley Wood Road, acting on instinct like a predator chasing its prey, Tom keyed his ignition, slammed the 'Cuda into drive and went after him.

Not many cars could escape the Barracuda, once it got going. And a military Defender, while it would leave him stranded and sinking up to his wheel-arches in the mud if he'd tried to pursue it in its natural element, wasn't going to win prizes in an on-road performance showdown against a seven-litre Hemi monster. Tom had to hang right back to avoid being seen as Kendrick led him eastwards across the county. He hit the southern bypass and then cruised at sixty-five along the A40 and A418 for about fifteen miles before turning off and slicing southwards through minor country roads for another four miles, where the twisty going forced Tom to stay closer to his tail in case he turned off one of the many side roads.

Kendrick led Tom to the tiny village of Great Haseley, a haven of expensive thatched cottages and listed country homes. Just beyond the village outskirts, a fancy big barn conversion, all windows and pointed stonework, came into view and Tom saw the Landy turn into its broad driveway into a large front yard. Tom held back, let the car sit idling and watched through a gap in trees and hedges where he could see Kendrick pull up in front of the big house, next to the yellow Porsche. He watched Kendrick climb out and disappear inside the house.

Tom gave it another three minutes, just enough time to allow Kendrick to get settled. When they were settled, they were off their guard. Then he gunned the motor and slewed into the driveway, cutting a crunching arc on the white gravel and pulling up between the Porsche and the Landy. Tom killed the engine and stepped out. A couple of centuries ago, Kendrick's home would have been a workmanlike little stone farmhouse with a big workmanlike outbuilding attached for keeping cows and storing hay, as well as providing a domain for rats and owls. Now the barn was the main part of the house and the property that had once provided a bare eking-out existence for a toothless old farmer was probably worth a million or two, and any concept of living the rural life was long gone. Through the immaculate glass frontage Tom caught a glimpse of the modern, minimalist interior, white wood, white walls.

He didn't know exactly what he'd come here to say or do, but there was no stopping now. He surged out of the car and strode fast towards the house. As he got closer he could hear loud rock music, fast and ultra-aggressive, the beat thumping insistently through the stone walls. Kendrick was visible inside, back on his phone, stomping about and looking very pissed off. It looked as if he was leaving another message, maybe for Desi again.

Tom pushed against the front door and found it open. As he shoved it wide the music suddenly redoubled in volume, hard-edged grinding guitar and thundering drums. The vocalist wasn't trying to sing. The sound of his voice was a raw, enraged, demented screaming. And there, suddenly, was Kendrick, appearing from a room down the hallway and freezing for an instant as he saw Tom framed in the doorway, his look of surprise quickly knitting into a hostile glare.

'Wha—' Kendrick started to say, but the pounding cacophony drowned him. He reached into his back pocket and took out a remote. He pointed it round behind him, aiming like a gun, thumbed a button and the pounding and screaming dropped a few points in volume.

'What do you want, McAllister?' He stepped closer to the doorway and stood blocking it with his arms folded.

Tom said, 'I want to talk to you.'

CHAPTER TWENTY-SEVEN

Kendrick said, 'Yeah? But here's the thing. I don't want to talk to you. So how about you piss off and leave me alone?' He started closing the door. Tom shoved his foot in it.

'You can't do that,' Kendrick said.

But Tom held his foot in the door. 'No?'

'I could break your leg,' Kendrick said.

'Oh, I'll bet you think you can.'

'What part of "I don't want to talk to you" don't you understand, McAllister?'

'Do you talk to your clients?' Tom asked.

Kendrick was thrown enough by the question to give an open reply. 'Of course.'

'What about?'

'Whatever they want. They're paying for the time.'

'Okay, then I just became your client.'

'I see. You want your picture taken?'

Tom said, 'You're a photographer, aren't you? You shoot, we'll talk.'

Kendrick glowered at him. 'I don't want to take your photo.'

'Maybe I'm not beautiful enough for you. Think of me as a nature shot, if you want. Something wild and unapproachable.'

'You couldn't afford me.'

'My birthday's coming up,' Tom said. 'I'm treating myself. You don't always get the chance to be snapped by a famous photographer. And you might not be around much longer.'

Kendrick's frown grew deeper. 'What's that supposed to mean?'

'You going to take my picture or not?'

'Maybe you'd like to pose next to that ridiculous cowboy wagon,' Kendrick said, pointing past Tom and out of the open doorway at the Barracuda in the front yard.

Tom shrugged. 'You're right,' he said. 'It is a ridiculous car. I won it off a guy who worked for the Swansea mafia. He used to garrotte people for a living.'

'Nice folks you hang out with.'

'He was a nicer person than me,' Tom said. 'A lot gentler. Less prone to sudden violence. I think you should let me in and take the picture.'

Kendrick looked as if he was going to make a stand, but then stepped back from the door. He glanced at his watch. 'If that's what you want, McAllister. But I have to be somewhere later, so you've got half an hour. Then you pay me and fuck off.'

Tom brushed past him into the airiness of the house. It seemed virtually empty next to the cosy clutter of his cottage. Heavy, dark beams running the length of the open-plan space were the only nods to its traditional, rustic origins. The floors were heavily waxed and squeaked underfoot. Through a high doorway was a dining area in white, sunlight streaming across a long table.

'Come this way.' Kendrick led him through a sitting area where two big leather sofas faced one another either side of a glass-topped table covered in photography magazines. On the walls were framed blow-ups, mostly black and white, big flashy prints of portraits of actors, models, and some nature shots. Hampton Burnley the film star was one face that Tom recognised. The furious, pounding music was softer now, but only a little. It seemed to come from every nook of the house. Hidden wireless speakers, all hooked up to the internet.

'What do you call this stuff?' Tom asked. 'Rage metal? Hate metal? Who do you think about when you're listening to it? Jesus Christ, no wonder you're depressed.'

'Depressed?' Kendrick said, pausing in his step. 'Who the hell said I'm depressed?'

Ignoring him, Tom pointed at a door beside a broad open-tread staircase. 'That your studio?'

'No, that's a basement boiler room. Be my guest, if you want to shut yourself up inside. It hasn't been used in months.'

'Well, lead on, then, smart guy.'

'This is it,' Kendrick said when they reached another door at the end of a hallway. 'Let's make this quick.'

The studio was dazzling white inside, with a large satiny cloth backdrop draped elegantly behind a stage area around which were arrayed a variety of lighting equipment and a collection of expensive-looking cameras with lenses of different lengths, mounted on tripods. Air conditioning whirred softly in the background. In the middle of the stage was a plain wooden stool. Kendrick pointed at it and said, 'Sit there.'

Tom sat, while Kendrick aimed a powerful bank of lights at him, making him blink. 'Watch it with that,' Tom warned.

'Stop moaning. And sit straight. You're slouching.'

Kendrick stepped behind a camera, framed Tom in the lens, then stepped away from it again with a frown and plucked some tissues from a box, balled them up and tossed them across. 'Wipe your face. You're sweating like a pig in a sauna.'

Tom dabbed his forehead. 'So tell me again how you met her.'

'How about you tell me why that's any of your bloody business?' Kendrick replied coolly, stepping back behind the camera.

'I'll tell you why. It's because that whole story about how you and she just happened to bump into one another that day in the botanical gardens is a pile of shit.'

'Really. You think that, do you?'

'Yeah, I do. I think you set the whole thing up so you could go over and talk to her.'

'You know what I think?' Kendrick said, snapping shots. 'I think you're without a doubt the ugliest thing I've ever seen through a camera lens. These are going to come out terrible.'

'So you're not denying it.'

'I wouldn't dignify it with a denial, because it's complete bollocks. Why the hell would I have set it up?'

Tom replied, 'I don't know. You tell me.'

Kendrick looked up from behind the camera, and shrugged. 'It's true that you don't know the whole story. But I don't think you want to.'

'Try me.'

'Fine, you asked for it,' Kendrick said. 'The way she and I met up in Oxford was just like she told you. But the fact is it wasn't just some cosy little social encounter. The attraction was there, right from the beginning. We went to an afternoon movie. You get the idea: back row, place almost empty, dark and as private as it gets in a public place. Have you ever tried to do it in a cinema, McAllister?'

Tom said nothing.

'Afterwards, I brought her back here. She left a trail of clothes all the way to that sofa.' Kendrick pointed. 'We did it three times. She said it was the best she'd had in years. She's had even better since.'

Tom was silent.

'You're slouching again,' Kendrick said, and then gave a

little smile. 'See, I told you you didn't want to hear the whole story. What else do you want to know about my private life?'

'What were you doing at her place today?' Tom asked.

Kendrick's eyes narrowed into slits. 'What? Have you been following me?'

'Not technically. I just happened to be there when you turned up.'

'So what were *you* doing there?'

'Paying her a visit.'

'She dumped you, or have you forgotten?'

'I wanted to talk to her.'

Kendrick snorted. 'Yeah, well, I've nothing to hide. You really want to know what I went round there for? I'd told her I knew where some kestrels are nesting. She said she'd love to see them, and we arranged a time for me to go and pick her up in the Landy. The nesting site's way off road in the middle of nowhere. But she wasn't at home. Fact is, I don't know where she is. Okay? End of story. Now I'm going to take another picture, so try not to sit bent over like the hunchback of Notre Dame.' He detached one lens and fitted another. Aimed the camera back at Tom, with his finger poised on the button. 'Smile. That's fine, then don't smile. You don't like me very much, do you?'

'You got that right,' Tom said. 'And I wasn't following you before, but you can be damn sure I'll be watching you now.'

'Is that a fact?'

'And here's another fact, Kendrick. You hurt her, even a little bit, and I'll end you. I'll flatten you into the dirt.'

Kendrick smiled. 'I get what this is about. You've got some kind of fantasy happening here, like you're the knight in shining armour saving the damsel. You think that if you turn her against me that she'll go running back to you, don't you? Well, you've got it all wrong. You were just her bit of rough.

She was just slumming it. She'll never go back to you, so get real, mate.'

'What was your unit?' Tom asked.

'What?'

'In the army. What was your unit?'

Kendrick dropped his gaze and went back to fiddling with the camera. 'What makes you think I was in the army?' he asked, in an altered voice.

'The Land Rover.'

'Ha. Pathetic. Anyone can buy a bloody Land Rover. The MoD auctions them off cheap. That the best you can do, detective?'

Tom stared at Kendrick. Hard. Harder than he'd stared at anyone for a long time. 'Tell the truth, Soldier Boy. Think I don't know the look of a squaddie when I see one? Didn't grow up in frigging Belfast for nothing.'

Kendrick turned off his camera and slapped on the lens cap. 'All right, we're done. I'm tired of this conversation.'

'Already? You only took a couple of shots. And you haven't answered the question.'

'Fuck your question. You owe me a thousand pounds.'

'That's a friend price, is it?'

'Call it eleven hundred.'

'Let's make a deal,' Tom said. 'That camera's worth, what, three grand? How about I *don't* smash it into tiny little pieces against your head before I leave here. Then we're even. Agreed?'

'I'm not afraid of you, you know.'

Tom stood up from the stool and replied, 'You should be.'

'You're not even a cop any more.'

'That's why you should be afraid of me,' Tom said.

They moved closer, one step each, like fighters squaring up.

'Go on, then,' Kendrick challenged him. 'Try your luck.'

Tom's fists were clenched tighter than rocks. But he thought of Desi, and relaxed them.

'Send me a bill,' he told Kendrick. Then he walked out of studio, out of the house and back to the Barracuda, and left deep trenches in the gravel driveway as he roared away.

Gordy Nash walked out of the gates into white light and tasted the free air for the first time in fourteen years. He stepped out onto the patchy grass in front of the prison, dropped the suitcase he was carrying in one hand and the jacket he was holding in the other, and raised his arms to embrace the freedom. He closed his eyes and felt the sun's heat on his face, feeling it soaking into him, burning orange through his closed eyelids.

He had enough cash in his pocket to feed himself for a couple of weeks and see him up north. No point wasting money on the train. He could hitch rides all the way up to Scotland. He had the whole thing figured out. Life was starting again, and it was sweet. The road ahead of him stretched on to infinity. No more bars, no more locked doors, no more of the slamming of steel on steel and clanking of keys that filled his head and made him want to smash his brains out against the wall. It was an open world now, and he intended to make the most of it, the only way he knew how.

Here I come, he thought.

Gordy picked up the battered case that contained all his worldly possessions, slung the leather jacket over his shoulder and started walking into the sun. It felt so good to be able to walk longer than the length of a prison corridor or an exercise yard without finding the way closed off ahead of you that he kept on walking for half a mile before he even thought about hitching his first lift.

The traffic was thin out here in the countryside. Gordy had expected to have to wait a while before anyone picked him up. A lone male hitch-hiking in the vicinity of a men's prison wasn't guaranteed a ride, even at the best of times. He was surprised when the very first car that came by stopped for him almost the moment he'd stuck out his thumb. He heard it slowing down behind him and turned to look. The sun was reflecting brightly on the windscreen, but through it he could see the driver waving at him.

He was even more surprised when he walked up to the little red sporty hatchback and got a clearer look at the driver as the window rolled down. She was young and blonde, with slim tanned arms bare to the shoulder and all the right curves in all the right places visible under the tight, short dress she was wearing. Her lips were the same colour as the car. And she was alone.

Wow.

Gordy leaned close to the window with a friendly smile, at an angle where he could see her long bare legs stretched out all the way to the pedals. Gordy hadn't seen a pair of legs like that for a very long time, and they were hard to take your eyes off.

The sunlight gleamed on her sunglasses. 'Where're you headed?' she asked, returning his smile. Dazzling.

'North,' Gordy replied.

'Hop in. You can chuck your case in the back.'

CHAPTER TWENTY-EIGHT

Back home, Tom spent a lot of time pacing and fretting before he finally picked up the phone to call Desi. Harvey had since migrated from the sofa to a lounger in the garden, where he sat under the shade of an oak tree slowly consuming bottle after bottle of Langtree Hundred. Radar lay watchfully nearby, not quite sure what to make of their new resident and possibly wondering for how much longer they were going to have the pleasure of his company.

For nearly two more hours, Tom kept getting Desi's voicemail, on both her landline and mobile. It wasn't until he'd started preparing a late lunch for himself and his houseguest – in his distracted state of mind he couldn't stretch to anything more involved than mushrooms with garlic and parsley, sliced thick and pan-fried until they reached the perfect point of juiciness, or that was the theory at any rate – that he finally got through to her.

'He's all wrong for you, Desi,' he said, standing there in his apron with a spatula in his hand and the sizzle of the mushrooms in the background. He was emboldened by half a bottle of Langtree, or else he'd never have had the courage to blurt the words out. 'I'm telling you, you don't know who this guy really is.'

She'd sounded unwilling to speak to him from the start, and there was a blaze of anger in her voice as she shot back, 'What did you think you were doing, confronting him like that? Were you going to thump him, too, like you did Ferguson?'

'So you heard about that, did you?'

'Heard it? I saw it on live TV, along with about a million other people. What's the matter with you?'

'Never mind me,' he replied gruffly. 'It's your boy Kendrick I'd be worried about. Where is he now?'

'He's gone to London,' she said after a beat. 'Got a photo shoot.'

Tom thought they must be making progress, for her to answer his questions at all. He was even slightly surprised that she wasn't more riled by his "your boy Kendrick" jab. 'Celebs, I suppose,' he said, laying the disapproval on all the more thickly, seeing as he could apparently get away with it.

'No, old soldiers,' she said. 'Some kind of regimental get-together thing.'

'Ha. I knew he was a soldier boy. He couldn't fool me.'

'You're always right, aren't you, Tom McAllister?'

'No,' he replied, in all earnestness. 'I'm not. I've been wrong more often than I can count, about all kinds of things. But I'm right about this, Desi. I swear I am.'

'What makes you so sure?' she demanded.

'I just feel it,' he replied. 'I wish you'd listen to me.'

'I have to go,' she said.

'Desi—' he began, but she was already gone.

That was when Tom smelled the mushrooms burning, put the phone down in a panic and whisked the pan off the heat, too late to rescue them. 'Ah, shit!'

Luckily the next day's lunch escaped being burned, and the next day's after that, with two fairly lavish dinners in between, all of which Tom shared with his visitor who wasn't yet showing any signs of wanting to leave. It had to be said that Harvey's company was much less scintillating than it might have been if not for his personal woes, though Tom liked having him around nonetheless. Maybe it was selfish to let a friend's troubles act as a distraction from your own, he thought. But having someone to cater for helped to take his mind off the thoughts of Desi that would otherwise have been eating away at him.

Meanwhile, with a greedy extra mouth to feed, early in the afternoon of the third day of Harvey's stay Tom noticed that his supply of Langtree Hundred was running dangerously low again, meaning that it was time to make the trip over to Bampton to stock up on a few cases. He hadn't seen Alfie Birtwhistle since getting suspended, but he was sure the old guy would've seen it on the news and would have plenty to say about it.

'You stay here and look after him,' Tom told Radar, pointing at Harvey who was curled up on the sofa, napping as he often did. Then he jumped in the car and sped off, leaving the reluctant shepherd to mind his flock of one.

Tom had been right: old Alfie had some pretty strong opinions to express, with a good deal of colourful language in condemnation of them good-for-nothing parcel of fucking arses in the police and much lavish praise for the dynamite right hook that had floored that bloody stuck-up professor so-and-so, who did he think *he* was, the best punch Alfie had seen on TV since Henry Cooper felled Ali at Wembley in '63. It was some time before Tom was able to extricate himself from Alfie's clutches. 'You give 'em what for, son, you give 'em what for,' the old man repeated with shrill indignation as Tom loaded the two crates of beer into the car.

'I will, Alfie. I will.' Though quite what it was he was supposed to do, Tom had no idea as he drove off again towards home.

By the time Tom rolled up outside the cottage he'd been away more than forty minutes, longer than he'd meant to – but then, who needed to be regulated by the clock any more? Shifting the first crate of Langtree from the car he noticed that the cottage door was hanging wide open. As he walked towards the doorway he called, 'Harvey? Harvey? You want another beer?' Not that he should encourage the guy to sit around drinking ale all day, he thought, but it was better than knocking back whisky, which he'd no doubt have been doing if left to his own devices at home.

There was no reply. Tom was entering the cottage when Radar suddenly emerged, tense and whingeing, and he knew instantly from the dog's behaviour that something was wrong. 'Radar, what is it?'

Then Tom walked inside with the crate still in his arms, and what he saw there made him drop it to the floor with a crash.

Harvey was lying sprawled out on the living room rug near the fireplace, inert, apparently dead. Blood was everywhere, leaking profusely from a gaping gash on his head and soaking into the rug. Tom rushed over to him, suddenly shaking, his legs turning to jelly.

'Harvey!'

No response. Tom crouched by the body and checked the pulse. It was there, but it was weak and fluttering.

Tom jumped to his feet, reaching for his phone to dial 999 for an ambulance and thinking that Harvey must have fallen and hit his head against something hard, like the corner of the fireplace. But then he saw the heavy iron poker lying on the floor a few feet away. Out of policeman's instinct he snatched the folded bed sheet from the nearby sofa, used that to pick up the fallen poker, and saw the fresh blood and strands of black hair stuck to the tip. This had been no accident. Someone had been inside the cottage and violently attacked his friend.

'Harvey! What happened? Talk to me!'

Harvey's eyes fluttered open and tried to focus. One pupil was dilated, the other shrunk to a pinhead. Signs of serious concussion. He managed to croak, 'Tom?'

'It's me, Harve,' Tom said urgently, gripping his hand. 'I'm here. Who did this to you?'

Harvey's voice was so weak and incoherent that it was hard to make out the words. 'There was . . . a robber. Black . . .'

'Black what, Harvey?'

'All in black. Couldn't . . . see . . . his face. Mask . . . he . . . hit . . .'

Then Harvey passed out again.

After calling for the ambulance Tom dialled Billie's number, which would get the cops here a lot faster than going through the call centre. 'It's me. Something's happened.'

Events moved quickly after that. Harvey had been drifting in and out of consciousness, and Tom was unable to get anything more out of him before the paramedics hustled him into the ambulance. Billie Flowers was already at the scene by then, taking charge of the two uniformed coppers who'd turned up soon afterwards. She tried to persuade Tom to ride with her to the hospital, but he insisted on driving himself. Billie used her blues and twos as they accompanied the ambulance in a speeding convoy that screeched up at the John Radcliffe ER soon afterwards. Nurses held Tom back as Harvey was wheeled urgently inside and disappeared through a swinging door.

'He's going to be okay,' Billie reassured Tom, close at his side and squeezing his arm.

'He'd better be.'

They spent the next hour in a waiting area, Tom too anxious and worked up to stay still, pacing the squeaky floor as Billie sat frowning. A distraught couple were seated nearby, waiting for news of their kid who'd been hit by a car. When a doctor came to say the kid was okay, the mother let out a wail of relief and they all hurried off, leaving Tom and Billie alone and able to resume their private conversation.

'A man all in black, with a mask on,' Billie said, speaking low. 'Are you absolutely sure?'

'I told you, that's what he said,' Tom replied grimly. 'That's all he *could* say.'

'A burglar? That's the obvious explanation.'

'A burglar doesn't dress up as a ninja assassin,' Tom said. 'Not in rural west Oxfordshire. Not in my experience. Or yours.'

'Then here's another possibility. Back at the cottage you told me the reason Harvey had come to stay with you was that he was upset about his divorce. But also that he was worried about debts. So I'm thinking, who does he owe money to? Is he in worse trouble than he let on?'

'Nobody knew he was with me,' Tom answered, still pacing. 'It doesn't make sense.'

'Then that rules out loony therapy clients, too, I suppose.'

'This wasn't aimed at Harvey,' Tom said, shaking his head. 'The poor guy was just in the wrong place at the wrong time. It was aimed at me.'

Billie was silent for a while, deep in thought with her brows furrowed and a vertical frown line cut deep between her eyes. 'I wish you'd stop pacing. You're making me dizzy, watching you.'

'I'm sorry,' he sighed, and slumped in a plastic seat next to her. He squeezed his eyes shut and pinched the bridge of his nose, hard, trying to calm his thoughts.

'I have another idea,' Billie said. 'You're not going to like it.'

'I don't like anything much at the moment.'

'I'm thinking that this masked man all in black sounds like the description that Toby Friar gave after the Port Meadow killing.'

Tom looked at her. 'You think the paedo killer came to the cottage to get me?'

'Maybe. It could make sense.'

'But why?'

'Because what if you were onto something?' she replied. 'What if you know something that makes you a threat to him, somehow?'

'I'm onto bugger all,' Tom said. 'I'm not even on the case any more. I don't have a clue what's happening with it.'

'Nothing, is the answer to that,' Billie sighed. 'No leads, no breakthroughs, no suspects. We're floundering. But you must know something, even if you don't know you do.'

'Story of my life,' he muttered darkly.

'And the killer knows you know.'

'You're tying my brain up in knots. How can the killer know something that I know that *I* don't know I know?'

'Think, Tom.'

'I am thinking.'

Billie paused a while longer, then a new idea came to her mind, taking her on a different tack. Tom had never known anyone else with Billie's ability to think sideways, as well as forwards and backwards. She asked, 'So, where was the dog when all this happened?'

'I left him at the cottage with Harvey. I was only gone thirty, forty minutes.'

Billie frowned again. 'So,' she said slowly, 'if the dog was at home, then how the hell did an intruder get in? I mean, who in their right mind's going to walk into someone else's house with that thing on guard? Does he normally just let masked strangers walk in and beat guests over the head?'

'He's a good watchdog,' Tom said. 'He'd eat them alive, so he would.'

'Unless . . .' she began, thinking aloud.

'Unless what?'

'Unless maybe the attacker was someone the dog knew.'

Tom was still digesting her words when a door swung open at the bottom of the corridor and the little Chinese doctor with the ponytail who'd been attending to Harvey came to tell them that he was out of surgery and stable. The concussion wasn't too serious and things were looking good for a full recovery. How long, they couldn't say, but they wanted to keep him in for observation a couple of days. All being well, he should be free to go home afterwards.

Relief flooded through Tom like warm milk and honey. 'Can we see him?'

'No, he's resting now. The best thing for you is to go home. We'll call you if there's any change.'

'I have to make tracks,' Billie said, looking at her watch when the doctor was gone. 'Try to get some rest, okay? Call me if you want to talk.'

'I will.'

They returned to their cars, and Tom drove slowly home. The cottage was a crime scene now, though a humble assault didn't warrant the kind of major fanfare that another paedo killing would have caused. While the police were hovering about and some assistants of Thins Waller's were gathering their evidence, Tom slipped away. He took a walk down by the river with Radar, then stood for a while under the beams of his roofless restaurant gazing at the lazy, splashing revolutions of the water wheel.

That was when his phone rang. It was Desi Fielding.

225

CHAPTER TWENTY-NINE

'You sound upset,' he said, at the sound of her voice.

'So do you.'

'It's not been a good day. Someone came to the cottage and bashed Harvey over the head.'

Desi gasped. 'Oh my God. Is he okay?'

'Just a bit of concussion, thank Christ. If I catch the bastard who . . .' Tom held back from saying more. Controlling his voice he said, 'It's good to hear from you, Desi. But what's the matter? Has something happened?'

'Well, yes, something has. I'm sorry you're having troubles. But I really need to talk to you, Tom.'

His muscles clenched tight. Without hesitation he replied, 'I'll come right over.'

'Not here,' she said. 'He might turn up.'

'Who might turn up?'

'Julian. That's what I need to talk to you about. I think you were right about him. I'm frightened, Tom.'

Tom felt a volcanic glow of heat spreading through his whole being. He ground the phone so tight against his ear that it hurt. 'Here's not a good place either. The cottage is swarming with cops.' Hearing himself talk like that made him realise that he barely even felt like one himself any more. 'You name the time and the place, and I'm there.'

'I'm in the middle of town right now. How about outside the Radcliffe Camera?'

'Give me twenty minutes.'

Tom roared into the City of Dreaming Spires with his foot to the floor. Hustling through the traffic to the centre, he jammed the 'Cuda into a parking space across from Blackwell's bookshop in Broad Street and ran around the corner of the Bodleian Library, past the Bridge of Sighs and Hertford College and up Catte Street to the circular, domed academic library that was one of Oxford's most iconic landmarks. The gradually lowering afternoon sun was shining pinkish-gold off the scrubbed limestone and glittering off a hundred leaded windows of the grand old building. A crowd of tourists were milling about, taking selfies and nattering in Japanese. Tom felt a jolt of excitement as he spotted the figure of Desi standing on the lawn gazing towards the High Street and looking pensive and anxious.

Tom was out of breath as he joined her. 'I got here as quickly as I could.' He wanted to hold her in his arms but stood back to give her space.

'I'm so shocked to hear about Harvey. Do you have any idea who—?'

'None,' Tom said. 'But I will. Tell me about Kendrick. What's he done to you?'

She shook her head. 'It isn't like that.'

'Tell me.'

'I think you were right about him, Tom. He isn't who he seems to be.' Glancing nervously around her she added, 'Can we go somewhere? I don't want to talk here.'

'Let's go for a coffee.'

They headed up the High Street to the Covered Market

227

and climbed the stairs into Georgina's café. It felt good to be with her, but Tom was itching to hear the rest of what she had to tell him. The place was in its last busy period before closing time, full of chatter with Edith Piaf warbling *Milord* in the background. At a small table in the corner Tom ordered them cappuccinos, and Desi began to talk.

'It happened last night. I woke up around three in the morning and his side of the bed was empty.'

A lancing ache went through Tom's skull and he tried to shut the image of the two of them together out of his head. 'I don't really want to hear about your sleeping arrangements with the guy, Desi.'

'Just listen, okay? I got up, and from the top of the stairs I could see light coming out from under the study door. I wondered what he was doing in there, so I went downstairs as quietly as I could. As I reached the door I heard movement from inside. Furtive, you know?'

'Go on.'

'So I opened the door and there he was, sitting at the desk looking at my laptop. I asked him what he was doing, and he told me he'd woken up remembering he needed to check his webmail. Some client in the States who contacts him at funny hours. That was the story, anyhow.'

'Why your laptop?' Tom asked. 'Couldn't he use his own phone, like everyone else?'

'I asked him that, and he said the battery was dead and he'd left the charger at home. Which is plausible enough in theory, but he was acting strange, sort of agitated and false. I got the feeling he was hiding something.'

'What?'

'Well, this morning, while he was in the shower, I found his phone in his jeans pocket and checked it. The battery was fine.'

'So he lied about his phone not working,' Tom said.

'But that's not all. Later, when he'd gone, I noticed that the key to my filing cabinet was in the wrong place. I always keep it in the right-hand drawer of my desk. It was in the left-hand drawer instead. And I know I didn't put it there.'

'The filing cabinet where you keep all your copies of client records?'

'And other even more confidential material from the Institute. I think that's what he was sneaking a look at. Why would he be interested in my private clients? Then when he heard me coming down the stairs he quickly put it all away, closed the filing cabinet and pretended to be looking at the laptop instead. But in his hurry he must have replaced the cabinet key in the wrong drawer.'

Tom asked, 'By "other confidential material", do you mean the files on newly released sex offenders?'

She nodded. 'It's all in there. Stuff that nobody outside the system is meant to see. It's extremely sensitive information, for obvious reasons.'

'Let me get this straight. You're saying that someone with access to those files would know exactly who's getting out, when, which prisons they did their time in, the details of the crimes they committed to get banged up in the first place, and where they're being relocated to for so-called rehabilitation in the community?'

'You don't have to knock my job, Tom. But yes, that's exactly what I'm saying. I'm certain that's what Julian was after. And it's not the first time it's happened. The other day I found some files that had been put in the wrong order. At the time, I thought it must've been me, though it would be very odd indeed for an organisational nerd like me to do something like that. Now I realise he's been sneaking into the study whenever I'm not around, to snoop through my papers.'

She paused for an agitated gulp of coffee, the fingers of both hands clasping the cup tightly as though she was afraid she might drop it. 'That's why I now believe you were right about him all along, Tom. That day when I first met him, I'm beginning to think it was all a set-up, just like you said it was. I think he made the whole thing up about meeting a client. I think he's been using me, just so that he could get to my information. I keep asking myself: why would he do that? The more I think about it, the more obvious it seems that there's only one possible conclusion I can draw. And the more it scares me to death.'

Tom said nothing. The interior of the café, the other customers, the buzz of conversation, the background music, the waiting staff weaving between the tables: they were all faded away to nothing, suddenly vanished from existence. Connections were flying together at light speed in his brain, neurons lighting up like a chain reaction inside a nuclear fission reactor in full meltdown. It all began to make sense now.

There are other things, too,' Desi said. 'Things he's said, things he does, the way he acts sometimes. Like that old basement in his house. He pretends that he never goes down there, but he does often, when he thinks you're not looking. I caught him at it once, and he got really furious. What's he trying to hide? What's his secret?'

'Oh, he's got a secret, all right,' Tom said. 'He's got plenty. Such as the fact that he's a soldier boy. Or was. He didn't deny it when I challenged him about it. I'm guessing he was in the New Zealand military.'

She frowned. 'He was. He told me, in confidence. I think he was a captain. But how did you know?'

'It was the day I went to your place and saw him.'

'When was that?'

'A couple of days after you dumped me for him,' Tom replied. 'I had to talk to you. Then Kendrick turned up in this bloody great army jeep, something about going to see a bird's nest. But you weren't at home. I was glad you stood him up like that.'

'Oh,' she said, nonplussed for a moment. 'I . . . something came up that I had to do that day.'

'Anyhow, that's when I knew. He's got the look. You can't mistake it. Now you've confirmed it. Which would mean the frigger is trained to shoot more than just a camera. A three-hundred-yard shot with a rifle would be nothing to him. Neither would blowing someone away at close quarters with a handgun or jamming a knife in their guts.'

Desi looked sickened and shook her head, not wanting to believe it. 'This whole thing is freaking me out. Could we be getting it all wrong, Tom? Is it possible that there's some other explanation?'

'Yeah? Like what?'

'I've no idea. It's so awful, I just don't know *what* to think.'

'I do,' he said, lowering his voice. 'Your man Julian Kendrick. He's the paedo killer. You told me yourself that time at the party, he hates them. I didn't make anything of it at the time, because why should I have? I thought it was weird that he even confided that in you. But now it all fits. He hates them so much, he wants to kill as many of them as he can before he's caught. Jameson, Blake, Moss, Gibson, he murdered them all. He would've killed Sweeney, too, if he hadn't slipped up. And then he almost killed Harvey.'

'I don't understand. Why Harvey?'

'Harvey wasn't the target. I was. Billie figured it out. She said I must know something that made the killer feel threatened. Truth is I didn't, not then. But the day I went around and confronted Kendrick, he must've thought I was onto him. And so he came around to the cottage to kill me.'

'How can you be so sure it was him?'

'Because it had to be someone the dog knew,' Tom said. 'Something else Billie figured out, except neither of us knew what it meant at the time. Radar took an instant liking to the frigger, the one time he met him. That's the only reason Kendrick was able to get inside the cottage without getting his arse ripped off. I was out at the time, but maybe he was planning on lying in wait until I came home, so he could bash my brains out, shoot me, stab me to death or whatever. Except by a fluke Harvey happened to be there instead, and he must've surprised him. It's just a miracle Harve didn't end up becoming victim number five.'

'Oh, my God.'

Tom sighed. 'Poor Harvey. The guy's a genius, so he is. He's the only one who saw the whole thing clearly, from the start. He knew the killer wasn't working alone. That was the only way to account for what happened to Vinnie Sweeney.'

Tom remembered what Harvey had said to him that day, months ago in the Claddagh, when he'd explained his Dracula and Renfield theory. *Perhaps Sweeney had outlived his usefulness. Vampires are fickle like that. He'll always be able to find another.'*

And Tom was certain that was exactly what he had done. That explained the lull in the spate of killings. The point when they'd restarted, with the murder of Adrian Gibson, coincided almost exactly with when Desi had started seeing Kendrick. The vampire had ditched his first helper in exchange for one far more useful.

Tom said, 'After Sweeney died everyone thought the killer was gone. Even I began to think it. But he was just looking for a new source, like Harvey predicted. He hooked up with you so that he could track down more targets. First he went after Gibson. Who's next?'

'We'd know that from my records,' Desi said. 'It means we could anticipate his next move. We could catch him in the attempt.'

Tom asked, 'These records that he's now had access to – do they cover just this region?'

'No. It's nationwide. The entire sex offender rehabilitation database.'

'And how many child abusers are due for release in the near future, across the whole country?'

She reflected. 'Off the top of my head, maybe eighteen or twenty, over the next few months.'

'Then it's needles and haystacks,' Tom said. 'Until now the killings were all restricted to the local area, but now he's playing on a much bigger field. He can pick his targets anywhere he likes, and his job gives him all the alibis he needs to travel all over the country. No telling where he'll strike next, or when. It could be tomorrow, or it could be in two months' time.'

'You're right,' she said, looking crestfallen.

'Which means you'd need to launch a country-wide sting operation, with eyes on every single possible victim, to have any chance of netting him. In any case, we can't report this to the cops. Not yet.'

'But why?'

'There's just not enough to go on. All the evidence is circumstantial and he hasn't left any real traces that can link him to the crime. If I went to Thames Valley about this, everyone would think it was just a personal thing, because I was jealous of the new man in your life. And they'd be dead right. I am, too.'

She touched his hand across the table. 'You've got nothing to be jealous about. And I'm sorry I hurt you. I really am. But what are we going to do?'

'Never mind the cops,' Tom said. 'I'm going to have it out with him. Let's see if I can't make him talk.'

'If we're right about this . . . it means he's dangerous, Tom.'

'So am I.'

CHAPTER THIRTY

Tom left Oxford and hit the ring road in a maelstrom of roaring speed, tearing past the traffic as though it were standing still. As he came skidding to a halt outside the cottage he knew what he had to do. Harvey Pepper was no doubt a much better psychotherapist than he gave himself credit for. But there were other ways besides therapy to achieve a certain peace of mind. Tom had had it for years already.

Passing by the kitchen, he tossed Radar a piece of fillet steak from his fridge that he'd been planning on cooking tonight: the beef Stroganoff for himself and Harvey that now wasn't going to happen. Then he stormed upstairs to his room, shunted his bed aside and prised up the loose floorboard hidden underneath. And here was his peace of mind: an Ithaca Featherlight twelve-gauge shotgun, cut off at both ends to make it as short and concealable as a pump-action combat shotgun had any right to be. Tom had won it in the same card game that netted him the Barracuda. The thug who'd previously owned both was long since dead, strangled with one of his own garrottes.

Just being in possession of the gun was enough to land Tom in jail for five years, if he'd been daft enough to be caught with it. It was stored away loaded, four in the tube plus one up the spout. Enough illegal, unregistered firepower to take down a brick wall with, though he'd never fired it and only kept it for that once-in-a-lifetime emergency you hope will never happen, but damn well want to be ready for if it does.

Hurrying back downstairs, he locked up the cottage with Radar posted on guard duty, slung the weapon in the Barracuda and took off so fast that the car's back end was swinging like a pendulum and spinning its wheels for the first hundred yards. Hitting the main roads he drove like a wild man, southwards across the county towards the village of Great Haseley. Woe betide the traffic cop who might've pulled him over on the way to Kendrick's, but none did.

When Tom arrived there, the ex-military Land Rover was parked up outside the house but the yellow Porsche was nowhere to be seen. He grabbed the shotgun from the car and walked up to Kendrick's front door with it on open display. He didn't care any more. The guy was a vicious and practised killer with an apparent history of eliminating his accomplices, who'd now tricked his way into the affections of the woman Tom loved. Tom would cheerfully blow Kendrick's damn head off and spend the rest of his days in prison for it, before he'd let him hurt her.

He walked a loop of the house banging on doors and windows until he was satisfied that Kendrick wasn't at home. Either way would have suited him fine, but the guy being out of the way made Tom's job easier. He let himself in the front door, with a hard kick that splintered the lock out of the frame. There was no alarm system. Inside, he looked around him. Something Desi had said earlier was still ringing in his head. *Things he's said, things he does, the way he acts sometimes. Like that old basement in his house. He pretends that he never goes down there, but he does often, when he thinks you're not looking. What's he trying to hide?'*

Tom remembered the basement room door from his first visit to Kendrick's place. He walked over to it, tried the handle and found it was locked. So he smashed that one in, too. The broken door crashed open to reveal a flight of descending concrete steps. Tom went down them into the basement. It was pretty much what Kendrick had said it was, an old boiler room, with a bare concrete floor showing a couple of damp spots and a lot of copper piping running up from the big oil-fired boiler and the hot water tank, and up through the ceiling into the rest of the house. At first glance there was nothing particularly unusual or incriminating about the place, but then in his experience there seldom was, until you probed a little deeper. It certainly gave the impression of being a room that was seldom used, with a thick layer of dust on everything.

Almost everything.

Casting his expert eye around every detail, Tom noticed the recent finger marks on the surface of the hot water tank, showing that someone had been here not very long ago. A plumber, maybe? But there were no signs of any of the piping being a recent replacement. It wasn't until Tom got down on his knees and looked behind the tank that he noticed the loose panel next to where it was mounted on the wall.

Aha.

With just a little effort, he was able to reach in and pull away the panel. And there it was. You couldn't fool a cop with half a lifetime of experience of hunting for stuff people didn't want him to find. Especially one who'd kept an illicit weapon successfully hidden in his own home for years.

Behind the loose panel, each wrapped up in a clear polythene bag, was a stash of guns. Three of them. The first one Tom pulled out and examined through the plastic was a bolt-action battle rifle that looked like it had seen heavy action a long time ago. The second was a nine-millimetre CZ75 pistol, fitted with a tubular sound suppressor and a case catcher, to avoid leaving spent cartridges behind. *One of the most classic military handguns of all time*, as Tom had described it himself to Desi. And the third was a modern semiautomatic rifle, sleek and black and well-oiled inside its wrapping. The expertise of Thins Waller would have to be called upon to verify it, but to Tom's eye the weapon looked very much like the .300 Blackout rifle that the police had been looking for since the start of all of this. The rifle used in the murders of Raymond Jameson and Eddie Blake.

More deacts, like Vinnie Sweeney's? Tom seriously doubted it. Especially when he dug another three plastic bags out of the recess behind the boiler and found that they all contained what looked suspiciously like live ammunition.

The question was, what to do now: should he act like a cop and call in Billie and the troops? Or tear up the last few pages of the rulebook that he hadn't already, wait for Kendrick to turn up, confront him and make him talk? The mood Tom was in, it wouldn't take much to make the guy put his hands up to the whole thing. Army captain or not. Tom would roll over him like a tidal wave.

In the event, he was still mulling over it when the decision was made for him. Hearing the sound of crunching tyres outside, he grabbed his shotgun and went bounding up the stairs to the broken front door. The Porsche was rolling into the drive with its windows open and Julian Kendrick at the wheel. Kendrick had already spotted the big black car parked in front of his house, and didn't look pleased to see it. Next his eyes opened wide at the sight of Tom standing there in the open doorway, and wider again when he saw the gun clenched in Tom's hands. The Porsche revved hard and its spinning tyres sprayed gravel as Kendrick slewed around in a tight U-turn and tore back out of his entrance and into the road, accelerating fast away.

Tom ran to his car, bundled the gun into the passenger footwell and took off in pursuit. No way was he going to let this dirtbag slip through his fingers. The roar of the Hemi V8 filled his ears as he hammered away from the house. He made it to the first twist in the narrow road in time to see the zipping tail end of the Porsche up ahead. Kendrick was really shifting it, using up the whole width of the twisting lane. The Plymouth was built for straight-ahead powerhouse speed on an oval racetrack, while the little sports car was as nimble and agile as it was lightning-quick, giving it the major advantage. Just as Tom was beginning to worry that Kendrick was going to lose him so soon into the chase, suddenly there was a car in the Porsche's path. Kendrick swerved and the oncoming vehicle had to duck into the verge to avoid a collision. Its horn blared angrily as the Porsche sped on by.

The near miss had allowed Tom to gain a few seconds on Kendrick. He pressed his foot down harder and the 'Cuda surged onwards with a throaty blast. The rear of the Porsche drew closer, closer; then Kendrick must have seen him looming larger in his mirrors, dropped a gear and punched the gas, because suddenly Tom found himself falling back again. Another bend came up, forcing him to brake and lose more ground. 'Come on!' he yelled, more at himself than at the car. He hadn't driven like this in years. His stomach was all knotted up and his fists were clenched tight on the wheel. He wasn't going to allow Kendrick to get away. He couldn't.

Leaving the village behind them now, and the open country road was faster and less twisty. Trees, signposts and houses flashed past in a blur. His tachometer needle flickered past the ninety mark, climbed closer to the hundred and hovered there. Now the big-bore brute power of the Barracuda was more in its element, and with his foot hard against the floor and the engine bellowing like a mad bull Tom was gradually reeling the Porsche in. Just how he planned on stopping the guy, he had no idea. But he was where he needed to be, right on Kendrick's tail with no intention of letting him out of his sight.

Vehicles hurtled by in the opposite direction. Seeing a long empty straight ahead, Tom saw his chance to overtake and cut in front of Kendrick, intending to force him to a halt. He kicked the pedal and the revs soared upwards a few tones with a fruity howl as the auto shifter cogged down a gear. Gas pedal all the way back down against the stops and the needle touching 130 miles an hour; and the screaming Barracuda began to gain faster on the tail of the Porsche. Tom was about to swerve out of lane and go for the mad, reckless overtake when Kendrick anticipated him and the Porsche veered crazily across the line to block the way. Tom had to stand on the brake to avoid piling into the back of him, and lost precious momentum. 'Shit!' Now it was the Porsche once again widening the gap between them; and the empty straight ahead was suddenly running out as they entered a long, sweeping bend.

Kendrick was so desperate to get away that he went piling into the turn too fast. Dropped back some fifty yards, Tom saw the Porsche get into trouble as Kendrick tried to scrub off speed mid-corner. The rear end of the Porsche wobbled and broke into a skid that suddenly escalated out of control and the car gyrated through a complete three-sixty before it ploughed a huge furrow in the verge, tore violently through a hedge and the barbed wire fence behind it, and mowed down a sixty-yard stretch of bright yellow rapeseed crop before it came to a bouncing, skidding halt in the field beyond. Only a miracle had saved it from going into a roll that would have totalled both car and driver.

The road was completely empty in both directions. Nobody else had witnessed the crash. And there was nobody around to witness Tom screech to a halt by the torn verge, fling open his door and march out with his shotgun in his hands. He scrambled through the ragged hole in the fence and ran along the flattened aisle of rapeseed to collar Kendrick before he could escape on foot.

Tom needn't have hurried. The exploding airbag had dazed Kendrick and he was sitting flopped forward in the driver's seat, nursing a bloody nose. The front end of the Porsche was crumpled and the windscreen was a mass of fissures. Tom ripped open the door, grabbed Kendrick by the neck, hauled him bodily out of the car and slammed him against its side. Kendrick tried to resist, but he was still too dazed to focus, and he didn't see Tom's clenched fist coming until the same right hook that had floored Professor Ferguson hammered him to the ground.

Before Kendrick could get up, the muzzle of Tom's shotgun was pointing in his face. Tom said, 'Are you going to come quietly, or what?'

Tom half-dragged, half-shoved Kendrick at gunpoint all the way back to the road and bundled him roughly into the passenger seat of the Barracuda. He carried a spare pair of police-issue handcuffs in the glove box. He took them out, clipped one end to Kendrick's wrist and the other to the tubular frame of the car seat. Then he slammed Kendrick's door, walked around the car to the driver's side and got in.

'What the hell are you doing?' Kendrick demanded angrily, beginning to come back to his senses. He wiped a dribble of blood from his nose with the back of his hand.

'What does it look like? I'm taking you in.'

'For what? I haven't done anything.'

'Says the man whose house I just found a stash of guns in.'

Kendrick's face flushed scarlet. 'What guns? I haven't touched a weapon since I quit the army!'

"'They're not mine." You actually think I haven't heard that one before? Innocent men don't try to run.'

'You were pointing a bloody sawn-off shotgun at me!'

'Always come prepared,' Tom replied. 'That's my motto.'

'So you're arresting me on some trumped-up charge for possession of firearms, is that right?'

'There's also the small matter of multiple murder. You're the paedo killer, Kendrick. Had a good run but it's over now. You might as well make it easy on yourself and come clean.'

'Oh, this is bullshit. Can't you see I'm being set up?'

Tom gave a snort. He'd heard that one before, too. 'Yeah? That why you were snooping through Desi's files, to find out who was framing you?'

'What files?' Kendrick's look of shock appeared quite genuine.

'You might be a better actor than the meathead movie stars you photograph, Kendrick, I'll give you that. But you don't fool me. I'm talking about the files that you've been sneaking looks at when you've been staying with her at night.'

'I've never been there overnight. Is that what she's told you? It's a lie!'

Kendrick was staring at Tom. Tom stared back. There was a lot of sincerity in the guy's eyes. But Tom still didn't trust a word he said.

'I wanted to,' Kendrick said. 'I'm crazy about her. Who wouldn't be? But she said she wanted to take it slow. What I told you the other day, that was all just to make you jealous. I swear nothing's happened between us, so how could I have been there at night?'

Tom had met a lot of blokes who would brag to you that they'd slept with a woman, when they hadn't. Few would tell you they hadn't, when in fact they had. It was a basic male principle.

'Bollocks,' he said, undeterred. 'Doesn't change a thing.'

'I swear it's the truth. Those are not my guns and I am not a murderer. You need to listen to me. Hear me out. That's the least you can do.'

'Why should I?'

'Because you might learn a thing or two,' Kendrick said. 'It concerns you, as well.'

'Damn right it does.'

'You don't understand. Please. Five minutes.'

Tom was silent for a beat. 'You've got three. And counting.'

'Then I'd better make it quick, hadn't I? Has she told you about her uncle?'

Tom remembered the elderly relative Desi had been so worried about. Taken aback, he replied, 'Her sick old uncle Hugh? What's he got to do with anything?'

'That would be Brigadier Underwood to you and me,' Kendrick said. 'He's not sick, he's as fit as a fiddle. Guy could probably still finish the Paras endurance march ahead of most guys a third of his age. If she told you he was ill, that was just another lie. She lies about everything. Don't you see?'

'She's not a liar,' Tom replied defensively.

'You think you know her, but you don't. You don't know the first thing about her.'

'And so how come you're so clued up about this uncle?' Tom demanded.

Kendrick replied, 'Because I've known him for twelve years.'

CHAPTER THIRTY-ONE

Tom was too bewildered to say anything for a moment. Kendrick explained: 'You called it right, McAllister. I *was* a soldier back in the day. It's not something I tell most people about. But that's how I first met Hugh Underwood, twelve years ago. We were on a joint New Zealand Defence Force and British Army operation in Afghanistan. He was a brigadier, just a few weeks away from retirement. I was a twenty-seven-year-old captain, newly promoted. Virtually at opposite ends of the officer ranks. If it hadn't been for the incident, we'd never even have known each other.'

Tom had no idea where any of this was leading. He frowned and asked, 'What incident?'

'We were on a counter-insurgent mission in Helmand Province when my unit set up camp near a village,' Kendrick said. 'There was a detachment of British troops with us. Late at night, I was having a smoke outside camp when I heard screaming among the rocks, and ran to see what was going on. I found these two squaddies trying to have it away with a young Afghan girl. She couldn't have been more than thirteen. Anyway, things got out of control and before I knew it I'd beaten the pair of them half to death. Men who mess with children are the worst kind of scumbags. They were lucky I didn't shoot them both.'

'British squaddies?'

Kendrick nodded. 'So, next thing you know, there's this major inter-forces flap going on. The girl had run off, of course, and the villagers were keeping well out of it. Meanwhile the two Brits were totally denying the whole thing, saying I attacked them unprovoked. Cut a long story short, the British army brass all circled their wagons except for Brigadier Underwood, who was the only one who believed me and tried to stand up for me. Didn't do much good, though. I got discharged from the NZDF over it. End of career.'

'Very noble of you,' Tom said. 'I'd have done the same thing. But what's this got to do with—?'

'I hadn't heard from Brigadier Underwood in all this time,' Kendrick went on. 'Then a few weeks ago, out of the blue, I get this email from the army press office inviting me up to London to do a shoot for a regimental reunion at the Royal Overseas League. That's a posh members' club in St James's, if you didn't know.'

'Not for the likes of me, you mean,' Tom muttered. 'Go on.'

'I took the job. Whatever bad blood there was between me and the British Army was a long time ago. Anyway, to my surprise, Brigadier Underwood was there. We didn't get much of a chance to talk, and as I was leaving afterwards he said he'd give me a call. I didn't know if he would or not. But then last night, the phone rang. I thought it was just going to be a quick catch-up-on-old-times kind of five-minute conversation. Turned out to be a lot more than that. He started off by asking me, did I wonder who'd set up the photo shoot? I replied that I'd been approached by some regimental admin person and had no clue whose idea it was to offer me the gig. He chuckled and said it was him. He'd often wondered what I was up to these days, and then by chance he saw the feature article on me in a back issue of the *Tatler*, and he pulled a couple of strings to get me the job.'

'The *Tatler*?'

'It was last year,' Kendrick said dismissively. 'Came about because I'd done a shoot for Baxter Burnett, while he was on location in London. I had a two-page spread and a big picture of me. I wish I hadn't done it now.'

'We said three minutes, Kendrick. You're running out of time. What's the connection?'

'I'm coming to that,' Kendrick said, speaking fast to try to cram it all in. 'So when the brigadier calls me yesterday evening, he happens to mention, "You have another fan." I asked who, and he replies, "My niece is a big admirer of your work. I had a copy of the magazine lying around in my living room, and she took a great interest in it." His niece.'

'I get who his niece is,' Tom said.

'You don't find it's a strange coincidence?'

'It's a small world,' Tom said. 'And she knows you. So what?'

Kendrick shook his head. 'No, you don't understand. This happened weeks before I ever met her. It was the last time she'd gone to visit him.'

Tom remembered Desi's visit to her uncle's place in Berkshire, earlier that summer, before Kendrick had come on the scene. But nothing was making sense to him. Confused by all the dates and chronology of events he said, 'You mean it happened weeks before you set her up to meet you.'

Kendrick sighed, exasperated. 'Please, just listen to me. So anyway, he's going on about his niece and of course at this point I have no idea who she is, okay? He said, "She's a wonderful girl. Well, I say 'girl' but she's a woman now. And a very brilliant and beautiful one, I might add." I replied, just jokingly, "Sounds great. You must introduce me sometime." To which he replied, "Oh, she'd love that. Her name's

245

Desdemona, but everyone calls her Desi." So I'm thinking, hey, what a coincidence that the old man's niece has the same name as the woman I'm involved with. Or trying to get involved with, at any rate. I said, "Oh, really? That's a nice name." So then he starts going on all proudly about how she's this successful clinical psychologist who works in Oxford. At this point I was beginning to realise it was the same woman. Then he drops the name, Dr Desi Fielding. I almost let go of the phone.'

Tom was blankly staring at him. Kendrick said, 'Don't you understand, you dummy? The point is that she'd already heard of me, before I ever met her. So how the hell could *I* have set *her* up?'

'You'd better not be jerking my chain, Kendrick.'

'Shut up and listen, okay? I couldn't say a word, but the old man goes on talking. Says, "If you wanted to meet her, why not come over to my place some weekend and have lunch with the two of us? Mrs Lovett makes a lovely Sunday roast." I said, "Who's Mrs Lovett?" He replied, "Clarissa Lovett. My housekeeper. She often cooks for me."'

'So?' Tom asked, getting totally baffled.

Kendrick said, 'Clarissa Lovett was the name of the client who'd booked me for a private photo shoot the day I met Desi at the botanic gardens. Except she never showed up.'

'The housekeeper?'

'Not the bloody housekeeper,' Kendrick said impatiently. 'She used the housekeeper's name. Do you get it? Do you see? I didn't set her up. *She* set *me* up.'

Tom said nothing as he struggled to process all this. Kendrick's three minutes had run out long ago.

'Confused?' Kendrick said. 'You will be. There's more. Lots more. The old man's so damn proud of his wonderful niece, the esteemed medical doctor and clinical psychologist, he couldn't stop waxing lyrical about her. Then he paused and said to me in a more serious tone, "Terrible thing, though. She's doing all right now, but she's had a very difficult life."'

'What terrible thing?'

'I wondered that too. Then he told me. Said, "She lost her only child, her lovely little boy Michael, just three years old when he was murdered. She and Craig never got over it." Craig – that was her husband, by the way,' Kendrick added.

Tom couldn't quite get a grip on what he was hearing. 'She told me . . .' his words faltered.

'That she'd never had time for marriage or kids?' Kendrick finished for him. 'Snap. She said the same thing to me.'

'*Murdered?*' Tom shook his head.

'At first I thought it must be bullshit,' Kendrick said. 'Or that the old guy's lost his marbles or something. But then I thought, no. I know him. He's as sharp as a knife. And she's all the family he has. Would he bullshit about something like that? I mean, would he?'

'What happened to the wee boy?'

'He wouldn't tell me any more,' Kendrick said. 'And I couldn't ask. I got the feeling I was touching a hell of a raw nerve. There are some dark, terrible secrets in that family, McAllister. And she's been lying to both of us.'

Kendrick sounded angry, but Tom couldn't feel that way about Desi. All he could feel was the deepest sadness for her, if this was true. 'People keep things hidden, Kendrick. Sometimes those are things from the past that are just too painful to talk about.'

'Except it's not just that, is it? What about all the other lies? When you put it all together, even you can't deny that there's something weird going on here.'

'But what?'

Kendrick let out a snort. 'You tell me. All I've been doing all day is just driving around, feeling pretty darn confused, trying to figure this out. I don't even know where I've been.

Next thing I know, you're coming out of my front door like a raging bull with a fucking great shotgun pointed at me, having apparently broken in, and now you're telling me there are hidden weapons in my house and I'm the paedophile killer. I'm being set up, McAllister. I don't know why, or by who, but I'm sure beyond a shadow of a doubt that Desi's somehow involved in it. So now I'd really, *really* like someone to explain this whole fucked-up thing to me.'

Tom looked at him and saw the haggard look of utter sincerity in his eyes. 'I don't know where you've been either, Kendrick, and I don't give a crap. But I know where you're going.'

Kendrick exploded with frustration. 'To the cops? But how can you . . . after all I just . . .?'

'Not to the cops,' Tom said. 'I need to know more about this. So you're going to pay a visit to the brigadier. And I'm coming with you.'

CHAPTER THIRTY-TWO

But before he could make the thirty-mile trip to the Berkshire village of Hurley, first Tom needed to make a detour back to Kendrick's house. There was no way he was leaving a bunch of firearms and live ammo unsecured and unattended in a house with a broken front door lock.

Tom pulled up to the house, killed the engine and plucked out the key with a dubious look at his prisoner.

'Really? How the hell do you think I'm going to drive off, when I'm chained to this bloody seat?' Kendrick muttered.

'Break anything inside my car and you're dead meat,' Tom told him, stepping out and grabbing his shotgun for safekeeping. 'I'll be right back.'

Inside, Tom first paid a visit to the kitchen where he found a roll of plastic bin liners. Back down in the boiler room he bundled each of the illicit packages into a bag, tied them up tight and then carried the heavy load upstairs and outside. He tossed his own weapon into the Barracuda's back seat where he could get to it, and locked the rest of the arsenal into the boot.

'How many times do I have to tell you, they're not mine,' Kendrick said wearily as Tom got back behind the wheel.

'Shut your hole. The only reason you're not already on your way to the cop shop is because I need to get to the bottom of this crap.'

'And then you're planning on marching me into the station with a sawn-off pump-action shotgun to my head? How's that going to fly with your superiors, *Inspector?*'

'That?' Tom said, pointing at the gun. 'It's not mine. Never saw it before. Must be one of yours.'

'You're a real piece of work, aren't you, McAllister. And who's going to pay for my front door?'

'Sue me,' Tom said, and took off.

Kendrick was shooting him resentful looks. 'We don't even know where he lives.'

'Trust me.'

'Trust you? That's a good one.'

Blasting out of Great Haseley for the second time that day, Tom pulled out his phone, speed-dialled Billie's number and couldn't help but smile when he heard her voice come on the line. 'It's me.'

'How's Harvey?' she asked anxiously.

'They'd have contacted me if anything was wrong,' Tom said. 'I wasn't calling about that. Can you pull up an address for a Hugh Underwood? It's in Hurley, Berkshire.'

'What are you up to?' she asked, instantly suspicious. 'On second thoughts, I don't want to know.'

'Nothing, I swear. It's only an address.'

'You're on suspension. I shouldn't.'

'Not even if I say pretty please?'

'No chance.' A pause. 'But for a pot of your special tiramisu, I just might.'

'A bucket of it. With extra chocolate grated on top.'

She said, 'Just so happens, I'm at my desk. As usual. Because I have no life. None.'

'Then a quick peek into the DVLA records wouldn't take you out of your way.'

She huffed. 'You'd better not make me regret this. Hold on a sec. Did you say the surname was "Underwood"? . . . Okay, got it.'

'Text it to me, would you? Just the street and number, that's all I need.'

'Jesus, Tom. All right, then. Stand by. Anything else you can do me for?'

'That'll do it,' he replied as her text message pinged into his inbox. 'You're a star.'

'Let me know if there's any news about Harvey, okay?'

'You can bet on it.'

'That's police corruption, McAllister,' Kendrick said when the call was finished. 'Prying into people's personal data is an abuse of power.'

'I know. I'm a disgrace to the force, so I am.'

The sun was close to setting by the time Tom rumbled into the scenic rural village of Hurley, with its pretty thatched cottages, rose gardens and riverside views. The address Tom had managed to blag from Billie was a large, fine Georgian house situated quarter of a mile past the edge of the village with no overlooking neighbours, behind a high ivied wall and a gateway guarded by stone lions.

'This is it,' Tom said as he pulled into the driveway. He flung open his door and piled out of the car, grabbing his shotgun from the back. Then marched around to the passenger side, unlocked Kendrick's handcuff from the seat, clipped the cuff to his other wrist, and hauled him out at gunpoint. 'Don't even think about trying to run.'

'Or what, you'll shoot me? How do you plan on squaring that with your colleagues?'

'I have an understanding boss,' Tom said. 'Now move it.'

The front entrance was a grand old affair with a massive

brass knocker on the door. Tom had manhandled Kendrick halfway there when the door flew open and an elderly man appeared, tall and trim. He was dressed in a way that would have been called casual fifty years earlier, the portrait of the retired military officer. His hair was gone on top, buzzed short and snow-white around the ears. He held himself very upright for his age. But the most noticeable thing about him was the old military pistol in his hand. It was a relic from a time long before his own service days. But it looked real, and it was pointed steadily at Tom in a way that suggested he knew how to use it. Tom guessed the old man must have seen them from a window. He obviously kept the pistol handy for emergencies.

'What the devil is going on here? Captain Kendrick, who is this man?'

'Brigadier Underwood, I presume,' Tom said.

The brigadier came on a step closer, staring red-faced at Tom, the pistol unwavering in his hand. 'How dare you come onto my property in this threatening manner? Put that gun down this instant, or I *will* shoot. Don't think I won't.'

'Hugh, for Christ's sake don't do anything stupid,' Kendrick said. 'He's a police officer.'

The brigadier's small, pale eyes scrutinised the weapon in Tom's hand. 'What kind of police officer brandishes a sawn-off shotgun at members of the public?'

'The kind who won't clipe on you, if you don't clipe on him,' Tom replied. 'Something tells me you don't have a licence for that, given it's a prohibited weapon. I suggest you put it away before you get yourself into trouble, eh?'

The brigadier hesitated, then lowered the pistol. Tom did the same.

'What do you want?' the old man blustered.

'We need information, Hugh,' Kendrick said. 'That's all, I swear.'

'You've got a strange bloody way of asking for it.

Information? Information about what? Why are you wearing handcuffs?'

'Let's talk inside the house,' Tom said.

The interior of the brigadier's home was the stylistic opposite of Kendrick's. Tapestries, dark wood panelling, oriental rugs, suits of armour and grandfather clocks, every corner cluttered with the collectables of a lifetime. Tom left his gun by the inside of the door and unfastened Kendrick's handcuffs, 'There. All friends now. Okay?'

'I told you I wasn't going to run,' Kendrick said bitterly, rubbing his chafed wrist. 'I've as much reason for wanting to come here as you do.'

The old man led them up a long hallway to a living room that had no television. Another long-case clock tick-tocked resonantly in a corner. Dust hovered in the rays of light shining in the leaded windowpanes and the glazed eyes of stuffed foxes and owls stared down from the walls.

The brigadier settled in a slightly threadbare armchair and motioned for his visitors to do the same. The illicit handgun seemed to have magically disappeared, but the deep scowl of consternation was still etched on his face. 'Now, gentlemen, perhaps someone would care to explain to me what the hell this is all about?'

Tom said, 'It's in connection with the little boy who was murdered. Your grandnephew.'

The old man shook his head in bewilderment that quickly gave way to mounting anger. 'Michael? But why? That case was closed long ago. The man who did it has been in prison for many years. What the hell do you need to come here asking questions about it for?'

'I want to know too, Hugh,' Kendrick said. 'Why wouldn't you tell me before?'

'Because it's too bloody personal,' the brigadier replied irritably. 'What has my niece's family past got to do with anyone? Besides, it's too painful to talk about, even after nearly fifteen years. Stirring up a lot of terrible memories, things that should be left where they are, forgotten. As much as anything so terrible can ever be forgotten.'

'I'm sorry for your pain, sir,' Tom said as gently as he could, when the next word inevitably had to be 'but'. 'But it's my job to ask questions, and I need to know what happened to Michael.'

'Do I really have to . . . I mean, aren't there case files or something you people can look up?'

'I'd sooner talk to you, if that's okay.'

The old man still wasn't convinced. 'But why is Captain Kendrick here? If this is police business—'

'Captain Kendrick is helping me with my inquiry.'

'Is that why he was in handcuffs?'

'Never mind the handcuffs,' Tom said. 'He's concerned about your niece.'

'But they don't even know one another,' the old man said, confused. He blinked at Kendrick. 'Do you?'

'It's complicated. Please.'

A new thought came into the old man's head, and he looked alarmed. 'Is something wrong? Has something happened?'

'For old times' sake, Hugh,' Kendrick said, evading the question. 'I'll explain afterwards.'

'And you owe me for turning a blind eye to that illegal handgun of yours,' Tom said. 'So let's have it.'

The old man puffed a sigh. 'Very well, then, I suppose. But I hope you aren't going to go stirring all this up with my niece. The poor girl's suffered enough.'

'Who killed the boy?' Tom asked.

'His name was Nash,' the brigadier replied in a tone of pure hatred. 'Gordon Nash. I say that *was* his name, although I suppose he must still be alive. God damn his rotten soul, that filthy pervert.'

'Pervert?' Tom's blood suddenly seemed to freeze to a standstill in his veins.

'I suppose you're not meant to use such language these days,' the old man said. 'Well I make no apology for it and I've no truck with all that political correctness nonsense. Call them what you like – sex offenders, child molesters, paedophiles – what's in a name? Sick men who commit abominations against children. If I had my way, they'd be strung up, one and all; no judge, no jury, no beating about the bush, straight to execution.'

'Michael was murdered by a paedophile,' Tom repeated, letting the words sink in. He felt numbed. He could sense the shockwaves of amazement coming off Kendrick, but didn't look at him.

'Indeed he was, the poor dear little boy,' the old man replied, shaking his head sadly. 'That child was the light of my life. And his mother's. His father's too, I expect, but *he* wasn't around for much longer afterwards. Couldn't cope with it all, went off to live in Canada. He was an architect. Don't know if he still is. Probably remarried by now, I should think. Decent enough chap, I always thought, but weak, terribly weak, should have been there for her instead of running off like that.'

'She must have had a tough time,' Tom said. Inside his head he was still wrestling with all the implications of this new information.

'That's putting it rather mildly,' the brigadier said, peering down his nose at Tom. 'Have you ever lost a child, Inspector?'

'Never even had one,' Tom replied.

'Then you have *no* idea, none at all, of what it did to her. I have seen men utterly destroyed, mentally and physically, by the ravages of war. But I've never seen a human being more smashed to pieces than she was. It tore her soul apart. She was only twenty-three when it happened, you know, little more than a child herself. The poor thing went completely off the rails for a time. Mental illness is a dreadful thing; wouldn't wish it on my worst enemy.'

The old man sighed at the painful memories it evoked. 'But then she began to pick herself up, as one does, in time. Became deeply involved in her career, and she's doing well now, God bless her. We never talk about the past. But I know she must still hurt awfully, because something like that . . . something like that, believe you me, it marks you for the rest of your life. For my part, there isn't a day I don't think about Michael. And I often look at the photographs.'

'May I, as well?' Tom asked.

'Can't see what harm it would do,' the brigadier said gruffly. 'Though I still don't have the faintest bloody idea what this is all about.'

He got up from his chair and went over to a sideboard, from whose cupboard he fetched an old shortbread tin. Sitting down with it on his knee, he prised off the lid. It was full of yellowed newspaper clippings and a collection of photograph prints, some of them faded with age. He picked out one of the clippings and offered it across for Tom to see. 'This is him. Nash.'

It was a police mugshot of the killer, taken at the time of his arrest. Nash had been in his twenties back then. Nothing remarkable about his face. He could have been anybody. In some ways that was the most frightening thing about these men.

The brigadier fished out an age-faded photograph and let Tom see. 'That's her with Michael, just a month before he was taken.'

The photo showed a very young, very pretty and happy-looking Desi with blond hair, smiling for the camera with a truly beautiful little golden-haired boy cradled in her arms.

They were sitting on a tartan picnic blanket in a flower meadow with a blue sky in the background. Tom couldn't recall having ever seen a more perfect picture.

He looked up and said, 'You said Michael was taken?'

'Kidnapped. That sick pervert abducted and strangled him. Don't ask me to talk about it, because I won't.'

Back in those days Tom had still been in uniform, working the beat. He was trying to remember the case, and was ashamed to admit to himself that he couldn't. There had been so many horrific stories. You soon learned to erase them from your memory, or you'd go mad. 'I'm sorry,' he replied, handing the photo back.

The old man replaced it carefully in the box, and took out another. 'Here's one of my niece when she was a child.'

'She was lovely,' Tom said. He almost added, 'She still is,' but caught himself in time.

'We've always been close,' the brigadier said with a tender look softening his eyes. 'She was like the little daughter I never had. And here's another. We'd just celebrated her ninth birthday.'

Tom took it, and suddenly found himself gaping.

CHAPTER THIRTY-THREE

In the photo Tom was holding, a young Desi, blond-haired like in the others and turning to flash the photographer the sweetest of smiles, was seated at a shooting bench holding some kind of Olympic-style target rifle that looked enormous in her skinny little arms. Her eyes were lit up with joy, as though nothing in the world could be as much fun.

'That's her about to win the junior county smallbore championship,' her uncle explained proudly. 'She went on to win it four times in a row. None of the other kids ever stood a chance against her.'

Stunned, Tom said, 'She could shoot?'

'Oh, she certainly could,' the brigadier replied with a smile. 'I should know, because I taught her. From an early age she showed an avid interest, not just in target sports, but in the mechanics of the weapon. By the time she was twelve, she could field-strip almost any firearm you care to name right down to its component parts and reassemble it virtually blindfold, then punch clover-leaf patterns on paper targets at a hundred metres. I had high hopes she might have a glittering career as a competitive shooter. That was all long ago, of course,' he added solemnly. 'Before the bad times in her life. Then later on she became focused on her medical studies. I was always trying to talk her into taking it up again, but she seemed to have lost interest. It was a shame, because talent like that doesn't fade.'

As the old man talked, Tom was having a mental flashback to that day, months earlier, when he'd sat with Desi in her study. The day she'd showed him the video footage of her interview with Vinnie Sweeney. The day he'd broken her coffee cup. Something she'd told him leaped into his mind, as fresh as though he'd heard it just minutes ago. *I dislike guns extremely and know nothing about them*, she'd said. The statement couldn't have been clearer or more precise.

But it had been a lie.

Tom exchanged glances with Kendrick, who was staring at him with wide eyes. Tom knew what he was thinking, because the same dizzying realisation was forming in his own mind. One he didn't want to face. But now, suddenly, there was no escaping it, and the nightmare truth was beginning to dawn over his horizon like the incandescent glow of a forest fire.

He handed the photo back to the brigadier and rose up from his chair. 'Excuse me for a moment. I'll be right back.'

Tom hurried from the room and ran out to the car. Evening had fallen while they'd been talking inside. Opening up the boot, he lifted out the plastic-wrapped weapons he'd taken from Kendrick's basement and carried them back into the house. His heart was thudding so hard that he felt light-headed.

'What on earth—?' the brigadier exclaimed as Tom dumped his load on the sideboard and started tearing off the plastic. The first he unwrapped was the .300 Blackout semiautomatic. Then the CZ pistol with its silencer.

'Do you recognise these?' Tom asked him.

The brigadier's mouth had dropped open and his face had

turned livid red with the same guilty expression of shock and horror that Tom had seen on the faces of a thousand criminals caught in possession of something they shouldn't have. 'They're mine,' he admitted. 'At least, they look like mine. B— but I don't understand. How . . .? Where did you . . .?'

Tom asked, 'Can you prove that they're yours?'

'I'm not sure I want to prove anything that could get me into deeper trouble.'

'You're not in any trouble,' Tom said. 'This is just between you and me. Okay? I only want to know the truth.'

'Yes, they're mine, all right,' the brigadier said, looking at them more closely. 'They're part of my little collection. But it's not possible. I keep them all safely locked away in the attic.'

'Except for that old pistol you were waving around earlier, you mean.'

'The Mauser? No, I keep that under my pillow. Lots of disreputable types around these days, you know.'

'Tell me about it,' Tom said. 'Now, show me this little collection of yours. Let's go.'

Brigadier Hugh Underwood was a man much more accustomed to giving orders than to receiving them. But there was no resisting the power of authority in Tom's voice. Without a word of protest the old man led them up three creaky flights of stairs, all the way to the very top of the house where the low-ceilinged attic space had long ago been converted into a living area, now filled with clutter. Among the piles of dusty old books and records, three-legged armchairs and forgotten memorabilia stood a pair of ancient glass-fronted gun cabinets with the keys in their locks.

'This is where I . . .' the brigadier began. Then he paused and stared and said, 'Good Lord, someone's been in here! But . . . but who?'

He was pointing a trembling finger at the empty spaces in his neat row of other illegal guns. Even though he was hardly an expert himself, Tom instantly recognised them all as prohibited, therefore unregistered, weapons. Some were obvious bring-backs from theatres of war around the world, things like Kalashnikovs and light machine guns. Others were revolvers and automatic pistols, from modern to semi-antique. Each had its own designated space, with a museum-style label marked with the gun's make, model and calibre.

The empty spaces matched perfectly with the guns Tom had found in Kendrick's basement.

Tom said, 'Who's been in here, Brigadier? Do you really need me to tell you?'

CHAPTER THIRTY-FOUR

Ten minutes later, Tom was back in his car and speeding through the night towards Oxford. He'd left Kendrick at the brigadier's place. What was coming next, he could only do alone.

As he drove he snatched out his phone and stabbed in Billie's mobile number. 'Still at your desk?'

'Until around ten tonight. Poor me. But something tells me you haven't called to find out how I am.'

He said urgently, 'I need whatever you can dig me up on one Gordy Nash. Guy's been doing time the last fifteen years for the abduction and murder of a child.'

'Tom—'

'Don't ask. Please. As a special favour to me, okay? But I need it quickly.'

Billie was stony silent for a few tense moments, and he was afraid she was going to say no. He wouldn't have blamed her. He was asking her to take a big career risk. If she was discovered feeding such privileged information to someone who, at this moment, was no longer a member of the force, she stood to lose everything.

'I'll call you back,' she said, after another beat.

Which she did, exactly eight minutes later. This time she sounded even more concerned. 'I have the information you wanted. But first you need to tell me. Just what the fuck are you into with this, Tom?' It was extremely unlike Billie Flowers to swear. When she did, you knew she was upset.

'I can't tell you yet,' Tom replied. 'Please just trust me, Billie.'

She sighed. 'All right. Anyway, it's like you said. Gordon James Nash, born 1980 in Chelmsford, has spent the last fifteen years in HMP Bullingdon for the kidnap and murder of a three-year-old boy, Michael Wilkins. He was sentenced to twenty-three years, but four months ago they knocked eight years off for good behaviour. He walked out of Bullingdon three days ago, current whereabouts unknown.'

A cold tremor shivered down Tom's back. But he could scarcely have felt any more shocked and numb than he already did. Three days ago was the day Desi had gone off unexpectedly and stood Kendrick up when he came to visit.

'Tom? Are you still there?'

'I'm here. Owe you one, Billie.'

'Bet your arse you do. And you still haven't ans—'

'Got to go.' Tom ended the call and immediately redialled, this time for the hospital to check on Harvey. After a minute's wait, he was told that the patient was doing fine and could come home in the morning. At least there was *some* good news, he thought, as he made another call, this time to Ken Sparrowhawk.

'Ken, it's me. Listen, I need to borrow your van.'

Sparrowhawk kept the old rustbucket of a VW parked near his riverboat mooring point, for those infrequent but necessary trips into civilisation, or 'going down among 'em' as Sparrowhawk liked to put it. With a chuckle he said, 'Don't tell me that Yank tank has let you down again. No problem, pal.

I'm downriver at the moment, but you know where it is. Keys are in it.'

Tom raced westwards into the countryside beyond the city and went bumping down a rutted track to the secluded Thames riverbank, where he found the van parked by the empty mooring point. Switching vehicles, he set off again, this time heading back east towards Kennington. The clapped-out van had an exhaust as holed as a colander and handled like a shopping trolley, but as long as the wheels kept turning it suited his purpose perfectly. Reaching Bagley Wood he threaded his way up the narrow lane past Desi's house, saw lights in the windows and her white Beemer parked in front. He turned around and pulled up in the shadow of an overhanging tree some distance beyond her gateway. Killed the lights and engine and sat in the darkness, watching the house. After a couple of minutes he took out his phone and called her.

'It's me. Just calling to see how you are.'

'I'm okay,' she said, sounding nervous. 'Did you talk to Julian?'

'He wasn't at home. But I will. Can I come round?'

'It'll have to wait until tomorrow. I'm working late at Metcalfe.'

'No worries,' he replied. 'I'll see you soon. Take care, Desi.'

With her lie, another piece fell into place and his hunch grew stronger. He didn't know exactly what he expected to happen, or what he was waiting for. But he'd wait all night if he had to, and all the next day too.

It didn't come to that. Shortly after ten-thirty, car headlights lit up Desi's gate entrance. Moments later, the white Beemer pulled out of her drive. By the lights of a car coming the other way, Tom was able to make out the familiar figure sitting alone at the wheel. She could have been going for some late-evening shopping, to pick up a takeaway or to meet a friend for a drink. Whatever the case, he wanted to stay close and track her movements.

Tom followed, hanging well back in the evening traffic but nonetheless grateful for the inconspicuous van. Desi headed into Oxford, cutting up Abingdon Road and over Folly Bridge, then up St Aldates and slicing left past the ice rink towards Botley and the ring road, the same route Tom had followed ten thousand times from the nearby police station. He was three cars behind on Botley Road when he saw the BMW turn sharply into a side street. Shadowing her car he saw her pull up in a dead end with rows of lockup rental garages either side. As he watched from a safe distance, Desi got out of the Beemer, walked to a lockup, hauled up the shutter door and disappeared inside. A moment later, a bright red old-model Mazda sports car reversed out of the lockup and stopped next to the BMW; Desi got out of the Mazda, into her normal car and rolled it into the garage. When it was locked inside, she got back in the Mazda and resumed her journey towards the ring road. He gave her a few moments to get a little way ahead, then continued following.

Covertly tailing a car in city traffic was easy, but became much trickier as they left Oxford behind them. Desi circled the city anti-clockwise towards the town of Burford, gradually picking up speed in the nifty little sports car until Tom began to worry he was going to lose her. He pushed Sparrowhawk's van harder and prayed it wouldn't break down. At the same time he reached once more for his phone and called Billie again.

'I was just about to go home,' she complained. 'What is it now?'

'Check this reg for me, will you?' He read off the number plate of the Mazda, and gave Billie a description of the vehicle make, model and colour.

Sounding resigned, she said, 'Might as well, seeing as I'm

already deep in the shit for helping you, if we get caught. Although I don't even know what I'm helping with.'

Three minutes later she called back with her search result. 'Are you sure you gave me the right registration? Because according to my screen, this one comes off a blue Suzuki Splash that was scrapped two years ago.'

Which came as no surprise to Tom, because all it did was to confirm his worst, darkest intuition. He hung up on Billie and stayed on the Mazda, staring fixedly at its taillights as it sped on into the night, deeper and deeper into the Cotswolds countryside. Signs for the town of Burford flashed past and were gone, replaced by fleeting glimpses of names of villages Tom had never heard of but were probably mentioned in the Domesday Book. He lost track of how long it was before the Mazda, now two hundred yards ahead of him on an almost completely deserted country road, finally slowed for a narrow lane on the left and darted into the sharp turn without indicating.

Tom waited until her taillights were out of sight over a rise before he followed up the lane. The moon was bright enough to see by, and so he turned off his headlamps so she wouldn't spot him behind her. A rusted metal sign on chains by the dilapidated gate said SLOCOCK FARM. The red dots of the Mazda's taillights kept appearing and disappearing as the lane twisted and wound, overhung by trees and filled with potholes. Barbed wire the colour of dead twigs sagged from rotted fence posts, and nothing lived in the neglected fields either side of the lane.

Nearly quarter of a mile further on, Tom came over another rise and saw the farm buildings: a lugubrious old house with broken windows, surrounded on three sides by corrugated sheds and stone barns that looked like ruins in the moonlight. The red Mazda was parked in the yard out front. As he watched, Desi got out and disappeared into the farmhouse.

Normally he would have been asking himself what the hell she was doing in such a place. But a terrible voice deep inside was already whispering the answer to him. Thinking of Vinnie Sweeney. The experiences the man had been through leading up to his escape, before the violent car smash that had ended him.

Tom slipped the van into neutral, shut off the engine and let it roll to a halt. He turned off the interior light, then silently opened his door and got out, taking his shotgun with him. His heart was in his mouth as he began walking down towards the buildings. The closer he got, the more abandoned and derelict the farm looked. From not too far away he heard the rumble of a diesel generator. This place's mains power had been shut off a long time ago.

Moving as stealthily as he knew how, he reached the farmhouse doorway he'd seen Desi disappear inside, and slipped through after her. The house was dark inside, forcing him to pause and blink until his night vision began to kick in. His nose twitched at the smell of rats and mould, and other things. Thinking that he'd heard a sound, he followed it through the darkness, groping his way cautiously with his free hand while clutching his gun in the other. His heart was thudding like a drum. A glimmer of light up ahead; he made his way towards it, and very nearly pitched headlong into empty space before he realised he'd come to the top of a descending stone stair. Had to be a basement or a cellar, he thought.

Down he went, following the light. The bad smell was growing stronger. The stench of human confinement. More sounds drifted up to meet his straining ears. He couldn't make them out. Another step down. Then another.

And now he was at a metal door. At the same moment he reached out with a tentative hand to nudge it open, he heard the scream from inside. It was the worst sound he'd ever known. A cry of terror and pain and pleading, all rolled together in one awful wail. It sounded barely human. But it had come from the voice of a man: the man Tom sensed, or somehow *knew*, was trapped down here. And had been, for the last three days.

The door slowly swung open. The stink was suddenly much stronger, pungent and sickening. Now Tom could see the source of the light he'd been able to make out from upstairs. The dim glow of a bare bulb, pooling on the concrete floor of the cellar or basement. Tom saw the glint of the steel bars, behind which hovered the cowed, shadowy shape of a man. Then the shape moved and he got a clear view of the ghastly, pallid face of the prisoner inside the metal cage.

Tom knew that face. It was an older version of the police mugshot in the fifteen-year-old newspaper clipping the brigadier kept in his shortbread tin.

Gordy Nash.

As Tom stood frozen near the doorway, unnoticed in the shadows, almost too frightened to breathe, the man in the cage let out another long, agonized wail of terror. This time it formed coherent words. '*Please no please don't please don't do this to me no please. No. NOOO!!!*'

Gordy Nash wasn't alone down here. Now Tom saw the other figure stepping into the dim light, a figure all in black. It wore a black ski mask over its face, and a bulky black jacket that covered much of its shape.

Covered *her* shape.

That was why no witness had ever seen a man leaving the scene of the crimes. Because it wasn't a man who had committed them. Nobody had been looking for a woman. The simplest thing, and it had fooled them all.

In one black-gloved hand she clutched a long, curved blade. As she stepped towards the bars of the cage her prisoner shrank away in horror, but the confines of his prison wouldn't let him get far enough away to escape the hurt that was coming. And there would be yet more to come, afterwards. Laid out on a table nearby were the rest of the torture implements she planned on using on her captive.

That was when Tom heard her voice, so familiar to him and yet so strange. He couldn't make out what she was saying at first – then he realised that she was crying. The sharp end of the long blade raked against the bars of the cage. 'You murdered my child,' he heard her say to Nash, in a terrible, hollow tone. 'This punishment has been coming to you a long time.'

And Tom stepped out of the shadows with the gun in his hands and said, 'Hold it there, Desi.'

CHAPTER THIRTY-FIVE

The sound of Tom's voice startled her like a wild animal. She whirled around and backed away, and the long bayonet she'd been tormenting her prisoner with fell from her grip with a clatter. But as her hand flew to her belt he realised that she was just exchanging one weapon for another. Suddenly there was a large service revolver in her fist, pointing unflinchingly right at him.

Tom was still clutching his shotgun – but in that moment he knew he could never use it against her, not even to save his own life. He let it drop to the ground. 'If you're going to shoot me, Desi, then you'd better shoot me.'

Desi said nothing. She pulled off her ski mask. Her hair was bedraggled and awry and her eyes blazed with a light that he'd never seen in the eyes of even the most desperate criminal.

Then she turned around, still without a word, and directed the handgun at Gordy Nash, who was standing there clutching at the bars of his cage in open-mouthed horror. By the time Tom realised what she was about to do, before he could rush forwards to stop her, it was already too late.

The sound of the shot was deafening in the cellar. Gordy

staggered, crumpled and folded to the floor of the cage. The muzzle of the revolver followed his descent and she fired and fired again, hammering bullets into his body until the cylinder was empty and the hammer was clicking on fired chambers and Gordy Nash lay twisted up in a spreading pool of dark blood.

Only then did Desi toss the weapon away, and then she spoke for the first time. 'There. You cheated me out of the revenge I wanted. Happy?'

'He's not going to get any deader,' Tom said.

'I wanted more than that. I wanted him to pay for what he did. You can't possibly even begin to understand.'

Tom said, 'But I do understand. I know what he did, Desi. I know what happened to Michael.'

'Michael . . .' she echoed. Her voice was suddenly soft, vulnerable, almost a sob.

'I know you've been planning all this for a long, long time,' Tom said. 'You were in the wilderness for a while, after it happened. Then you came out of it, but you were a different person. Your blood had turned cold. You made a vow to stay close to the paedophiles and the rapists so you could take your revenge on the man who murdered your son. It's why you trained to become a doctor and then a psychiatrist, to get inside the system. You were just patiently waiting, all this time. You still had eight years to go before Gordy Nash was due to go free. But then all that changed when they decided to give him early release. You were on the clock now, gearing up for action. That's when you took the guns from your uncle's place. Then you kidnapped Vinnie Sweeney and held him here.'

She nodded. 'Figured it all out, haven't you, Tom?' she replied. Her voice was stronger again, and her face was almost expressionless in the dim light. 'It was easy, kidnapping Sweeney. I lured him, drugged him, made him get into the cage at gunpoint. He was my prisoner for a long time.'

'Your original fall guy. Right down to his DNA on the cartridge cases.'

'A known paedophile hater like him had all the motive to make it plausible. But that's not the only reason I brought him here. I needed someone to practise on.'

Tom suddenly realised the cold, brutal methodology of her plan. 'That's what the others all were, practice. That's why you didn't just wait for Gordy Nash to come out.'

'Have you ever killed anyone, Tom?' When he made no reply she went on, 'No, of course you haven't. Take it from someone who has, it doesn't come naturally. Not to me, anyway. Even though I made my mind up many years ago what I was going to do to Nash. No matter how badly I wanted him to suffer for taking my little boy away from me. I had to build up my courage, step by step. That's why I started from a distance first. It makes it a lot easier when you're just watching them through a rifle scope. Even then, I was sick for days after that first one. But it gets easier each time.'

Tom said, 'And then you started getting closer.'

She nodded. 'First the pistol. Then the knife. Working my way up to it in stages. I'm there now. I don't feel a thing any longer. If you hadn't turned up, I was ready to torture him to death.'

'I can't believe I'm hearing you say that.'

'No? You said yourself, it's been my whole life for fifteen years. I had it all planned to the smallest detail. I'd always suspected that Nash would get early release. Some of the most evil men are also the cleverest. He'd been doing all the right things, pressing all the right buttons, manipulating the prison authorities into thinking he was a reformed character. So I got ready early. I bought the two cars I'd figured I would need to move around incognito, and fitted them with plates from old wrecks. I rented this farm. Took a welding course so I could build this cage myself. I'd thought of everything. And it almost worked, didn't it? But it seems I didn't reckon on you, Tom.'

'All those private clients in your diary, they never even existed, did they? They were all made up, to cover your tracks while you were hunting down your victims and coming here to feed the animals.'

'It's true. I only work a few hours a week. This was my real job.'

'And to think I was so worried you were working yourself too hard.'

'What was I supposed to tell you, the truth?'

He looked down at the dead body in the cage. 'That day Kendrick came by, wanting to show you the nesting birds of prey, but you stood him up. That was the day you kidnapped Nash.'

'Yes. His early release date was brought forward another week. I only found out about it at the last minute, or I'd have missed him and he would have been off to Scotland. All my hard work would have been wasted.'

'Scotland?'

Desi explained, 'He was trying to hitch a ride near the prison when I stopped to give him a lift, all tarted up in my blond wig and my sexy dress. Just like I did with Sweeney. They were both too busy gawping at my legs to recognise Dr Fielding from the therapy sessions at Metcalfe House and the prison. In the car, Nash told me he was heading up north, planning on getting into some small community there. He said he loved working with children, that was what he wanted to do. That's when I stuck him with the needle.'

'Jesus.'

'Something you said to me the very first day we met, Tom. You said these people can't be cured. I pretended to disagree, but I've always known it was true. Gordy Nash was already a registered paedophile, loose in the community, when he kidnapped and murdered my little boy. Killing them is the only way to make them stop. They have it coming. They all have it coming. They're monsters.'

'Harvey Pepper isn't a monster,' Tom said. 'He's one of the good guys. But you put him in the hospital. Didn't you? That was you at the cottage.'

Desi shook her head vehemently and her eyes gleamed with tears. 'But I swear to you that I never intended to hurt him. I'd watched you leave the cottage and I thought it was empty, apart from Radar. He knows me, so I wasn't afraid of him. The door was open. I know you never lock it half the time anyway. I soon found what I was looking for, and I was just about to leave when Harvey suddenly appeared. He was drunk, yelling, "Hey, who are you?" and tried to hit me with the bottle he was drinking out of. And so I picked up the nearest thing and lashed out in a panic. I didn't mean it to happen.'

'You say you were looking for something. Looking for what?'

'It was the books I was after, Tom. Not Harvey. And certainly not you.'

He didn't understand. 'What books?'

She replied, 'The two that you borrowed from me. I found them in your living room, buried under a stack of newspapers.'

Tom blinked. He'd completely forgotten about it. 'I never got around to reading them.'

'If you had, you'd have seen the dedication inside the copy of *The Master of Ballantrae*. You'd have known my secret. You, of all people. You might easily have put two and two together, being a copper. You might even have known the case.'

'How would I have found out your secret from a book?' he asked, still confused.

'It was a birthday present from Craig, just two months

before Michael died. My little boy was very precocious, already learning to write. Under where Craig had written, "To my darling Desi, happy birthday", Michael added a line saying "For Mummy with love from Michael".' Desi blinked away the tears that came back from the memory. 'I know I've made mistakes. But that slip with the book was one of the worst. I was distracted that day, thanks to you.'

'Why thanks to me?'

'Because those times we had together were the nearest thing I'd had to being happy in a long, long while,' she replied. 'It wasn't until weeks afterwards that I suddenly realised which book you had. I had to get it back before you discovered my secret. What else was I supposed to do? We'd already broken up by then. It would have seemed strange, me turning up at the cottage as myself. And what excuse would I have had to start rummaging around looking for it?'

'You could have just asked me for it back.'

'Then I'd have risked drawing attention to it,' she replied. 'I had no choice but to do what I did. I hope Harvey's all right. The last thing I'd ever want to do is hurt an innocent person.'

'You mean an innocent person like Julian Kendrick? He might be a gobshite, but he's not a murderer. Yet you'd have happily framed him up to take the fall. After you got Nash and you didn't need the guns any more, you planted them at Kendrick's place and laid a trail to make sure I'd find them.'

Desi nodded. 'Yes, I know, and I'm sorry about that, too. Julian just happened to come along at the right time. Everything was going wrong. I was forced to come up with a whole new plan.'

Tom said, 'You're talking about when Sweeney escaped.'

'I thought I had it all under control. But he was cunning, and then I let my stupid guard down with him. When he got away, that changed everything.'

'Good thing for you that he got totalled in the car smash.'

'I wasn't as worried about that. He couldn't have identified me. I doubt he could even have remembered where this place was, not with all the drugs in his system. But all the same it was a disaster, even with him dead.'

'And so that's where Kendrick came into it,' Tom said. 'Thanks to a magazine feature, you'd found your replacement fall guy.'

'When I saw the article about him and my uncle told me the whole story about why he was thrown out of the army, I knew he was the perfect choice for me to pin my crimes on. I was lucky. And desperate.'

'Did you sleep with him?'

She flushed. 'No. Never. I'm a killer. I'm not a whore.'

Tom fell silent for a moment. He could almost have marvelled at how good her plan was, if he hadn't been caught up in it like meat in a grinder. 'You broke my heart, you know that? You used me, right from the beginning. Hooking me in and then dumping me in cold blood. You *wanted* me to get jealous of Kendrick, so that later on you could make me suspect him too. It was all calculated. You never cared for me at all.'

'That's not true, Tom. I might have had to lie to you about a lot of things, but my feelings were real. I never thought I would ever care for anyone again. I truly thought my heart was dead. But you showed me I was wrong. Breaking up with you was the hardest thing I've ever had to do. It was harder than killing. Harder even than having to sit face to face with my son's murderer in Bullingdon Prison, pretending I was there to help him, when all I wanted was his blood on my knife.'

Tom looked at her for the longest time. Then he asked her, 'If I hadn't come here tonight, what next?'

'You mean, after I'd finished taking my time with this piece of trash? I was going to torch this house. Burn it to the ground so there was nothing left. Everything I need is all set up in the kitchen, right above us. Nobody would have missed the place. I rent it from the alcoholic son of the old farmer who lived here alone before he was finally put in a care home years ago. The son doesn't care about it, and £350 a month pays for enough gin to keep him blotto. The insurance would be worth more to either of them than the house.'

'And then you were just going to go back to your life? Like nothing had happened?'

'I was going to go back to medicine,' she said. 'No more working with monsters. I wanted to be able to help people who needed and deserved my help. To be able to make a real difference to their lives. But that future is all gone now, isn't it? Now you've found me, I suppose you're going to have me arrested, and I'll be going to prison for a long time.'

Tom said nothing.

'Well, congratulations, Inspector. You're the hero who caught the paedo killer. Even your friend Forbes will have to shake your hand. They won't just give you your job back, they'll give you a nice promotion. A bigger salary and a cushy pension to match, if you decided to take early retirement. Your dream of the Three Bay Leaves restaurant has just come a step closer.'

'No, it hasn't, Desi.' He shook his head. 'You want me to tell you why?'

She was peering at him curiously, eyes narrowed, trying to gauge what he was thinking.

Tom said, 'Because all the years that Gordy Nash has sat in that jail for what he did, you've been locked in a cage of your own. His had steel bars, but yours was made of grief and hatred. That's a much worse place to be than any prison. I don't want you to have to spend another day behind bars, because the way I see it, you've already done your time. That's why I'm going to set you free.'

Desi was quiet. A tear welled up in her eye and rolled down her face.

'You should know one thing, though,' he said. 'If you'd hurt Harvey worse than you did, if you'd killed him, then I'd be thinking about this differently. I'd let them take you away and bang you up for evermore.'

She nodded, and more tears ran down both cheeks. 'You're an amazing man, Tom McAllister.'

'But a lousy cop,' he replied.

They left Nash's body where it lay, and he followed her back up the dingy stairway. Neither of them spoke as she led him to the kitchen and turned on a light, another grimy bare bulb that flickered with the uneven power of the generator. The room was full of red steel propane gas bottles that she'd spent months collecting and transporting to the farm. Next to those was a row of metal jerrycans. On the dusty kitchen worktop was an electric toaster, plugged into a cable running from the generator. A rolled-up newspaper was stuffed into each of its toasting slots. It was a crude but effective fuse.

'Are you sure you want to do this?' she asked him uncertainly. 'You'll be making yourself an accomplice.'

'Nobody will ever know, Desi.'

'What about Julian?'

'He doesn't have enough to put it together. Not all of it.'

'Then he'll make it his business to find out the rest. Out of revenge against me, for what I put him through.'

'He'll just be happy for all this to go away,' Tom said. 'Trust me, I'll make sure of that.'

She nodded, reassured. 'All right. And then?'

'And then we're done,' Tom told her. 'You have to go away too, far away. Sell the house. Leave the county. Leave the country if you can. Go to America or Europe. Not many people get a second chance at life, Desi. Make the best of it.'

'I won't ever see you again, will I?'

He smiled. 'Come on. We've got work to do.'

They poured the petrol into the collection of shallow dishes, roasting trays, saucepans, anything she'd been able to find, and left them all around the house until the fumes were dizzying. With a wet towel wrapped over his face, Tom sloshed more fuel all over the cellar, splashing it on the cage floor and the body of Gordy Nash, more of it on the cellar steps. He dragged a couple of gas bottles down there and turned the valves so that the gas started hissing out. Back in the kitchen, he and Desi opened up the valves on the rest of the propane bottles, and soon the hiss was loud and filling the air with the stink of gas.

He asked, 'Ready?'

'I've been ready for fifteen years,' she replied.

'Then here we go.' He pressed down the switch on the toaster, activating the makeshift fuse. Soon the rolled-up newspapers would begin to smoulder. The moment they burst into flame and touched off the escaping gas, this whole place would turn into a big incendiary bomb.

They hurried out of the farmhouse, into the sultry night. 'I'd suggest you get out of here,' Tom said, pointing at her Mazda parked nearby. 'Things are going to heat up a little in a minute.'

She hesitated. 'Tom—'

'No goodbyes, Desi. I can't do it. Just go.'

She said, 'I love you.' Then before he could reply, she hurried to her car, fired it up and took off.

Tom watched her taillights recede up the farm track. They faded into little red pinpricks. Then into nothing at all. And with that, Desi Fielding was gone from his life forever.

He murmured, 'I love you too.'

He was walking back towards Sparrowhawk's van when the house exploded. The violent blast rocked the ground under his feet. Flames erupted from the shattered windows and a leaping fireball tore up through the roof and lit up the night.

Tom stood there for a while, watching the inferno rip through the whole place and the black smoke rising up to blot out the moon and stars.

Then he got into the van, turned it around on the track and drove away.

AUTHOR'S NOTE

Thank you for having purchased *The Cage*. I hope you enjoyed reading it as much as I enjoyed writing it. It was a story in development for many years and it's been a pleasure making it finally happen.

A big part of the enjoyment of crafting this tale has been that it enabled me to return, in spirit at least, to my old stamping grounds in and around Oxford. I will confess to having played fast and loose with a few of the story's locations: for instance, the Oxfordshire village of Whitlington, where DI Tom McAllister finds Terry Brennan, is fictitious. And don't go searching for Tom and Harvey's favourite haunt, the Claddagh pub on Cowley Road, because you won't find it. I've invented the place as a nostalgic tribute to the grand old Bullingdon Arms, east Oxford's legendary and much-missed Irish pub, where I spent many a happy hour in the early nineties.

Likewise, Tom McAllister's favourite real ale, Langtree Hundred, is a figment of this writer's imagination, so vivid I can taste it! But please don't be disappointed if you can't find any to buy.

If you liked *The Cage*, please check out my website, www.scottmariani.com, for information about all my other books.

Scott Mariani

ABOUT THE AUTHOR

Scott Mariani is best known for the bestselling thriller series featuring ex-SAS hero Ben Hope. Scott's novels have topped the charts in his native Britain and are translated into 25 languages. He has been described as 'perhaps the best living exponent of the classic chase thriller'.

Scott was born in Scotland, later studied at Oxford and ended up living there. Deciding after university that a career in academia didn't suit him, he pursued his ambition to write for a living. During what turned out to be a long process of reaching that goal, he worked in various jobs from teaching English and music, running a burger bar, and playing in bands. Eventually leaving Oxfordshire and moving to the tranquil and beautiful setting of rural west Wales, the idea for the Ben Hope character came to him while hiking in the countryside with his dogs. The first Ben Hope book, *The Alchemist's Secret*, went on to spend six straight weeks at #1 in the charts and sell publishing rights across the world. Every book since has been a bestseller, and there is no end in sight for the Ben Hope series.

When he isn't hard at work on his next book, Scott can be found (and sometimes heard) pursuing his other interests which include shooting, archery and astronomy.

ALSO BY SCOTT MARIANI

BEN HOPE SERIES: